A TIME OF CHANGES

A TIME
OF CHANGES

ROBERT SILVERBERG

NELSON DOUBLEDAY, Inc.

GARDEN CITY, NEW YORK

A TIME OF CHANGES

This book was first serialized in "Galaxy Magazine."

For
Terry and Carol Carr

A TIME OF CHANGES

1

I AM KINNALL DARIVAL and I mean to tell you all about myself.

That statement is so strange to me that it screams in my eyes. I look at it on the page, and I recognize the hand as my own—narrow upright red letters on the coarse gray sheet—and I see my name, and I hear in my mind the echoes of the brain-impulse that hatched those words. *I am Kinnall Darival and I mean to tell you all about myself.* Incredible.

This is to be what the Earthman Schweiz would call an autobiography. Which means an account of one's self and deeds, written by one's own self. It is not a literary form that we understand on our world. I must invent my own method of narrative, for I have no pecedents to guide me. But this is as it should be. On this my planet I stand alone, now. In a sense, I have invented a new way of life; I can surely invent a new sort of literature. They have always told me I have a gift for words.

So I find myself in a clapboard shack in the Burnt Lowlands, writing obscenities as I wait for death, and praising myself for my literary gifts.

I am Kinnall Darival.

Obscene! Obscene! Already on this one sheet I have used the pronoun "I" close to twenty times, it seems. While also casually dropping such words as "my," "me," "myself," more often than I care to count. A torrent of shamelessness. I I I I I. If I exposed my manhood in the Stone Chapel of Manneran on Naming Day, I would be doing nothing so foul as I am doing here. I could almost laugh. Kinnall Darival practicing a solitary vice. In this miserable lonely place he massages his stinking ego and shrieks offensive pronouns into the hot wind, hoping they will sail on the gusts and soil his fellowmen. He sets down sentence after sentence in the naked syntax of madness. He would, if he could, seize you by the wrist and pour cascades of filth into your unwilling ear. And why? Is proud Darival in fact insane? Has his sturdy spirit entirely collapsed under the gnawing of mindsnakes? Is nothing left but the shell of him, sitting in this dreary hut, obsessively titillating himself with disreputable language, muttering "I" and "me" and "my" and "myself," blearily threatening to reveal the intimacies of his soul?

No. It is Darival who is sane and all of you who are sick, and though I know how mad that sounds, I will let it stand. I am no lunatic muttering filth to wring a feeble pleasure from a chilly universe. I have passed through a time of changes, and I have been healed of the sickness that affects those who inhabit my world, and in writing what I intend to write I hope to heal you as well, though I know you are on your way into the Burnt Lowlands to slay me for my hopes.

So be it.

I am Kinnall Darival and I mean to tell you all about myself.

2

LINGERING VESTIGES of the customs against which I rebel still plague me. Perhaps you can begin to comprehend what an effort it is for me to frame my sentences in this style, to twist my verbs around in order to fit the first-person construction. I have been writing ten minutes and my body is covered with sweat, not the hot sweat of the burning air about me but the dank, clammy sweat of mental struggle. I know the style I must use, but the muscles of my arm rebel against me, and fight to put down the words in the old fashion, saying, *One has been writing for ten minutes and one's body is covered with sweat,* saying, *One has passed through a time of changes, and he has been healed of the sickness that affects those who inhabit his world.* I suppose that much of what I have written could have been phrased in the old way, and no harm done; but I do battle against the self-effacing grammar of my world, and if I must, I will joust with my own muscles for the right to arrange my words according to my present manner of philosophy.

In any case, however my former habits trick me into misconstructing my sentences, my meaning will blaze through the screen of words. I may say, "I am Kinnall Darival and I mean to tell you all about myself," or I may say, "One's name is Kinnall Darival and he means to tell you all about himself," but there is no real difference. Either way, the content of Kinnall Darival's statement is—by your standards, by the standards I would destroy—disgusting, contemptible, obscene.

3

ALSO I AM TROUBLED, at least in these early pages, by the identity of my audience. I assume, because I must, that I will have readers. But who are they? Who are you? Men and women of my native planet, perhaps, furtively turning my pages by torchlight, dreading the knock at the door? Or maybe otherworlders, reading for amusement, scanning my book for the insight it may give into an alien and repellent society? I have no idea. I can establish no easy relationship with you, my unknown reader. When I first conceived my plan of setting down my soul on paper, I thought it would be simple, a mere confessional, nothing but an extended session with an imaginary drainer who would listen endlessly and at last give me absolution. But now I realize I must take another approach. If you are not of my world, or if you are of my world but not of my time, you may find much here that is incomprehensible.

Therefore I must explain. Possibly I will explain too much, and drive you off by pounding you with the obvious. Forgive me if I instruct you in what you already know. Forgive me if my tone and mode of attack show lapses of consistency and I seem to be addressing myself to someone else. For you will not hold still for me, my unknown reader. You wear many faces for me. Now I see the crooked nose of Jidd the drainer, and now the suave smile of my bondbrother Noim Condorit, and now the silkiness of my bondsister Halum, and now you become the tempter Schweiz of pitiful Earth, and now you are my son's son's son's son's son, not to be born for a cluster of years and eager to know what manner of man your ancestor was, and now you are some stranger of a different planet, to whom we of Borthan are grotesque, mysterious, and baffling. I do not know you, and so I will be clumsy in my attempts to talk to you.

But, by Salla's Gate, before I am done you will know me, as no man of Borthan has ever been known by others before!

4

I AM A MAN of middle years. Thirty times since the day of my birth has Borthan traveled around our golden-green sun, and on our world a man is considered old if he has lived through fifty such circuits, while the most ancient man of whom I ever heard died just short of his eightieth. From this you may be able to calculate our spans in terms of yours, if otherworlder you happen to be. The Earthman Schweiz claimed an age of forty-three years by his planet's reckoning, yet he seemed no older than I.

My body is strong. Here I shall commit a double sin, for not only shall I speak of myself without shame, but I shall show pride and pleasure in my physical self. I am tall: a woman of normal height reaches barely to the lower vault of my chest. My hair is dark and long, falling to my shoulders. Lately streaks of gray have appeared in it, and likewise in my beard, which is full and thick, covering much of my face. My nose is prominent and straight, with a wide bridge and large nostrils; my lips are fleshy and give me, so it is said, a look of sensuality; my eyes are deep brown and are set somewhat far apart in my skull. They have, I am given to understand, the appearance of the eyes of one that has been accustomed all his life to commanding other men.

My back is broad and my chest is deep. A dense mat of coarse dark hair grows nearly everywhere on me. My arms are long. My hands are large. My muscles are well developed and stand out prominently beneath my skin. I move gracefully for a man my size, with smooth coordination; I excel in sports, and when I was younger I hurled the feathered shaft the entire length of Manneran Stadium, a feat that had never been achieved until then.

Most women generally find me attractive—all but those who prefer a flimsier, more scholarly looking sort of man and are frightened of strength and size and virility. Certainly the political power I have held in my time has helped to bring many partners to my couch, but no doubt they were drawn to me as much by the look of my body as by anything more subtle. Most of them have been disappointed in me. Bulging muscles and a hairy hide do not a skilled lover make, nor is a massive genital member such as mine any guarantee of ecstasy. I am no champion of copulation. See: I hide nothing from you. There is in me a certain constitutional impatience that expresses itself outwardly only during the carnal act; when I enter a woman I find myself swiftly swept away, and rarely can I sustain the deed until her pleasure comes. To no one, not even a drainer, have I confessed this failing before, nor did I ever expect that I would. But a good many women of Borthan have learned of this my great flaw in the most immediate possible way, to their cost, and doubtless some of them, embittered, have circulated the news in order that they might enjoy a scratchy joke at my expense. So I place it on the record here, for perspective's sake. I would not have you think of me as a hairy mighty giant without also your knowing how often my flesh has betrayed my lusts. Possibly this failing of mine was among the forces that shaped my destinies toward this day in the Burnt Lowlands, and you should know of that.

5

My FATHER WAS hereditary septarch of the province of Salla on our eastern coast. My mother was daughter to a septarch of Glin; he met her on a diplomatic mission, and their mating was, it was said, ordained from the moment they beheld one another. The first child born to them was my brother Stirron, now septarch in Salla in our father's place. I followed two years later; there were three more after me, all of them girls. Two of these still live. My youngest sister was slain by raiders from Glin some twenty moontimes ago.

I knew my father poorly. On Borthan everyone is a stranger to everyone, but one's father is customarily less remote from one than others; not so with the old septarch. Between us lay an impenetrable wall of formality. In addressing him we used the same formulas of respect that subjects employed. His smiles were so infrequent that I think I can recall each one. Once, and it was unforgettable, he took me up beside him on his rough-hewn blackwood throne, and let me touch the ancient yellow cushion, and called me fondly by my child-name; it was the day my mother died. Otherwise he ignored me. I feared and loved him, and crouched trembling behind pillars in his court to watch him dispense justice, thinking that if he saw me there he would have me destroyed, and yet unable to deprive myself of the sight of my father in his majesty.

He was, oddly, a man of slender body and modest height, over whom my brother and I towered even when we were boys. But there was a terrible strength of will in him that led him to surmount every challenge. Once in my childhood there came some ambassador to the septarchy, a hulking sun-blackened westerner who stands in my memory no smaller than Kongoroi Mountain; probably he was as tall and broad as I am now. At feasting-time the ambassador let too much blue wine down his throat, and said, before my father and his courtiers and his family, "One would show his strength to the men of Salla, to whom he may be able to teach something of wrestling."

"There is one here," my father replied in sudden fury, "to whom, perhaps, nothing need be taught."

"Let him be produced," the huge westerner said, rising and peeling back his cloak. But my father, smiling—and the sight of that smile made his courtiers quake—told the boastful stranger it would not be fair to make him compete while his mind was fogged with wine, and this of course maddened the ambassador beyond words. The musicians came in then to ease the tension, but the anger of our visitor did not subside, and, after an hour, when the drunkenness had lifted somewhat from him, he demanded again to meet my father's champion. No man of Salla, said our guest, would be able to withstand his might.

Whereupon the septarch said, "I will wrestle you myself."

That night my brother and I were sitting at the far end of the long table, among the women. Down from the throne-end came the stunning word "I" in my father's voice, and an instant later came "myself." These were obscenities that Stirron and I had often whispered, sniggering, in the darkness of our bedchamber, but we had never imagined we would hear them hurled forth in the feasting-hall from the septarch's own lips. In our shock we reacted differently, Stirron jerking convulsively and knocking over his goblet, myself letting loose a half-suppressed shrill giggle of embarrassment and delight that earned me an instant slap from a lady-in-waiting. My laughter was merely the mask for my inner horror. I could barely believe that my father knew those words, let alone that he would say them before this august company. *I will wrestle you myself.* And while the reverberations of the forbidden forms of speech still dizzied me, my father swiftly stepped forward, dropping his cloak, and faced the great hulk of an ambassador, and closed with him, and caught him by one elbow and one haunch in a deft Sallan hold, and sent him almost immediately toppling to the polished floor of gray stone. The ambassador uttered a terrible cry, for one of his legs was sticking strangely out at a frightening angle from his hip, and in pain and humiliation he pounded the flat of his hand again and again against the floor. Perhaps diplomacy is practiced in more sophisticated ways now in the palace of my brother Stirron.

The septarch died when I was twelve and just coming into the first rush of my manhood. I was near his side when death took him. To escape the time of rains in Salla he would go each year to hunt the hornfowl in the Burnt Lowlands, in the very district where now I hide and wait. I had never gone with him, but on this occasion I was permitted to accompany the hunting party, for now I was a young prince and must learn the skills of my class. Stirron, as a future septarch, had other skills to master; he remained behind as regent in our father's absence from the capital. Under a bleak and heavy sky bowed with rainclouds the expedition of some twenty groundcars rolled westward out of Salla City and through the flat, sodden, winter-bare countryside. The rains were merciless that year, knifing away the precious sparse topsoil and laying bare the rocky bones of our province. Everywhere the farmers were repairing their dikes, but to no avail; I could see the swollen rivers running yellow-brown with Salla's lost wealth, and I nearly wept to think of such treasure being carried into the sea. As we came into West Salla, the narrow road began to climb the foothills of the Huishtor Range, and soon we were in drier, colder country, where the skies gave snow and not rain, and the trees were mere bundles of sticks against the blinding whiteness. Up we went into the Huishtors, following the

7

Kongoroi Road. The countryfolk came out to chant welcomes to the septarch as he passed. Now the naked mountains stood like purple teeth ripping the gray sky, and even in our sealed groundcars we shivered, although the beauty of this tempestuous place took my mind from my discomforts. Here great flat shields of striated tawny rock flanked the rugged road, and there was scarcely any soil at all, nor did trees or shrubs grow except in sheltered places. We could look back and see all of Salla like its own map below us, the whiteness of the western districts, the dark clutter of the populous eastern shore, everything diminished, unreal. I had never been this far from home before. Though we were now deep into the uplands, midway, as it were, between sea and sky, the inner peaks of the Huishtors still lay before us, and to my eye they formed an unbroken wall of stone spanning the continent from north to south. Their snow-crowned summits jutted raggedly from that continuous lofty breast-works of bare rock: were we supposed to go over the top, or would there be some way through? I knew of Salla's Gate, and that our route lay toward it, but somehow the gate seemed mere myth to me at that moment.

Up and up and up we rode, until the generators of our groundcars were gasping in the frosty air, and we were compelled to pause frequently to defrost the power conduits, and our heads whirled from shortness of oxygen. Each night we rested at one of the camps maintained for the use of traveling septarchs, but the accommodations were far from regal, and at one, where the entire staff of servants had perished some weeks before in a snowslide, it was necessary for us to dig our way through mounds of ice in order to enter. We were all of us in the party men of the nobility, and all of us wielded shovels except the septarch himself, for whom manual labor would have been sinful. Because I was one of the biggest and strongest of the men I dug more vigorously than anyone, and because I was young and rash I strained myself beyond my strength, collapsing over my shovel and lying half dead in the snow for an hour until I was noticed. My father came to me while they were treating me, and smiled one of his rare smiles; just then I believed it was a gesture of affection, and it greatly sped my recovery, but afterward I came to see it was more likely a sign of his contempt.

That smile buoyed me through the remainder of our ascent of the Huishtors. No longer did I fret about getting over the mountains,

8

for I knew that I would, and on the far side my father and I would hunt the hornfowl in the Burnt Lowlands, going out together, guarding one another from peril, collaborating ultimately on the tracking and on the kill, knowing a closeness that had never existed between us in my childhood. I talked of that one night to my bond-brother Noim Condorit, who rode with me in my groundcar, and who was the only person in the universe to whom I could say such things. "One hopes to be chosen for the septarch's own hunt-group," I said. "One has reason to think that one will be asked. And an end made to the distance between father and son."

"You dream," said Noim Condorit. "You live in fantasies."

"One could wish," I replied, "for warmer encouragement from one's bondbrother."

Noim was ever a pessimist; I took his dourness in stride, and counted the days to Salla's Gate. When we reached it, I was unprepared for the splendor of the place. All morning and half an afternoon we had been following a thirty-degree grade up the broad breast of Kongoroi Mountain, shrouded in the shadow of the great double summit. It seemed to me we would climb forever and still have Kongoroi looming over us. Then our caravan swung around to the left, car after car disappearing behind a snowy pylon on the flank of the road, and our car's turn came, and when we had turned the corner I beheld an astonishing sight: a wide break in the mountain wall, as if some cosmic hand had pried away one corner of Kongoroi. Through the gap came daylight in a glittering burst. This was Salla's Gate, the miraculous pass across which our ancestors came when first they entered our province, so many hundreds of years back, after their wanderings in the Burnt Lowlands. We plunged joyously into it, riding two and even three cars abreast over the hardpacked snow, and before we made camp for the night we were able to see the strange splendor of the Burnt Lowlands spread out astonishingly below us.

All the next day and the one that followed we rode the switchbacks down Kongoroi's western slope, creeping at a comical pace along a road that had little room to spare for us: a careless twitch of the stick and one's car would tumble into an infinite abyss. There was no snow on this face of the Huishtors, and the raw sunpounded rock had a numbing, oppressive look. Ahead everything was red soil. Down into the desert we went, quitting winter and entering a stifling world where every breath tingled in the lungs, where dry winds lifted the ground in clouds, where odd twisted-looking beasts scampered in terror from our oncoming cavalcade. On the sixth day we reached the hunting-grounds, a place of ragged escarpments far below sea level. I am no more than an hour's ride from that place now. Here the hornfowl have their nests; all day long they range the baking plains, seeking meat, and at twilight they return, collapsing groundward in weird spiraling flight to enter their all but inaccessible burrows.

In the dividing of personnel I was one of thirteen chosen for the septarch's companions. "One shares your joy," Noim told me solemnly, and there were tears in his eyes as well as in mine, for he knew what pain my father's coldness had brought me. At daybreak the hunt-groups set out, nine of them, in nine directions.

To take a hornfowl near its nest is deemed shameful. The bird returning is usually laden with meat for its young, and it therefore is clumsy and vulnerable, shorn of all its grace and power. Killing one as it plummets is no great task, but only a craven self-barer would attempt it. (*Self-barer!* See, how my own pen mocks me! I, who have bared more self than any ten men of Borthan, still unconsciously use the term as a word of abuse! But let it stand.) I mean to say that the virtue in hunting lies in the perils and difficulties of the chase, not in the taking of the trophy, and we hunt the hornfowl as a challenge to our skills, not for its dismal flesh.

Thus hunters go into the open Lowlands, where even in winter the sun is devastating, where there are no trees to give shade or streams to ease the thirst. They spread out, one man here, two men there, taking up stations in that trackless expanse of barren red soil, offering themselves as the hornfowl's prey. The bird cruises at inconceivable heights, soaring so far overhead that it can be seen only as a black scratch in the brilliant dome of the sky; it takes the keenest vision to detect one, though a hornfowl's wingspread is twice the length of a man's body. From its lofty place the hornfowl scans the desert for incautious beasts. Nothing, no matter how small, escapes its glossy eyes; and when it detects good quarry it comes down through the turbulent air until it hovers house-high above the ground. Now it commences its killing-flight, flying low, launching itself on a series of savage circles, spinning a death-knot around its still unsuspecting victim. The first swing may sweep over the equivalent of half a province's area, but each successive circuit is tighter and tighter, while acceleration mounts, until ultimately the hornfowl has made itself a frightful engine of death that comes roaring in from the horizon at nightmarish velocity. Now the quarry learns the truth, but it is knowledge not held for long: the rustle of mighty wings, the hiss of a slim powerful form cleaving the hot sluggish air, and then the single long deadly spear sprouting from the bird's bony forehead finds its mark, and the victim falls, enfolded in the black fluttering wings. The hunter hopes to bring down his hornfowl while it cruises, almost at the limits of human sight; he carries a weapon designed for long-range shooting, and the test is in the aim, whether he can calculate the interplay of trajectories at such vast distances. The peril of hunting hornfowl is this, that one never knows if one is the hunter or the hunted, for a hornfowl on its killing-flight cannot be seen until it strikes its stroke.

So I went forth. So I stood from dawn to midday. The sun worked its will on my winter-pale skin, such of it as I dared to expose; most of me was swaddled in hunting clothes of soft crimson leather, within which I boiled. I sipped from my canteen no more often than survival demanded, for I imagined that the eyes of my comrades were upon me and I would reveal no weaknesses to them. We were arrayed in a double hexagon with my father alone between the two groups. Chance had it that I drew the point of my hexagon closest to him, but it was more than a feathered shaft's toss from his place to mine, and all the morning long the septarch and I exchanged not a syllable. He stood with feet planted firm, watching the skies, his weapon at ready. If he drank at all as he waited, I did not see him do it. I too studied the skies, until my eyes ached for it, until I felt twin strands of hot light drilling my brain and hammering against the back wall of my skull. More than once I imagined I saw the dark splinter of a hornfowl's shape drifting into view up there, and once in sweaty haste I came to the verge of raising my gun to it, which would have brought me shame, for one must not shoot until one has established priority of sighting by crying one's claim. I did not fire, and when I blinked and opened my eyes I saw nothing in the sky. The hornfowl seemed to be elsewhere that morning.

At noon my father gave a signal, and we spread farther apart over the plain, maintaining our formation. Perhaps the hornfowl found us too closely clustered, and were staying away. My new position lay atop a low earthen mound, in the form almost of a woman's breast, and fear took hold of me as I took up my place on it. I supposed myself to be terribly exposed and in imminent peril of hornfowl attack. As fright crept through my spirit I became convinced that a hornfowl was even now flying its fatal circuits around my hummock, and that at any moment its lance would pierce my kidneys while I gazed stupidly at the metallic sky. The premonition grew so strong that I had to struggle to hold my ground; I shivered, I stole wary peeks over my shoulders, I clenched the stock of my gun for comfort, I strained my ears for the sound of my enemy's approach, hoping to whirl and fire before I was speared. For this cowardice I reproached myself severely, even offering thanks that Stirron had been born before me, since obviously I was unfit to succeed to the septarchy. I reminded myself that not in three years had a hunter been killed in this way. I asked myself if it was plausible that I should die so young, on my first hunt, when there were others like my father who had hunted for thirty seasons and gone unscathed. I demanded to know why I felt this overwhelming fear, when all my tutors had labored to teach me that the self is a void and concern for one's person a wicked sin. Was not my father in equal jeopardy, far across the sun-smitten plain? And had he not much more than I to lose, being a septarch and a prime septarch at that, while I was only a boy? In this way I cudgeled the fear from my damp soul, and studied the sky without regard for the spear that might be aimed at my back, and in minutes my former fretting seemed an absurdity to me. I would stand here for days, if need be, unafraid. At once I had the reward of this triumph over self: against the shimmering fierceness of the sky I made out a dark floating form, a notch in the heavens, and this time it was no illusion. for my youthful eyes spied wings and horn. Did the others see it? Was the bird mine to attempt? If I made the kill, would the septarch pound my back and call me his best son? All was silence from the other hunters.

"One cries claim!" I shouted jubilantly, and lifted my weapon, and eyed the sight, remembering what I had been taught, to let the inner mind make the calculations, to aim and fire in one swift impulse before the intellect, by quibbling, could spoil the intuition's command.

And in the instant before I sent my bolt aloft there came a ghastly outcry from my left, and I fired without aiming at all, turning in the same instant toward my father's place, and seeing him half hidden beneath the madly flapping form of another hornfowl that had gored him from spine to belly. The air about them was clouded with red sand as the monster's wings furiously slapped the ground; the bird was struggling to take off, but a hornfowl cannot lift a man's weight, though this does not prevent them from attacking us. I ran to aid the septarch. He still was shouting, and I saw his hands clutching for the hornfowl's scrawny throat, but now there was a liquid quality about his cries, a bubbling tone, and when I reached the scene—I was the first one there—he lay sprawled and quiet, with the bird still rammed through him and covering his body like a black cloak. My blade was out; I slashed the hornfowl's neck as if it were a length of hose, kicked the carcass aside, began to wrench desperately at the demonic head mounted so hideously upon the septarch's upturned back. Now the others came; they pulled me away; someone seized me by the shoulders and shook me until my fit was past. When I turned to them again, they closed their ranks, to keep me from seeing my father's corpse, and then, to my dismay, they dropped to their knees before me to do homage.

But of course it was Stirron and not I who became septarch in Salla. His crowning was a grand event, for, young though he was, he would be the prime septarch of the province. Salla's six other septarchs came to the capital—only on such an occasion were they ever to be found at once in the same city—and for a time everything was feasting and banners and the blare of trumpets. Stirron was at the center of it all, and I on the margins, which was as it should be, though it left me feeling more like a stableboy than a prince. Once he was enthroned Stirron offered me titles and land and power, but he did not really expect me to accept, and I did not. Unless a septarch is a weakling, his younger brothers had best not stay nearby to help him rule, for such help is not desired often. I had had no living uncles on my father's side of the family, and I did not care to have Stirron's sons be able to make the same statement; therefore I took myself quickly from Salla once the time of mourning was ended.

I went to Glin, my mother's land. There, however, things were unsatisfactory for me, and after a few years I moved on to the steamy province of Manneran, where I won my wife and sired my sons and became a prince in more than name, and lived happily and sturdily until my time of changes began.

6

Perhaps I should set down some words concerning my world's geography.

There are five continents on our planet of Borthan. In this hemisphere there are two, Velada Borthan and Sumara Borthan, which is to say, the Northern World and the Southern World. It is a long sea journey from any shore of these continents to the continents of the opposite hemisphere, which have been named merely Umbis, Dabis, Tibis, that is, One, Two, Three.

Of those three distant lands I can tell you very little. They first were explored some seven hundred years ago by a septarch of Glin, who laid down his life for his curiosity, and there have not been five seeking-parties to them in all the time since. No human folk dwell in that hemisphere. Umbis is said to be largely like the Burnt Lowlands, but worse, with golden flames bursting from the tormented land in many places. Dabis is jungles and fever-ridden swamps, and someday will be full of our people hoping to prove manhood, for I understand it is thick with dangerous beasts. Tibis is covered with ice.

We are not a race afflicted with the wanderlust. I myself was never a voyager until circumstances made me one. Though the blood of the ancient Earthmen flows in our veins, and they were wanderers whose demons drove them out to prowl the stars, we of Borthan stay close to home. Even I who am somewhat different from my comrades in my way of thinking never hungered to see the snowfields of Tibis or the marshes of Dabis, except perhaps when I was a child and eager to gobble all the universe. Among us it is considered a great thing merely to journey from Salla to Glin, and rare indeed is the man who has crossed the continent, let alone ventured to Sumara Borthan, as I have done.

As I have done.

Velada Borthan is the home of our civilization. The mapmakers' art reveals it to be a large squarish landmass with rounded corners. Two great V-shaped indentations puncture its periphery: along the northern coast, midway between the eastern and western corners, there is the Polar Gulf, and, due south on the opposite coast, there is the Gulf of Sumar. Between those two bodies of water lie the Lowlands, a trough that spans the entire continent from north to south. No point in the Lowlands rises higher above sea level than the height of five men, and there are many places, notably in the Burnt Lowlands, that are far below sea level.

There is a folktale we tell our children concerning the shape of Velada Borthan. We say that the great iceworm Hrungir, born in the waters of the North Polar Sea, stirred and woke one day in sudden appetite, and began to nibble at the northern shore of Velada Borthan. The worm chewed for a thousand thousand years, until it had eaten out the Polar Gulf. Then, its voracity having made it somewhat ill, it crawled up on the land to rest and digest what it had devoured. Uneasy at the stomach, Hrungir wriggled southward, causing the land to sink beneath its vast weight and the mountains to rise, in compensation, to the east and west of its resting-place. The worm rested longest in the Burnt Lowlands, which accordingly were depressed more deeply than any other region. In time the worm's appetite revived, and it resumed its southward crawl, coming at last to a place where a range of mountains running from east to west barred its advance. Then it chewed the mountains, creating Stroin Gap, and proceeded toward our southern coast. In another fit of hunger the worm bit out the Gulf of Sumar. The waters of the Strait of Sumar rushed in to fill the place where the land had been, and the rising tide carried Hrungir to the continent of Sumara Borthan, where now the iceworm lives, coiled beneath the volcano Vashnir and emitting poisonous fumes. So the fable goes.

The long narrow basin that we think of as Hrungir's track is divided into three districts. At the northern end we have the Frozen Lowlands, a place of perpetual ice where no man ever is seen: legend has it that the air is so dry and cold that a single breath will turn a man's lungs to leather. The polar influence reaches only a short distance into our continent, however. South of the Frozen Lowlands lie the immense Burnt Lowlands, which are almost totally without water, and on which the full fury of our sun constantly falls. Our two towering north-south mountain ranges prevent a drop of rain from entering the Burnt Lowlands, nor do any rivers or streams reach it. The soil is bright red, with occasional yellow streaks, and this we blame on the heat of Hrungir's belly, though our geolo-

15

gists tell another tale. Small plants live in the Burnt Lowlands, taking their nourishment from I know not where, and there are many kinds of beasts, all of them strange, deformed, and unpleasant. At the southern end of the Burnt Lowlands there is a deep east-west valley, several days' journey in breadth, and on its far side lies the small district known as the Wet Lowlands. Northerly breezes coming off the Gulf of Sumar carry moisture through Stroin Gap; these winds meet the fierce hot blasts out of the Burnt Lowlands and are forced to drop their burden not far above the Gap, creating a land of dense, lush vegetation. Never do the water-laden breezes from the south succeed in getting north of the Wet Lowlands to bathe the zone of red soil. The Frozen Lowlands, as I have said, go forever unvisited, and the Burnt Lowlands are entered only by hunters and those who must travel between the eastern and western coasts, but the Wet Lowlands are populated by several thousand farmers, who raise exotic fruits for the city folk. I am told that the constant rain rots their souls, that they have no form of government, and that our customs of self-denial are imperfectly observed. I would be among them now, to discover their nature at first hand, if only I could slip through the cordon that my enemies have set up to the south of this place.

The Lowlands are flanked by two immense mountain ranges: the Huishtors in the east, the Threishtors in the west. These mountains begin on Velada Borthan's northern coast, virtually at the shores of the North Polar Sea, and march southward, gradually curving inland; the two ranges would join not far from the Gulf of Sumar if they were not separated by Stroin Gap. They are so high that they intercept all winds. Therefore their inland slopes are barren, but the slopes facing the oceans enjoy fertility.

Mankind in Velada Borthan has carved out its domain in the two coastal strips, between the oceans and the mountains. In most places the land is at best marginal, so that we are hard put to have all the food we need, and life is constant struggle against hunger. Often one wonders why our ancestors, when they came to this planet so many generations ago, chose Velada Borthan as their settling-place; the farming would have been far easier in the neighboring continent of Sumara Borthan, and even swampy Dabis might have offered more cheer. The explanation we are given is that our forefathers were stern, diligent folk who relished challenge, and feared to let their children dwell in a place where life might be insufficiently harsh.

Velada Borthan's coasts were neither uninhabitable nor unduly comfortable; therefore they suited the purposes. I believe this to be true, for certainly the chief heritage we have from those ancient ones is the notion that comfort is sin and ease is wickedness. My bondbrother Noim, though, once remarked that the first settlers chose Velada Borthan because that was where their starship happened to come down, and, having hauled themselves across all the immensities of space, they lacked the energy to travel onward even one more continent in quest of a better home. I doubt it, but the slyness of the idea is characteristic of my bondbrother's taste for irony.

The firstcomers planted their initial settlement on the western coast, at the place we call Threish, that is, the place of the Covenant. They multiplied rapidly, and, because they were a stubborn and quarrelsome tribe, they splintered early, this group and that going off to live apart. Thus the nine western provinces came into being. To this day there are bitter border disputes among them.

In time the limited resources of the west were exhausted, and emigrants sought the eastern coast. We had no air transport then, not that we have a great deal now; we are not a mechanically minded people, and we lack natural resources to serve as fuel. Thus they went east by groundcar, or whatever served as groundcars then. The three Threishtor passes were discovered, and the bold ones bravely entered the Burnt Lowlands. We sing long mythic epics of the hardships of these crossings. Getting over the Threishtors into the Lowlands was difficult, but getting out on the far side was close to impossible, for there is only one route over the Huishtors out of the red-soil country fit for humans, and that is by way of Salla's Gate, the finding of which was no small task. But they found it and poured through, and established my land of Salla. When the quarreling came, a good many went north and founded Glin, and later others went south to settle in holy Manneran. For a thousand years it was sufficient to have but three provinces in the east, until in a new quarrel the small but prosperous maritime kingdom of Krell carved itself out of a corner of Glin and a corner of Salla.

There also were some folk who could not abide life in Velada Borthan at all, and put to sea from Manneran, sailing off to settle in Sumara Borthan. But one need not speak of them in a geography lesson; I will have much to say of Sumara Borthan and its people when I have begun to explain the changes that entered my life.

7

THIS CABIN where I hide myself now is a shabby thing. Its clapboard walls were indifferently put together to begin with, and now are crazed, so that gaps yawn at the joins and no angle is true. The desert wind passes through here unhindered; my page bears a light coating of red soil, my clothes are caked with it, even my hair has a red tinge. Lowlands creatures crawl freely in with me: I see two of them moving about the earthen floor now, a many-legged gray thing the size of my thumb and a sluggish two-tailed serpent not so long as my foot. For hours they have circled one another idly, as though they wish to be mortal foes but cannot decide which of them is to eat the other. Dry companions for a parched time.

I should not mock this place, though. Someone troubled to drag its makings here, in order that weary hunters might have shelter in this inhospitable land. Someone put it together, doubtless with more love than skill, and left it here for me, and it serves me well. Perhaps it is no fit home for a septarch's son, but I have known my share of palaces, and I no longer need stone walls and groined ceilings. It is peaceful here. I am far from the fishmongers and the drainers and the wine-peddlers and all those others whose songs of commerce clang in the streets of cities. A man can think; a man can look within his soul, and find those things that have been the shaping of him, and draw them forth, and examine them, and come to know himself. In this our world we are forbidden by custom to make our souls known to others, yes, but why has no one before me observed that that same custom, without intending it, keeps us from coming to know ourselves? For nearly all my life I kept the proper social walls between myself and others, and not till the walls were down did I see I had walled myself away from myself as well. But here in the Burnt Lowlands I have had time to contemplate these matters and to arrive at understanding. This is not the place I would have chosen for myself, but I am not unhappy here.

I do not think they will find me for some while yet.

Now it is too dark in here to write. I will stand by the cabin door and watch the night come rolling across the Lowlands toward the Huishtors. Perhaps there will be hornfowl drifting through the dusk, heading home from an empty hunt. The stars will blaze. Schweiz once tried to show me the sun of Earth from a mountaintop in Sumara Borthan, and insisted he could see it, and begged me to squint along the line of his pointing hand, but I think he was playing a game with me, I think that that sun may not be seen at all from our sector of the galaxy. Schweiz played many a game with me when we traveled together, and perhaps he will play more such games one day, if ever we meet again, if still he lives.

8

LAST NIGHT in a dream my bondsister Halum Helalam came to me.

With her there can never be more games, and only through the slippery-walled tunnel of dreams is she apt to reach me. Therefore while I slept she glowed in my mind more brightly than any star that lights this desert, but waking brought me sadness and shame, and the memory of my loss of her who is irreplaceable.

Halum of my dream wore only a light filmy veil through which her small rosy-tipped breasts showed, and her slim thighs, and her flat belly, the belly of an unchilded woman. It was not the way she often dressed in life, especially when paying a call on her bondbrother, but this was the Halum of my dream, made wanton by my lonely and troubled soul. Her smile was warm and tender and her dark shining eyes glistened with love.

In dreams one's mind lives on many levels. On one level of mine I was a detached observer, floating in a haze of moonlight somewhere near the roof of my hut, looking down upon my own sleeping body. On another level I lay asleep. The dream-self that slept did not perceive Halum's presence, but the dream-self that watched was aware of her, and I, the true dreamer, was aware of them both, and also aware that all I saw was coming to me in a vision. But inevitably there was some mingling of these levels of reality, so that I could not be sure who was the dreamer and who the dreamed, nor was I certain that the Halum who stood before me in such radiance was a creature of my fantasy rather than the living Halum I once had known.

"Kinnall," she whispered, and in my dream I imagined that my sleeping dream-self awoke, propping himself upon his elbows, with Halum kneeling close beside his cot. She leaned forward until her breasts brushed the shaggy chest of that man who was I, and touched her lips to mine in a flick of a caress, and said, "You look so weary, Kinnall."

"You should not have come here."

"One was needed. One came."

"It is not right. To enter the Burnt Lowlands alone, to seek out one who has brought you only harm—"

"The bond that links one to you is sacred."

"You've suffered enough for that bond, Halum."

"One has not suffered at all," she said, and kissed my sweaty fore-head. "How *you* must suffer, hiding in this dismal oven!"

"It is no more than one has earned," I said.

Even in my dream I spoke to Halum in the polite grammatical form. I had never found it easy to use the first person with her; certainly I never used it before my changes, and afterward, when no reason remained for me to be so chaste with her, I still could not. My soul and my heart had yearned to say "I" to Halum, and my tongue and lips were padlocked by propriety.

She said, "You deserve so much more than this place. You must come forth from exile. You must guide us, Kinnall, toward a new Covenant, a Covenant of love, of trust in one another."

"One fears he has been a failure as a prophet. One doubts the value of continuing such efforts."

"It was all so strange to you, so new!" she said. "But you were able to change, Kinnall, and to bring changes to others—"

"To bring grief to others and to oneself."

"No. No. What you tried to do was right. How can you give up now? How can you resign yourself to death? There's a world out there in need of being freed, Kinnall!"

"One is trapped in this place. One's capture is inevitable."

"The desert is wide. You can slip away from them."

"The desert is wide, but the gates are few, and all of them are watched. There's no escape."

She shook her head, and smiled, and pressed her hands urgently against my hips, and said, in a voice thick with hope, "I will lead you to safety. Come with me, Kinnall."

The sound of that *I* and the *me* that followed it, out of Halum's imagined mouth, fell upon my dreaming soul like a rainfall of rusted spikes, and the shock of hearing those obscenities in her sweet voice nearly awakened me. This thing I tell you to make it clear that I am not fully converted to my own changed way of life, that the reflexes of my upbringing still govern me in the deepest corners of my soul. In dreams we reveal our true selves, and my reaction of numb dismay to the words that I had placed (for who else could have done it?) in the dream-Halum's mouth told me a great deal about my innermost attitudes. What happened next was also revealing, though far less subtle. To urge me from my cot Halum's hands slipped over my body, working their way through the tangled thatch over my gut, and her cool fingers seized the stiffened rod of my sex. Instantly my heart thundered and my seed spurted, and the ground heaved as though the Lowlands were splitting apart, and Halum uttered a little cry of fear. I reached for her, but she was growing indistinct and insubstantial, and in one terrible convulsion of the planet I lost sight of her and she was gone. And there was so much I had wanted to say to her, so many things I had meant to ask. I woke, coming up through the levels of my dream. I found myself alone in the hut, of course, sticky-skinned with my outpourings and sickened by the villainies that my shameful mind, allowed to roam the night unfettered, had concocted.

"Halum!" I cried. "Halum, Halum, Halum!"

My voice made the cabin quiver, but she did not return. And slowly my sleep-fogged mind grasped the truth, that the Halum who had visited me had been unreal.

We of Borthan do not take such visions lightly, however. I rose, and went from my cabin into the darkness outside, and walked about, scuffing at the warm sand with my bare toes as I struggled to excuse my inventions to myself. Slowly I calmed. Slowly I came to equilibrium. Yet I sat by my doorstep unsleeping for hours, until dawn's first green fingers crept upon me.

Beyond doubt you will agree with me that a man who has been apart from women some time, living under the tensions I have known since my flight into the Burnt Lowlands, will occasionally experience such sexual eruptions in his sleep, nor is there anything unnatural about them. I must maintain also, though I have little enough evidence to prove it, that many men of Borthan find themselves giving way in slumber to expressions of desire for their bondsisters, simply because such desires are so rigidly repressed in the waking time. And further, although Halum and I enjoyed intimacies of soul far beyond those which men customarily enjoy with their bondsisters, never once did I seek her physically, nor did such a union ever occur. Take this on faith, if you will: in these pages I tell you so much that is discreditable to me, making no attempt to conceal that which is shameful, that if I had violated Halum's bond I would tell you that as well. So you must believe that it was not a deed I did. You may not hold me guilty of sins committed in dreams.

Nevertheless I held myself guilty through the waning of the night and into this morning, and only as I purge myself now by putting the incident on paper does the darkness lift from my spirit. I think what has really troubled me these past few hours is not so much my sordid little sexual fantasy, for which even my enemies would probably forgive me, as it is my belief that I am responsible for Halum's death, for which I am unable to forgive myself.

9

Possibly I should say that every man of Borthan, and by the same token every woman, is sworn at birth or soon thereafter to a bondsister and bondbrother. No member of any such tripling may be blood-kin to any other. The bondings are arranged soon after a child is conceived, and often are the subject of intricate negotiation, since one's bondbrother and bondsister are customarily closer to one than one's own family-by-blood; hence a father owes it to his child to make the bondings with care.

Because I was to be a septarch's second son, arranging my bondings was a matter of high circumstance. It might have been good democracy, but poor sense, to bond me to a peasant's child, for one must be reared on the same social plane as one's bond-kin if any profit is to come from the relationship. On the other hand I could not be bonded to the kin of some other septarch, since fate might one day elevate me to my father's throne, and a septarch must not be tangled in ties of bonding to the royal house of another district lest he find his freedom of decision circumscribed. Thus it was necessary to make bondings for me with the children of nobility but not of royalty.

The project was handled by my father's bondbrother, Ulman Kotril; it was the last aid he ever gave my father, for he was slain by bandits from Krell not long after my birth. To find a bondsister for me, Ulman Kotril went down into Manneran and obtained bonding with the unborn child of Segvord Helalam, High Justice of the Port. It had been determined that Helalam's child was to be female; hence my father's bondbrother returned to Salla and completed the tripling by compacting with Luinn Condorit, a general of the northern patrol, for his coming son.

Noim, Halum, and I were born all the same week, and my father himself performed the service of bonding. (We were known by our child-names then, of course, but I ignore that here to simplify things.) The ceremony took place in the septarch's palace, with proxies standing in for Noim and Halum; later, when we were old enough to travel, we repledged our bonds in each other's presence, I going to Manneran to be bonded to Halum. Thereafter we were only infrequently apart. Segvord Helalam had no objection to letting his daughter be raised in Salla, for he hoped she would strike a glittering marriage with some prince at my father's court. In this he was to be disappointed, for Halum went unmarried, and, for all I know, virgin, to her grave.

This scheme of bondings allows us a small escape from the constricting solitude in which we of Borthan are expected to live. You must know by now—even if you who read this be a stranger to our planet—that it has long been forbidden by custom for us to open our souls to others. To talk excessively of oneself, so our forefathers believed, leads inevitably to self-indulgence, self-pity, and self-corruption; therefore we are trained to keep ourselves to ourselves, and, so that the prisoning bands of custom may be all the more steely, we are prohibited even from using such words as "I" or "me" in polite discourse. If we have problems, we settle them in silence; if we have ambitions, we fulfill them without advertising our hopes; if we have desires, we pursue them in a selfless and impersonal way. To these harsh rules only two exceptions are made. We may speak our hearts freely to our drainers, who are religious functionaries and

23

mere hirelings; and we may, within limits, open ourselves to our bond-kin. These are the rules of the Covenant.

It is permissible to confide almost anything to a bondsister or a bondbrother, but we are taught to observe etiquette in going about it. For example, proper people consider it improper to speak in the first person even to one's bond-kin. It is not done, ever. No matter how intimate a confession we make, we must couch it in acceptable grammar, not in the vulgarities of a common self-barer.

(In our idiom a *self-barer* is one who exposes himself to others, by which is meant that he exposes his soul, not his flesh. It is deemed a coarse act and is punished by social ostracism, or worse. Self-barers use the censured pronouns of the gutter vocabulary, as I have done throughout what you now read. Although one is allowed to *bare* one's *self* to one's bond-kin, one is not a *self-barer* unless one does it in tawdry blurtings of "I" and "me.")

Also we are taught to observe reciprocity in our dealings with bond-kin. That is, we may not overload them with our woes, pouring into their ears a torrential gush of self, while failing to ease them of their own burdens. This is plain civility: the relationship depends on mutuality, and we may make use of them only if we are careful to let them make use of us. Children are often one-sided in their dealings with bond-kin; one may dominate his bondbrother, and chatter endlessly at him without pausing to heed the other's woes. But such things usually come into balance early. It is an unpardonable breach of propriety to show insufficient concern for one's bond-kin; I know no one, not even the weakest and most slovenly among us, who is guilty of that sin.

Of all the prohibitions having to do with bonding the most severe is the one against physical relationships with our bond-kin. In sexual matters we are generally quite free, only we dare not do this one thing. This struck at me most painfully. Not that I yearned for Noim, for that has never been my path, nor is it a common one among us; but Halum was my soul's desire, and neither as wife nor as mistress could she ever comfort me. Long hours we sat up together, her hand in mine, telling one another things we could tell no one else, and how easy it would have been for me to draw her close, and part her garments, and slip my throbbing flesh inside hers. I would not attempt it. My conditioning held firm; and, as I hope to survive long enough to tell you, even after Schweiz and his potion had changed my soul, still did I respect the sanctity of Halum's body, although I was able to enter her in other ways. But I will not deny my desire for her. Nor can I forget the shock I felt when I learned in boyhood that of all Borthan's women only Halum, my beloved Halum, was denied to me.

I was extraordinarily close to Halum in every but the physical way, and she was for me the ideal bondsister: open, giving, loving, serene, radiant, adaptable. Not only was she beautiful—creamy-skinned, dark-eyed and dark of hair, slender and graceful—but also she was remarkable within herself, for her soul was gentle and sleek and supple, a wondrous mixture of purity and wisdom. Thinking of her, I see the image of a forest glade in the mountains, with black-needled evergreen trees rising close together like shadowy swords springing from a bed of newly fallen snow, and a sparkling stream dancing between sun-spattered boulders, everything clean and untainted and self-contained. Sometimes when I was with her I felt impossibly thick and clumsy, a hulking lumbering mountain of dull meat, with an ugly hairy body and stupid ponderous muscles; but Halum had the skill of showing me, with a word, with a laugh, with a wink, that I was being unjust to myself when I let the sight of her lightness and gaiety lead me to wish I was woman-soft and woman-airy.

On the other side I was equally close to Noim. He was my foil in many ways: slender where I am burly, crafty where I am direct, cautious and calculating where I am rash, bleak of outlook where I am sunny. With him as with Halum I frequently felt awkward, not really in any bodily sense (for, as I have told you, I move well for a man my size) but in my inward nature. Noim, more mercurial than I, livelier, quicker of wit, seemed to leap and cavort where I merely plodded, and yet the prevailing pessimism of his spirit made him appear deeper than I as well as more buoyant. To give myself credit, Noim looked with envy on me just as I did on him. He was jealous of my great strength, and furthermore he confessed that he felt mean-souled and petty when he peered into my eyes. "One sees simplicity and power there," he admitted, "and one is aware that one often cheats, that one is lazy, that one breaks faith, that one does a dozen wicked things daily, and none of these things is any more natural to you than dining on your own flesh."

You must understand that Halum and Noim were no bond-kin to one another, and were linked only by way of their common relationship to me. Noim had a bondsister of his own, a certain Thirga, and Halum was bonded to a girl of Manneran, Nald by name. Through such ties the Covenant creates a chain that clasps our society together, for Thirga had a bondsister too, and Nald a bondbrother, and each of them was bonded in turn on the other side, and so on and so on to form a vast if not infinite series. Obviously one comes in contact often with the bond-kin of his own bond-kin, though one is not free to assume with them the same privileges one has with those of his own bonding; I frequently saw Noim's Thirga and Halum's Nald, just as Halum saw my Noim and Noim saw my Halum, but there was never anything more than nodding friendship between me and Thirga or me and Nald, while Noim and Halum took to each other with immediate warmth. Indeed I suspected for a time that they might marry one another, which would have been uncommon but not illegal. Noim, though, perceived that it would disturb me if my bondbrother shared my bondsister's bed, and took care not to let the friendship ripen into love of that sort.

Halum now sleeps forever under a stone in Manneran, and Noim has become a stranger to me, perhaps even an enemy to me, and the red sand of the Burnt Lowlands blows in my face as I set down these lines.

10

AFTER MY BROTHER STIRRON became septarch in Salla, I went, as you know, to the province of Glin. I will not say that I *fled* to Glin, for no one openly compelled me to leave my native land; but call my departure a deed of tact. I left in order to spare Stirron the eventual embarrassment of putting me to death, which would have weighed badly upon his soul. One province cannot hold safely the two sons of a late septarch.

Glin was my choice because it is customary for exiles from Salla to go to Glin, and also because my mother's family held wealth and power there. I thought, wrongly as it turned out, that I might gain some advantage from that connection.

I was about three moontimes short of the age of thirteen when I took my leave of Salla. Among us that is the threshold of manhood; I had reached almost my present height, though I was much more slender and far less strong than I would soon become, and my beard had only lately begun to grow full. I knew something of history and government, something of the arts of warfare, something of the skills of hunting, and I had had some training in the practice of the law. Already I had bedded at least a dozen girls, and three times I had known, briefly, the tempests of unhappy love. I had kept the Covenant all my life; my soul was clean and I was at peace with our gods and with my forefathers. In my own eyes at that time I must have seemed hearty, adventurous, capable, honorable, and resilient, with all the world spread before me like a shining high-way, and the future mine for the shaping. The perspective of thirty years tells me that that young man who left Salla then was also naïve, gullible, romantic, over-earnest, and conventional and clumsy of mind: quite an ordinary youth, in fact, who might have been skin-ning seapups in some fishing village had he not had the great good fortune to be born a prince.

The season of my going was early autumn, after a springtime when all Salla had mourned my father and a summer when all Salla had hailed my brother. The harvest had been poor—nothing odd in Salla, where the fields yield pebbles and stones more graciously than they do crops—and Salla City was choked with bankrupt husband-men, hoping to catch some largess from the new septarch. A dull hot haze hung over the capital day after day, and above it lay the first of autumn's heavy clouds, floating in on schedule from the eastern sea. The streets were dusty; the trees had begun to drop their leaves early, even the majestic firethorns outside the septarch's palace; the dung of the farmers' beasts clogged the gutters. These were poor omens for Salla at the beginning of a septarch's reign, and to me it seemed like a wise season for getting out. Even this early Stirron's temper was fraying and unlucky councilors of state were going off to dungeons. I still was cherished at court, coddled and complimented, plied with fur cloaks and promises of baronies in the mountains, but for how long, how long? Just now Stirron was troubled with guilt that he had inherited the throne and I had nothing, and so he treated me softly, but let the dry summer give way to a bitter winter of famine and the scales might shift; envying me my freedom from responsibility, he might well turn on me. I had studied the annals of royal houses well. Such things had happened before.

Therefore I readied myself for a hasty exit. Only Noim and Halum knew of my plans. I gathered those few of my possessions that I had no wish to abandon, such things as a ring of ceremony bequeathed by my father, a favorite hunting jerkin of yellow leather, and a double-cameo amulet bearing the portraits of my bondsister and bondbrother; all my books I relinquished, for one can get more books wherever one goes, and I did not even take the hornfowl spear, my trophy of my father's death-day, that hung in my palace bedchamber. There was to my name a fairly large amount of money, and this I handled in what I believed was a shrewd manner. It was all on deposit in the Royal Salla Bank. First I transferred the bulk of my funds to the six lesser provincial banks, over the course of many days. These new accounts were held jointly with Halum and Noim. Halum then proceeded to make withdrawals, asking that the money be paid into the Commercial and Seafarers Bank of Manneran, for the account of her father Segvord Helalam. If we were detected in this transfer, Halum was to declare that her father had undergone financial reverses and had requested a loan of short duration. Once my assets were safely on deposit in Manneran, Halum asked her father to transfer the money again, this time to an account in my name in the Covenant Bank of Glin. In this zigzag way I got my cash from Salla to Glin without arousing the suspicions of our Treasury officials, who might wonder why a prince of the realm was shipping his patrimony to our rival province of the north. The fatal flaw in all this was that if the Treasury became disturbed about the flow of capital to Manneran, questioned Halum, and then made inquiries of her father, the truth would emerge that Segvord prospered and had had no need of the "loan," which would have led to further questions and, probably, to my exposure. But my maneuvers went unnoticed.

Lastly I went before my brother to ask his permission to leave the capital, as courtly etiquette required.

This was a tense affair, for honor would not let me lie to Stirron, yet I dared not tell him the truth. Long hours I spent with Noim, first, rehearsing my deceptions. I was a slow pupil in chicanery; Noim spat, he cursed, he wept, he slapped his hands together, as time and again he slipped through my guard with a probing question. "You were not meant to be a liar," he told me in despair.

"No," I agreed, "this one never was meant to be a liar."

Stirron received me in the northern robing chamber, a dark and somber room of rough stone walls and narrow windows, used mainly for audiences with village chieftains. He meant no offense by it, I think; it was merely where he happened to be when I sent in my equerry with word that I wished a meeting. It was late afternoon; a thin greasy rain was falling outside; in some far tower of the palace a carillonneur was instructing apprentices, and leaden bell-tones, scandalously awry, came humming through the drafty walls. Stirron was formally dressed: a bulky gray robe of stormshield furs, tight red woolen leggings, high boots of green leather. The sword of the Covenant was at his side, the heavy glittering pendant of office pressed against his breast, rings of title cluttered his fingers, and if memory does not deceive me he wore yet another token of power around his right forearm. Only the crown itself was missing from his regalia. I had seen Stirron garbed this way often enough of late, at ceremonies and meetings of state, but to find him so enveloped in insignia on an ordinary afternoon struck me as almost comical. Was he so insecure that he needed to load himself with such stuff constantly, to reassure himself that he was indeed septarch? Did he feel that he had to impress his own younger brother? Or did he, child-like, take pleasure in these ornaments for pleasure's own sake? No matter which, some flaw in Stirron's character was revealed, some inner foolishness. It astounded me that I could find him amusing rather than awesome. Perhaps the genesis of my ultimate rebellion lies in that moment when I walked in on Stirron in all his splendor and had to fight to hold my laughter back.

Half a year in the septarchy had left its mark on him. His face was gray and his left eyelid drooped, I suppose from exhaustion. He held his lips tightly compressed and stood in a rigid way with one shoulder higher than the other. Though only two years separated us in age, I felt myself a boy beside him, and marveled how the cares of office can etch a young man's visage. It seemed centuries since Stirron and I had laughed together in our bedchambers, and whispered all the forbidden words, and bared our ripening bodies to one another to make the edgy comparisons of adolescence. Now I offered formal obeisance to my weary royal brother, crossing my arms over my breast and flexing my knees and bowing my head as I murmured, "Lord septarch, long life be yours."

Stirron was man enough to deflect my formality with a brotherly grin. He gave me a proper acknowledgment of my greeting, yes, arms raised and palms turned out, but then he turned it into an embrace, swiftly crossing the room and seizing me. Yet there was something artificial about his gesture, as though he had been studying how to show warmth to his brother, and quickly I was released. He wandered away from me, eyeing a nearby window, and his first words to me were, "A beastly day. A brutal year."

"The crown lies heavy, lord septarch?"

"You have leave to call your brother by his name."

"The strains show in you, Stirron. Perhaps you take Salla's problems too closely to heart."

"The people starve," he said. "Shall one pretend that is a trifling thing?"

"The people have always starved, year upon year," I said. "But if the septarch drains his soul in worry over them—"

"Enough, Kinnall. You presume." Nothing brotherly about the tone now; he was hard put to hide his irritation with me. He was plainly angered that I had so much as noticed his fatigue, though it was he who had begun our talk with lamenting. The conversation had veered too far toward the intimate. The condition of Stirron's nerves was no affair of mine: it was not my place to comfort him, he had a bondbrother for that. My attempted kindness had been improper and inappropriate. "What do you seek here?" he asked roughly.

"The lord septarch's leave to go from the capital."

He whirled away from the window and glared at me. His eyes, dull and sluggish until this moment, grew bright and harsh, and flickered disturbingly from side to side. "To go? To go where?"

"One wishes to accompany one's bondbrother Noim to the northern frontier," I said as smoothly as I could manage. "Noim pays a call on the headquarters of his father, General Luinn Condorit, whom he has not seen this year since your lordship's coronation, and one is asked to travel northward with him, for bondlove and friendship."

"When would you go?"

"Three days hence, if it please the septarch."

"And for how long a stay?" Stirron was virtually barking these questions at me.

"Until the first snow of winter falls."

"Too long. Too long."

"One might be absent then a shorter span," I said.

"Must you go at all, though?"

My right leg quivered shamefully at the knee. I struggled to be calm. "Stirron, consider that one has not left Salla City for so much as an entire day since you assumed the throne. Consider that one cannot justly ask one's bondbrother to journey uncomforted through the northern hills."

"Consider that you are the heir to the prime septarchy of Salla," Stirron said, "and that if misfortune comes to your brother while you are in the north, our dynasty is lost."

The coldness of his voice, and the ferocity with which he had questioned me a moment earlier, threw me into panic. Would he oppose my going? My fevered mind invented a dozen reasons for his hostility. He knew of my transfers of funds, and had concluded I was about to defect to Glin; or, he imagined that Noim and I, and Noim's father with his troops, would stir up an insurrection in the north, the aim being to place me on the throne; or, he had already resolved to arrest and destroy me, but the time was not yet ripe for it, and he wished not to let me get far before he could pounce; or—but I need not multiply hypotheses. We are a suspicious people on Borthan, and no one is less trusting than one who wears a crown. If Stirron would not release me from the capital, and it appeared that he would not, then I must sneak away, and I might not succeed at that.

I said, "No misfortunes are probable, Stirron, and even so, it would be no large task to return from the north if something befell you. Do you fear usurpation so seriously?"

"One fears everything, Kinnall, and leaves little to chance."

He proceeded then to lecture me on necessary caution, and on the ambitions of those who surrounded the throne, naming a few lords as possible traitors whom I would have placed among the pillars of the realm. As he spoke, going far beyond the strictures of the Covenant in exposing his uncertainties to me, I saw with amazement what a tortured, terrified man my brother had become in this short time of septarchy; and I realized, too, that I was not going to be granted my leave. He went on and on, fidgeting as he spoke, rubbing his talismans of authority, several times picking up his scepter from where it lay on an ancient wood-topped table, walking to the window and coming back from it, pitching his voice now low and now high as though searching for the best septarchical resonances. I was frightened for him. He was a man of my own considerable size, and at that time much thicker in body and greater in strength than I, and all my life I had worshiped him and modeled myself upon him; and here he was corroded with terror and committing the sin of *telling me about it.* Had just these few moontimes of supreme power brought Stirron to this collapse? Was the loneliness of the septarchy that awful for him? On Borthan we are born lonely, and lonely we live, and lonely we die; why should wearing a crown be so much more difficult than bearing the burdens we inflict upon ourselves each day? Stirron told me of assassins' plots and of revolution brewing among the farmers who thronged the town, and even hinted that our father's death had been no accident. I tried to persuade myself that hornfowl could be trained to slay a particular man in a group of thirteen men, and would not swallow the notion. It appeared that royal responsibilities had driven Stirron mad. I was reminded of a duke some years back who displeased my father, and was sent for half a year to a dungeon, and tortured each day that the sun could be seen. He had entered prison a sturdy and vigorous figure, and when he emerged he was so ruined that he befouled his own clothes with his dung, and did not know it. How soon would Stirron be brought to that? Perhaps it was just as well, I thought, that he was refusing me permission to go away, for it might be better that I remain at the capital, ready to take his place if he crumbled beyond repair.

But he amazed me at the finish of his rambling oration; for it had taken him clear across the room, to an alcove hung with dangling silver chains, and at the end, suddenly bunching the chains and yanking a dozen of them from their mountings, he swung round to face me and cried hoarsely, "Give your pledge, Kinnall, that you will come back from the north in time to attend the royal wedding!"

I was doubly pronged. For the last several minutes I had begun to make plans on the basis of staying in Salla City; now I found I could depart after all, and was not sure I should, in view of Stirron's deterioration. And then too he demanded from me a promise of swift return, and how could I give the septarch such a promise without lying to him, a sin I was not prepared to commit? So far all that I had told him was the truth, though only part of the truth; I *did* plan to travel north with Noim to visit his father, I *would* remain in northern Salla until winter's first snow. How though could I set a date for my coming back to the capital?

My brother was due to marry, forty days hence, the youngest daughter of Bryggil, septarch of Salla's southeastern district. It was a cunning match. So far as the traditional order of primacy went, Bryggil stood seventh and lowest in the hierarchy of Salla's septarchs, but he was the oldest, the cleverest, and the most respected of the seven, now that my father was gone. To combine Bryggil's shrewdness and stature with the prestige that accrued to Stirron by virtue of his rank as prime septarch would be to cement the dynasty of our family to the throne. And no doubt sons shortly would come marching out of Bryggil's daughter's loins, relieving me of my position as heir apparent: her fertility must have passed the necessary tests, and of Stirron's there could be no question, since he had already scattered a litter of bastards all over Salla. I would have certain ceremonial roles to play at the wedding as brother to the septarch.

I had wholly forgotten the wedding. If I skipped out of Salla before it came about, I would wound my brother in a way that saddened me. But if I stayed here, with Stirron in this unstable state, I had no guarantee of being a free man when the nuptial day arrived, or even of still owning my head. Nor was there any sense in going north with Noim if I bound myself to return in forty days. It was a hard choice: to postpone my departure and run the risks of my brother's royal whims, or to leave now, knowing I was taking on myself the stain of breaking a pledge to my septarch.

The Covenant teaches us that we should welcome dilemmas, for it toughens character to grapple with the insoluble and find a solution. In this instance events made a mockery of the Covenant's lofty moral teachings. As I hesitated in anguish, Stirron's telephone summoned him; he snatched its handpiece, jabbed at the scrambler, and listened to five minutes of gibberish, his face darkening and his eyes growing fiery. At length he broke the contact and peered up at me as though I were a stranger to him. "They are eating the flesh of the newly dead in Spoksa," he muttered. "On the slopes of the Kongoroi they dance to demons in hopes of finding food. Insanity! Insanity!" He clenched his fists and strode to the window, and thrust his face to it, and closed his eyes, and I think forgot my presence for a time. Again the telephone asked for him. Stirron jerked back like one who has been stabbed, and started toward the machine. Noticing me standing frozen near the door, he fluttered his hands impatiently at me and said, "Go, will you? Off with your bond-brother, wherever you go. This province! This famine! Father, father, father!" He seized the handpiece. I started to offer a genuflection of parting, and Stirron furiously waved me from the room, sending me unpledged and unchecked toward the borders of his realm.

11

NOIM AND I set forth three days afterward, just the two of us and a small contingent of servants. The weather was bad, for summer's dryness had given way not merely to the thick dreary gray clouds of autumn but to a foresampling of winter's heavy rains. "You'll be dead of the mildew before you see Glin," Halum told us cheerfully. "If you don't drown in the mud of the Grand Salla Highway."

She stayed with us, at Noim's house, on the eve of our departure, sleeping chastely apart in the little chamber just under the roof, and joined us for breakfast as we made ready to go. I had never seen her looking lovelier; that morning she wore a bloom of shimmering beauty that cut through the murk of the drizzly dawn like a torch in a cave. Perhaps what enhanced her so greatly then was that she was about to pass from my life for an unknown length of time, and, conscious of my self-inflicted loss, I magnified her attractiveness. She was clad in a gown of delicate golden chainmesh, beneath which only a gossamer wrap concealed her naked form, and her body, shifting this way and that under its flimsy coverings, aroused in me thoughts that left me drenched in shame. Halum then was in the ripeness of early womanhood, and had been for several years; it had already begun to puzzle me that she remained unwed. Though she and Noim and I were of the same age, she had leaped free of childhood before us, as girls will do, and I had come to think of her as older than the two of us, because for a year she had had breasts and the monthly flow, while Noim and I were still without hair on cheek or body. And while we had caught up to her in physical maturity, she was still more adult in her bearing than my bondbrother or I, her voice more smoothly modulated, her manner more poised, and it was impossible for me to shake off that notion that she was senior sister to us. Who soon must accept some suitor, lest she become overripe and sour in her maidenhood; I was suddenly certain that Halum would marry while I was off hiding in Glin, and the thought of some sweaty stranger planting babies between her thighs so sickened me that I turned away from her at the table, and lurched to the window to gulp the humid air into my throbbing lungs.

"Are you unwell?" Halum asked.

"One feels a certain tension, bondsister."

"Surely there's no danger. The septarch's permission has been granted for you to go north."

"There is no document to show it," Noim pointed out.

"You are a septarch's son!" Halum cried. "What guardian of the roads would dare to trifle with you?"

"Exactly," I said. "There is no cause for fear. One feels only a sense of uncertainty. One is beginning a new life, Halum." I forced a faint smile. "The time of going must be here."

"Stay a while longer," Halum begged.

But we did not. The servants waited in the street. The groundcars were ready. Halum embraced us, clasping Noim first, then me, for I was the one who would not be returning, and that called for a longer farewell. When she came into my arms I was stunned by the intensity with which she offered herself: her lips to my lips, her belly to my belly, her breasts crushed against my chest. On tiptoes she strained to press her body into mine, and for a moment I felt her trembling, until I began myself to tremble. It was not a sisterly kiss and certainly not a bondsisterly kiss; it was the passionate kiss of a bride sending her young husband off to a war from which she knows there is no coming back. I was singed by Halum's sudden fire. I felt as though a veil had been ripped away and some Halum I had not known before had flung herself against me, one who burned with the needs of the flesh, one who did not mind revealing her forbidden hunger for a bondbrother's body. Or did I imagine those things in her? It seemed to me that for a single protracted instant Halum repressed nothing and allowed her arms and lips to tell me the truth about her feelings; but I could not respond in kind—I had trained myself too well in the proper attitudes toward one's bondsister—and I was distant and cool as I clasped her. I may even have thrust her back a little, shocked by her forwardness. And, as I say, there may have been no forwardness at all except in my overwrought mind, but only legitimate grief at a parting. In any event the intensity went quickly from Halum; her embrace slackened and she released me, and she appeared downcast and chilled, as if I had rebuffed her cruelly by being so prim when she was giving so much.

"Come, now," Noim said impatiently, and, trying somehow to rescue the situation, I lifted Halum's hand and touched my palm lightly to her cool palm, and smiled an awkward smile, and she smiled even more awkwardly, and perhaps we would have said a stumbling word or two, but Noim caught me by the elbow and stolidly led me outside to begin my journey away from my homeland.

12

I INSISTED on opening myself to a drainer before leaving Salla City. I had not planned on doing so, and it irritated Noim that I took the time for it; but an uncontrollable yearning for the comforts of religion rose up in me as we neared the outskirts of the capital.

We had been traveling almost an hour. The rain had thickened, and gusty winds slammed it against the windscreens of our ground-cars, so that cautious driving was in order. The cobbled streets were slippery. Noim drove one of the cars, I sitting sullenly beside him; the other, with our servants, followed close behind. The morning was young and the city still slept. Each passing street was a surgery to me, for a segment of my life was ripped off by it: there goes the palace compound, there go the spires of the House of Justice, there the university's great gray blocky buildings, there the godhouse where my royal father brought me into the Covenant, there the Museum of Mankind that I visited so often with my mother to stare at the treasures from the stars. Circling through the fine residential district that borders the Skangen Canal, I even spied the ornate townhouse of the Duke of Kongoroi, on whose handsome daughter's silken bedsheets I had left my virginity in a clammy puddle, not too many years before. In this city I had lived all my life, and I might never see it again; my yesterdays were washing away, like the topsoil of Salla's sad farms under the knives of the winter rains. Since boyhood I had known that one day my brother would be septarch and this city would cease to have a place for me, but yet I had denied that to myself, saying, "It will not happen soon, perhaps it will not happen at all." And my father lay dead in his firethorn coffin, and my brother crouched beneath the awful weight of his crown, and I was fleeing from Salla before my life had fairly begun, and such a mood of self-pity came over me that I did not dare even to speak to Noim, though what is a bondbrother for if not to ease one's soul? And when we were driving through the ramshackle streets of Salla Old Town, not far from the city walls, I spied a dilapidated godhouse and said to Noim, "Pull up at the corner here. One must go within to empty himself."

Noim, fretful, did not want to spare the time, and made as if to drive on. "Would you deny one the godright?" I asked him hotly, and only then, simmering and cross, did he halt the car and back it up to let me out by the godhouse.

Its façade was worn and peeling. An inscription beside the door was illegible. The pavement before it was cracked and tilted. Salla Old Town has a pedigree of more than a thousand years; some of its buildings have been continuously inhabited since the founding of the city, though most are in ruins, for the life of that district ended, in effect, when one of the medieval septarchs chose to move his court to our present palace atop Skangen Hill, much to the south. At night Salla Old Town comes alive with pleasure-seekers, who guzzle the blue wine in cellar cabarets, but at this misty hour it was a grim place. Blank stone walls faced me from every building: we have a fashion of making mere slits serve for windows in Salla, but here they carried it to an extreme. I wondered if the godhouse could have a scanning machine in working order to watch my approach. Yes, as it happened. When I neared the godhouse door, it swung partly open, and a scrawny man in drainer's robes looked out. He was ugly, of course. Who ever saw a handsome drainer? It is a profession for the ill-favored. This one had greenish skin, heavily pocked, and a rubbery snout of a nose, and a dimness in one eye: standard for his trade. He gave me a fishy stare and, by his wariness, seemed to be regretting having opened the door.

"The peace of all gods be on you," I said. "Here is one in need of your craft."

He eyed my costly costume, my leather jerkin and my heavy jewelry, and studied the size and swagger of me, and evidently concluded I was some young bully of the aristocracy out to stir trouble in the slums. "It is too early in the day," he said uneasily. "You come too soon for comfort."

"You would not refuse a sufferer!"

"It is too early."

"Come, come, let one in. A troubled soul stands here."

He yielded, as I knew he must, and with many a twitch of his long-nosed face he admitted me. Within there was the reek of rot. The old woodwork was impregnated with the damp, the draperies were moldering, the furniture had been gnawed by insects. The lighting was dim. The drainer's wife, as ugly as the drainer himself, skulked about. He led me to his chapel, a small sweaty room off the living-quarters, and left me kneeling by the cracked and yellowing mirror while he lit the candles. He robed himself and finally came to me where I knelt.

He named his fee. I gasped.

"Too much by half," I said.

He reduced it by a fifth. When I still refused, he told me to find my priesting elsewhere, but I would not rise, and, grudgingly, he brought the price of his services down another notch. Still it was probably five times what he charged the folk of Salla Old Town for the same benefit, but he knew I had money, and, thinking of Noim fuming in the car, I could not bring myself to haggle.

"Done," I said.

Next he brought me the contract. I have said that we of Borthan are suspicious people; have I indicated how we rely on contracts? A man's word is merely bad air. Before a soldier beds a whore they come to the terms of their bargain and scrawl it on paper. The drainer gave me a standard form, promising me that all I said would be held in strictest confidence, the drainer merely acting as intermediary between me and the god of my choice, and I for my part pledging that I would hold the drainer to no liability for the knowledge he would have of me, that I would not call him as witness in a lawsuit or make him my alibi in some prosecution, et cetera, et cetera. I signed. He signed. We exchanged copies and I gave him his money.

"Which god would you have preside here?" he asked.

"The god who protects travelers," I told him. We do not call our gods aloud by their names.

He lit a candle of the appropriate color—pink—and put it beside the mirror. By that it was understood that the chosen god would accept my words.

"Behold your face," the drainer said. "Put your eyes to your eyes."

I stared at the mirror. Since we shun vanity, it is not usual to examine one's face except on these occasions of religion.

"Open now your soul," the drainer commanded. "Let your griefs and dreams and hungers and sorrows emerge."

"A septarch's son it is who flees his homeland," I began, and at once the drainer jerked to attention, impaled by my news. Though I did not take my eyes from the mirror, I guessed that he was scrabbling around to look at the contract and see who it was that had signed it. "Fear of his brother," I continued, "leads him to go abroad, but yet he is sore of soul as he departs."

I went on in that vein for some while. The drainer made the usual interjections every time I faltered, prying words out of me in his craft's cunning way, and shortly there was no need for such midwifery, for the words gushed freely. I told him of my desire for my bondsister and how her embrace had unsettled me; I told him how close I had come to lying to Stirron; I confessed that I would miss the royal wedding and give my brother injury thereby; I admitted several small sins of self-esteem, such as anyone commits daily.

The drainer listened.

We pay them to listen and to do nothing but listen, until we are drained and healed. Such is our holy communion, that we lift these toads from the mud, and set them up in their godhouses, and buy their patience with our money. It is permitted under the Covenant to say anything to a drainer, even if it is drivel, even if it is a shameful catalog of throttled lusts and hidden filth. We may bore a drainer as we have no right to bore our bond-kin, for it is the drainer's obligation by contract to sit with the patience of the hills as we speak of ourselves. We need not worry what the drainer's problems may be, nor what he thinks of us, nor whether he would be happier doing something else. He has his calling and he takes his fee, and he must serve those who have need of him. There was a time when I felt it was a miraculously fine scheme, to give us drainers in order that we might rid our hearts of pain. Too much of my life was gone before I realized that to open oneself to a drainer is no more comforting than to make love to one's own hand: there are better ways of loving, there are happier ways of opening.

But I did not know that then, and I squatted by the mirror, getting the best healing that money could buy. Whatever residue of wrongness was in my soul came forth, syllable smoothly following syllable, the way sweet liquor will flow when one taps the thorny flanks of the gnarled and repellent-looking flesh-trees that grow by the Gulf of Sumar. As I spoke the candles caught me in their spell, and by the flickering of them I was drawn into the curved surface of the mirror so that I was drawn out of myself; the drainer was a mere blur in the darkness, unreal, unimportant, and I spoke now directly to the god of travelers, who would heal me and send me on my way. And I believed that this was so. I will not say that I imagined a literal god-place where our deities sit on call to serve us, but I had then an abstract and metaphorical understanding of our religion by which it seemed to me, in its way, as real as my right arm.

My flow of words halted and the drainer made no attempt to renew the outpour. He murmured the phrases of absolution. I was done. He snuffed the god-candle between two fingers and rose to doff his robes. Still I knelt, weak and quivering from my draining, lost in reveries. I felt cleansed and purified, stripped of my soul's grit and debris, and, in the music of that moment, was only dimly aware of the squalor about me. The chapel was a place of magic and the drainer was aflame with divine beauty.

"Up," he said, nudging me with the tip of his sandal. "Out. Off about your journeys."

The sound of his splintery voice doused all the wonder. I stood up, shaking my head to cure it of its new lightness, while the drainer half pushed me into the corridor. He was no longer afraid of me, that ugly little man, even though I might be a septarch's son and could kill him with one wad of my spittle, for I had told him of my cowardice, of my forbidden hunger for Halum, of all the cheapnesses of my spirit, and that knowledge reduced me in his eyes: no man newly drained can awe his drainer.

The rain was even worse when I left the building. Noim sat scowling in the car, his forehead pressed to the steering-stick. He looked up and tapped his wrist to tell me I had dallied too long at the godhouse.

"Feel better now that your bladder's empty?" he asked.

"What?"

"That is, did you have a good soul-pissing in there?"

"A foul phrase, Noim."

"One grows blasphemous when his patience is extended too far."

He kicked the starter and we rolled forward. Shortly we were at the ancient walls of Salla City, by the noble tower-bedecked opening known as Glin Door, which was guarded by four sour-faced and sleepy warriors in dripping uniforms. They paid no heed to us. Noim drove through the gate and past a sign welcoming us to the Grand Salla Highway. Salla City dwindled swiftly behind us; northward we rushed toward Glin.

13

THE GRAND SALLA HIGHWAY passes through one of our best farming districts, the rich and fertile Plain of Nand, which each spring receives a gift of topsoil stripped from the skin of West Salla by our busy streams. At that time the septarch of the Nand district was a notorious coinclutcher, and thanks to his penury the highway was in poor repair there, so, as Halum had predicted in jest, we were hard put to wallow through the mud that clogged the road. It was good to finish with Nand and enter North Salla, where the land is a mixture of rock and sand and the people live on weeds and on scuttling things that they take from the sea. Groundcars are unusual sights in North Salla, and twice we were stoned by hungry and sullen townsfolk, who found our mere passage through their unhappy place an insult. But at least the road was free of mud.

Noim's father's troops were stationed in extreme North Salla, on the lower bank of the River Huish. This is the grandest of Velada Borthan's rivers. It begins as a hundred trifling brooks trickling down the eastern slopes of the Huishtors in the northern part of West Salla; these brooks merge in the foothills to become a swift stream, gray and turbulent, that rushes through a narrow granite canyon marked by six great steplike plunges. Emerging from those wild cascades onto its alluvial plain, the Huish proceeds more serenely on a northeastern course toward the sea, growing wider and wider in the flatlands, and splitting ultimately so that, at its broad delta, it gives itself to the ocean through eight mouths. In its rapid western reaches the Huish forms the boundary between Salla and Glin; at its placid easternmost end it divides Glin from Krell.

For all its length the great river is unbridged, and one might think little need exists to fortify its banks against invaders from the far side. But many times in Salla's history have the men of Glin crossed the Huish by boat to make war, and just as many times have we of Salla gone to ravage Glin; nor is the record of neighborliness between Glin and Krell any happier. So all along the Huish sprout military outposts, and generals like Luinn Condorit consume their lives studying the riverfogs for glimpses of the enemy.

I stayed a short while at Noim's father's camp. The general was not much like Noim, being a large-featured, heavy man whose face, eroded by time and frustration, was like a contour map of bouldery North Salla. Not once in fifteen years had there been any significant clash along the border he guarded, and I think that idleness had chilled his soul: he said little, scowled often, turned every statement into a bitter grumble, and retreated speedily from conversation into private dreams. They must have been dreams of war; no doubt he could not glance at the river without wishing that it swarmed with the landing-craft of Glin. Since men like him surely patrol the Glin side of the river as well, it is a wonder that the border guards do not trespass on one another out of sheer boredom, every few years, and embroil our provinces in pointless conflict.

A dull time we had of it there. Noim was bound by filial ties to call upon his father, but they had nothing to say to one another, and the general was a stranger to me. I had told Stirron I would stay with Noim's father until the first snow of winter fell, and I was true to that, yet luckily it was no lengthy visit I made; winter comes early in the north. On my fifth day there white sprinkles fluttered down and I was released from my self-imposed pledge.

Ferries, shuttling between terminals in three places, link Salla to Glin except when there is war. Noim drove me to the nearest terminal one black dawn, and solemnly we embraced and made our farewells. I said I would send my address, when I had one in Glin, so that he could keep me informed of doings in Salla. He promised to look after Halum. We talked vaguely of when he and she and I would meet again; perhaps they would visit me in Glin next year, perhaps we would all three go on holiday in Manneran. We made these plans with little conviction in our voices.

"This day of parting should never have come," Noim said.

"Partings lead only to reunions," I told him jauntily.

"Perhaps you could have come to some understanding with your brother, Kinnall—"

"There was never hope of that."

"Stirron has spoken warmly of you. Is he then insincere?"

"He means his warmth, just now. But it would not be long before it became inconvenient for him to have a brother dwelling by his side, and then embarrassing, and then impossible. A septarch sleeps best when there is no potential rival of the royal blood close at hand."

The ferry beckoned me with a bellow of its horn.

I clasped Noim's arm and we made farewells again, hurriedly. The last thing I said to him was, "When you see the septarch, tell him that his brother loves him." Then I went aboard.

The crossing was too quick. Less than an hour and I found myself on the alien soil of Glin. The immigration officials examined me brusquely, but they thawed at the sight of my passport, bright red to denote my place in the nobility, with a golden stripe to show that I was of the septarch's family. At once I had my visa, good for an indefinite stay. Such officials are a gossipy sort; beyond question they were on the telephone the instant I left them, sending word to their government that a prince of Salla was in the land, and I suppose that not much later that bit of information was in the hands of Salla's diplomatic representatives in Glin, who would relay it to my brother for his displeasure.

Across the way from the customs shed I came upon a branch of the Covenant Bank of Glin, and changed my Salla money for the currency of the northerners. With my new funds I hired a driver to take me to the capital city, which they call Glain, half a day's journey north of the border.

The road was narrow and winding, and traversed a bleak countryside where winter's touch had long ago pulled the leaves from the trees. Dirty snow was banked high. Glin is a frosty province. It was settled by men of a puritan nature, who found the living too easy in Salla, and felt that if they remained there, they might be tempted away from the Covenant; failing to reform our forefathers into greater piety, they left, crossing the Huish by rafts to hack out a livelihood in the north. Hard folk for a hard land; however poor the farming is in Salla, it is twice as unrewarding in Glin, and they live there mainly by fishing, by manufacturing, by the jugglements of commercial dealings, and by piracy. But that my mother had sprung from Glin, I would never have chosen it for my place of exile. Not that I gained anything from my family ties.

14

Nightfall saw me in Glain. A walled city it is, like Salla's capital, but otherwise not much like it. Salla City has grace and power; its buildings are made of great blocks of substantial stone, black basalt and rosy granite quarried in the mountains, and its streets are wide and sweeping, affording noble vistas and splendid promenades. Apart from our custom of letting narrow slits stand in place of true windows, Salla City is an open, inviting place, the architecture of which announces to the world the boldness and self-sufficiency of its citizens. But that dismal Glain! Oh!

Glain is fashioned of scruffy yellow brick, here and there trimmed with miserable poor pink sandstone that rubs to particles at a finger's nudge. It has no streets, only alleyways; the houses jostle one another as if afraid that some interloper may try to slip between them if they relax their guard. An avenue in Glain would not impress a gutter in Salla. And the architects of Glain have created a city fit only for a nation of drainers, since everything is lopsided, awry, uneven, and coarse. My brother, who had once been to Glain on a diplomatic errand, had described the place to me, but I put his harsh words off to mere patriotic prejudice; now I saw that Stirron had been too kind.

Nor were the folk of Glain more lovely than their city. On a world where suspicion and secrecy are godly virtues, one expects to find charm in short supply; yet I found the Glainish virtuous beyond all necessity. Dark clothes, dark frowns, dark souls, closed and shrunken hearts. Their speech itself displays their constipation of spirit. The language of Glin is the same as that of Salla, though the northerners have pronounced accents, clipping their syllables and shifting their vowels. That did not disturb me, but their syntax of self-effacement did. My driver, who was not a city man and therefore seemed almost friendly, left me at a hostelry where he thought I would have kind treatment, and I entered and said, "One would have a room for tonight, and for some days beyond this one, perhaps." The innkeeper stared balefully at me as if I had said, "I would have a room," or something equally filthy. Later I discovered that even our usual

44

polite circumlocution seems too vain for a northerner; I should not have said, "One would have a room," but rather, "Is there a room to be had?" At a restaurant it is wrong to say, "One will dine on thus and thus," but rather, "These are the dishes that have been chosen." And so on and so on, twisting everything into a cumbersome passive form to avoid the sin of acknowledging one's own existence.

For my ignorance the innkeeper gave me his meanest room, and charged me twice the usual tariff. By my speech I had branded myself a man of Salla; why should he be courteous? But in signing the contract for my night's lodgings I had to show him my passport, which made him gasp when he saw that he was host to a visiting prince; he softened more than a little, asking me if I would have wine sent to my room, or maybe a buxom Glainish wench. I took the wine but declined the wench, for I was very young and overly frightened of the diseases that might lurk in foreign loins. That night I sat alone in my room, watching snowflakes drowning in a murky canal below my window, and feeling more isolated from humanity than ever before, ever since.

15

OVER A WEEK PASSED before I found the courage to call upon my mother's kin. I strolled the city for hours every day, keeping my cloak wrapped close against the winds and marveling at the ugliness of all I beheld, people and structures. I located the embassy of Salla, and lurked outside it, not wishing to go in but merely cherishing the link to my homeland that the squat grim building provided. I bought heaps of cheaply printed books and read far into the night to learn something of my adopted province: there was a history of Glin, and a guidebook to the city of Glain, and an interminable epic poem dealing with the founding of the first settlements north of the Huish, and much else. I dissolved my loneliness in wine—not the wine of Glin, for none is made there, but rather the good sweet golden wine of Manneran, that they import in giant casks. I slept poorly. One night I dreamed that Stirron had died of a fit and a search was being made for me. Several times in my sleep I saw the hornfowl strike my father dead; this is a dream that still haunts me, coming twice or thrice a year. I wrote long letters to Halum and Noim, and tore them up, for they stank of self-pity. I wrote one to Stirron, begging him to forgive me for fleeing, and tore that up too. When all else failed, I asked the innkeeper for a wench. He sent me a skinny girl a year or two older than I, with odd large breasts that dangled like inflated rubber bags. "It is said you are a prince of Salla," she declared coyly, lying down and parting her thighs. Without replying I covered her and thrust myself into her, and the size of my organ made her squeal with fear and pleasure both, and she wriggled her hips so fiercely that my seed burst from me within half a moment. I was angered at myself for that, and turned my wrath on her, pulling free and shouting, "Who told you to start moving? I wasn't ready to have you move! I didn't want you to!" She ran from my room still naked, terrified more, I think, by my obscenities than by my wrath. I had never said "I" in front of a woman before. But she was only a whore, after all. I soaped myself for an hour afterward. In my naïveté I feared that the innkeeper would evict me for speaking so vulgarly to her, but he said nothing. Even in Glin, one need not be polite to whores.

I realized that there had been a strange pleasure in shouting those words at her. I yielded to curious reveries of fantasy, in which I imagined the big-breasted slut naked on my bed, while I stood over her crying, "I! I! I! I! I!" Such daydreams had the power to make my maleness stand tall. I considered going to a drainer to get rid of the dirty notion, but instead, two nights later, I asked the innkeeper for another wench, and with each jab of my body I silently cried "I! Me! I! Me!"

Thus I spent my patrimony in the capital of puritan Glin, wenching and drinking and loitering. When the stench of my own idleness offended me, I put down my timidity and went to see my Glainish relatives.

My mother had been a daughter of a prime septarch of Glin; he was dead, as was his son and successor; now his son's son, Truis, my mother's nephew, held the throne. It seemed too forward to me to go seeking preferment from my royal cousin directly. Truis of Glin would have to weigh matters of state as well as matters of kinship, and might not want to aid the runaway brother of Salla's prime septarch, lest it lead him into friction with Stirron. But I had an aunt, Nioll, my mother's younger sister, who had often been in Salla City in my mother's lifetime, and who had held me fondly when I was a babe; would she not help me?

She had married power to power. Her husband was the Marquis of Huish, who held great influence at the septarch's court, and also —for in Glin it is not thought unseemly for the nobility to dabble in commerce—controlled his province's wealthiest factor-house. These factor-houses are something akin to banks, but of another species; they lend money to brigands and merchants and lords of industry, only at ruinous rates, and always taking a slice of ownership in any enterprise they aid; thus they insinuate their tentacles into a hundred organizations and attain immense leverage in economic matters. In Salla the factor-houses were forbidden a century ago, but in Glin they thrive almost as a second government. I had no love for the system, but I preferred joining it to begging.

Some inquiries at the inn gained me directions to the palace of the marquis. By Glainish standards it was an imposing structure of three interlocking wings beside a mirror-smooth artificial lake, in the aristocrats' sector of the city. I made no attempt to talk my way inside; I had come prepared with a note, informing the marquise that her nephew Kinnall, the septarch's son of Salla, was in Glain and wished the favor of an audience; he could be found at such-and-such a hostelry. I returned to my lodgings and waited, and on the third day the innkeeper, popeyed with awe, came to my room to tell me I had a visitor in the livery of the Marquis of Huish. Nioll had sent a car for me; I was taken to her palace, which was far more lavish within than without, and she received me in a great hall cunningly paneled with mirrors set at angles to other mirrors to create an illusion of infinity.

She had aged greatly in the six or seven years since I last had seen her, but my amazement at her white hair and furrowed face was swallowed up in her astonishment over my transformation from tiny child to hulking man in so short a time. We embraced in the style of Glin, fingertips to fingertips; she offered condolences on the death of my father, and apologies for not having attended Stirron's coronation; then she asked me what brought me to Glin, and I explained, and she showed no surprise. Did I propose to dwell permanently here? I did, I said. And how would I support myself? By working in the factor-house of her husband, I explained, if such a position could be procured for me. She did not act as though she found my ambition unreasonable, but merely asked if I had any skills that might recommend me to the marquis. To this I replied that I had been trained in the lawcodes of Salla (not mentioning how incomplete my training was) and might be of value in the factor-house's dealings with that province; also, I said, I had connections of bonding to Segvord Helalam, High Justice of the Port in Manneran, and could serve the firm well in its Manneran business; lastly, I remarked, I was young and strong and ambitious, and would place myself wholly in the service of the factor-house's interests, for our mutual advantage. These statements seemed to sit smoothly with my aunt, and she promised to gain for me an interview with the marquis himself. I left her palace much pleased with my prospects.

Several days later came word to the hostelry that I should present myself at the offices of the factor-house. My appointment, however, was not with the Marquis of Huish; rather, I was to see one of his executives, a certain Sisgar. I should have taken that as an omen. This man was smooth to the point of oiliness, with a beardless face and no eyebrows and a bald head that looked as if it had been waxed, and a dark green robe that was at once properly austere and subtly ostentatious. He questioned me briefly about my training and experience, discovering in some ten queries that I had had little of the former and none of the latter; but he exposed my failings in a gentle and amiable way, and I assumed that despite my ignorance, my high birth and kinship to the marquise would gain me a post. Alas for complacency! I had begun to hatch a dream of climbing to great responsibilities in this factor-house when I caught with only half an ear the words of Sisgar, telling me, "Times are hard, as surely your grace comprehends, and it is unfortunate that you come to us at a time when retrenching is necessary. The advantages of giving you employment are many, yet the problems are extreme. The marquis wishes you to know that your offer of service was greatly appreciated, and it is his hope to bring you into the firm when economic conditions permit." With many bows and a pleasant smile of dismissal he drove me from his office, and I was on the street before I realized how thoroughly I had been destroyed. They could give me nothing, not even a fifth assistant clerkship in some village office! How was this possible? I nearly rushed back within, planning to cry, "This is a mistake, you deal with your septarch's cousin here, you reject the nephew of the marquise!" But they knew those things, and yet they shut their doors to me. When I telephoned my aunt to express my shock, I was told that she had gone abroad, to pass the winter in leafy Manneran.

16

EVENTUALLY what had occurred became clear to me. My aunt had spoken of me to the marquis, and the marquis had conferred with the septarch Truis, who, concluding that it might embarrass him with Stirron to allow me any kind of employ, instructed the marquis to turn me away. In my fury I thought of going straight to Truis to protest, but I saw the futility of that soon enough, and since my protector Nioll had plainly gone out of Glin to shake herself free of me, I knew there was no hope in that direction. I was alone in Glain with the winter coming on, and no position in this alien place, and my lofty birth worse than useless to me.

Harder blows followed.

Presenting myself at the Covenant Bank of Glin one morning to withdraw funds for living expenses, I learned that my account had been sequestered at the request of the Grand Treasurer of Salla, who was investigating the possibility of an illegal transfer of capital out of that province. By blustering and waving my royal passport about, I managed to break loose enough money for seven days' food and lodging, but the rest of my savings was lost to me, for I had no stomach for the kind of appeals and maneuvers that might free it.

Next I was visited at my hostelry by a diplomat of Salla, a jackal of an undersecretary who reminded me, with many a genuflection and formula of respect, that my brother's wedding would shortly take place and I was expected to return and serve as ring-linker. Knowing that I would never leave Salla City again if ever I gave myself into Stirron's hands, I explained that urgent business required me to remain in Glain during the season of the nuptials, and asked that my deep regrets be conveyed to the septarch. The undersecretary received this with professional grace, but it was not hard for me to detect the savage gleam of pleasure beneath his outer mask: I was buying me trouble, he was telling himself, and he would gladly help me close the contract.

On the fourth day thereafter my innkeeper came to tell me that I could no longer stay at the hostelry, for my passport had been revoked and I had no legal status in Glin.

This was an impossibility. A royal passport such as I carried is granted for life, and is valid in every province of Velada Borthan except in times of war, and there was no war at the moment between Salla and Glin. The innkeeper shrugged away my words; he showed me his notice from the police, ordering him to evict his illegal alien, and he suggested that if I had objections I should take the matter up with the appropriate bureau of the Glinish civil service, for it was beyond his scope. I regarded filing such an appeal as unwise. My eviction had not come about by accident, and should I appear at any government office I was likely to find myself arrested and hustled across the Huish into Stirron's grasp forthwith.

Seeing such an arrest as the most probable next development, I wondered how to elude the government agents. Now I sorely felt the absence of my bondbrother and bondsister, for where else could I turn for help and advice? Nowhere in Glin was there anyone to whom I might say, "One is frightened, one is in grave peril, one asks assistance of you." Everyone's soul was walled against me by stony custom. In all the world were only two whom I could regard as confidants, and they were far away. I must find my own salvation.

I would go into hiding, I decided. The innkeeper granted me a few hours to prepare myself. I shaved my beard, traded my royal cloak for the dim rags of another lodger nearly my height, and arranged the pawn of my ring of ceremony. My remaining possessions I bundled together to serve as a hump on my back, and I hobbled out of the hostelry doubled up, with one eye sealed shut and my mouth twisted far around to one side. Whether it was a disguise that could have fooled anyone, I cannot say; but no one waited to arrest me, and thus uglified I walked out of Glain under a cold, thin rain that soon turned to snow.

17

Outside the city's northwestern gate (for it was there my feet had taken me) a heavy truck came rumbling by me, and its treads rolled through a pool of half-frozen slush, spraying me liberally. I halted to scrape the chilly stuff from my leggings; the truck halted too, and the driver clambered down, exclaiming, "There is cause for apology here. It was not intended to douse you so!"

This courtesy so astounded me that I stood to my full height, and let the distortions slip from my features. Evidently the driver had thought me a feeble, bent old man; he showed amazement at my transformation, and laughed aloud. I knew not what to say. Into my gaping silence he declared, "There is room for one to ride, if you have the need or the whim."

Into my mind sprang a bright fantasy: he would drive me toward the coast, where I would sign on aboard a merchant vessel bound for Manneran, and in that happy tropical land I would throw myself on the mercies of my bondsister's father, escaping all this harrassment.

"Where are you bound?" I asked.

"Westward, into the mountains."

So much for Manneran. I accepted the ride all the same. He offered me no contract of defined liabilities, but I let that pass. For some minutes we did not speak; I was content to listen to the slap of the treads on the snowy road, and think of the distance growing between myself and the police of Glain.

"Outlander, are you?" he said at length.

"Indeed." Fearing that some alarm might be out for a man of Salla, I chose belatedly to adopt the soft slurred speech of southern folk, that I had learned from Halum, hoping he would come to believe that I had not spoken first to him with Sallan accents. "You travel with a native of Manneran, who finds your winter a strange and burdensome thing."

"What brought you north?" he asked.

"The settlement of one's mother's estate. She was a woman of Glain."

"Did the lawyers treat you well, then?"

"Her money melted in their hands, leaving nothing."

"The usual story. You're short of cash, eh?"

"Destitute," I admitted.

"Well, well, one understands your situation, for one has been there oneself. Perhaps something can be done for you."

I realized from his phrasing, from his failure to use the Glinish passive construction, that he too must be an outlander. Swinging round to face him, I said, "Is one right that you likewise are from elsewhere?"

"This is true."

"Your accent is unfamiliar. Some western province?"

"Oh, no, no."

"Not Salla, then?"

"Manneran," he said, and burst into hearty laughter, and covered my shame and confusion by telling me, "You do the accent well, friend. But you needn't make the effort longer."

"One hears no Manneran in your voice," I mumbled.

"One has lived long in Glin," he said, "and one's voice is a soup of inflections."

I had not fooled him for a moment, but he made no attempt to penetrate my identity, and seemed not to care who I might be or where I came from. We talked easily a while. He told me that he owned a lumber mill in western Glin, midway up the flanks of the Huishtors where the tall yellow-needled honey-trees grow; before we had driven much farther along he was offering me a job as a logger in his camp. The pay was poor, he said, but one breathed clean air there, and government officials were never seen, and such things as passports and certificates of status did not matter.

Of course I accepted. His camp was beautifully situated, above a sparkling mountain lake which never froze, for it was fed by a warm spring whose source was said to be deep beneath the Burnt Lowlands. Tremendous ice-topped Huishtor peaks hung above us, and not far away was Glin Gate, the pass through which one goes from Glin to the Burnt Lowlands, crossing a bitter corner of the Frozen Lowlands on the way. He had a hundred men in his employ, rough and foul-mouthed, forever shouting "I" and "me" without shame, but they were honest and hardworking men, and I had never been close to their sort before. My plan was to stay there through the winter, saving my pay, and go off to Manneran when I had earned the price of my passage. Some news of the outer world reached the camp from time to time, though, and I learned in this way that the Glinish authorities were seeking a certain young prince of Salla, who was believed to have gone insane and was wandering somewhere in Glin; the septarch Stirron urgently wished the unhappy young man to be returned to his homeland for the medical care he so desperately needed. Suspecting that the roads and ports would be watched, I extended my stay in the mountains through the spring, and, my caution deepening, I stayed the summer also. In the end I spent something more than a year there.

It was a year that changed me greatly. We worked hard, felling the huge trees in all weathers, stripping them of boughs, feeding them to the mill, a long tiring day and a chilly one, but plenty of hot wine at night, and every tenth day a platoon of women brought in from a nearby town to amuse us. My weight increased by half again, all of it hard muscle, and I grew taller until I surpassed the tallest logger in the camp, and they made jokes about my size. My beard came in full and the planes of my face changed as the plumpness of youth went from me. The loggers I found more likable than the courtiers among whom all my prior days had been passed. Few of them were able even to read, and of polite etiquette they knew nothing, but they were cheerful and easy-spirited men, at home in their own bodies. I would not have you think that because they talked in "I" and "me" they were open-hearted and given to sharing of confidences; they kept the Covenant in that respect, and might even have been more secretive than educated folk about certain things. Yet they seemed more sunny of soul than those who speak in passives and impersonal pronouns, and perhaps my stay among them planted in me that seed of subversion, that understanding of the Covenant's basic wrongness, which the Earthman Schweiz later guided into full flowering.

I told them nothing of my rank and origin. They could see for themselves, by the smoothness of my skin, that I had not done much hard labor in my life, and my way of speaking marked me as an educated man, if not necessarily one of high birth. But I offered no revelations of my past, and none were sought. All I said was that I came from Salla, since my accent marked me as Sallan anyway; they granted me the privacy of my history. My employer, I think, guessed early that I must be the fugitive prince whom Stirron sought, but he never queried me about that. For the first time in my life, then, I had an identity apart from my royal status. I ceased to be Lord Kinnall, the septarch's second son, and was only Darival, the big logger from Salla.

From that transformation I learned much. I had never played one of your swaggering, bullying young nobles; being a second son instills a certain humility even in an aristocrat. Yet I could not help feeling set apart from ordinary men. I was waited on, bowed to, served and pampered; men spoke softly to me and made formal gestures of respect, even when I was a child. I was, after all, the son of a septarch, that is to say a king, for septarchs are hereditary rulers and thus are part of mankind's procession of kings, a line that goes back to the dawn of human settlement on Borthan and beyond, back across the stars to Earth itself, to the lost and forgotten dynasties of her ancient nations, ultimately to the masked and painted chieftains enthroned in prehistoric caves. And I was part of that line, a man of royal blood, somehow superior by circumstance of birth. But in this logging camp in the mountains I came to understand that kings are nothing but men set high. The gods do not anoint them, but rather the will of men, and men can strip them of their lofty rank; if Stirron were to be cast down by insurrection, and in his place that loathsome drainer from Salla Old Town became septarch, would not the drainer then enter that mystic procession of kings, and Stirron be relegated to the dust? And would not that drainer's sons become blood-proud, even as I had been, although their father had been nothing for most of his life, and their grandfather less than that? I know, I know, the sages would say that the kiss of the gods had fallen upon that drainer, elevating him and all his progeny and making them forever sacred, yet as I felled trees on the slopes of the Huishtors I saw kingship with clearer eyes, and, having been cast down by events myself, I realized that I was no more than a man among men, and always had been. What I would make of myself depended on my natural gifts and ambitions, not upon the accident of rank.

So rewarding was that knowledge, and the altered sense of self it brought me, that my stay in the mountains ceased to seem like an exile, but more like a vocation. My dreams of fleeing to a soft life in Manneran left me, and, even after I had saved more than enough to pay my passage to that land, I found myself with no impulse to move onward. It was not entirely fear of arrest that kept me among the loggers, but also a love of the crisp clear cold Huishtor air, and of my arduous new craft, and of the rough but genuine men among whom I dwelled. Therefore I stayed on, through summer and into autumn, and welcomed the coming of a new winter, and gave no thought to going.

I might be there yet, only I was forced into flight. One woeful winter afternoon, with the sky like iron and the threat of a blizzard over us like a fist, they brought the whores up from town for our regularly appointed night of frolic, and this time there was among them a newcomer whose voice announced her place of birth to be Salla. I heard her instantly as the women came cavorting into our hall of sport, and would have crept away, but she spied me and gasped and cried out on the spot: "Look you there! For sure that is our vanished prince!"

I laughed and tried to persuade everyone that she was drunk or mad, but my scarlet cheeks gave me the lie, and the loggers peered at me in a new way. A prince? A prince? Was it so? They whispered to one another, nudging and winking. Recognizing my peril, I claimed the woman for my own use and drew her aside, and when we were alone, I insisted to her she was mistaken: I am no prince, I said, but only a common logger. She would not have it. "The Lord Kinnall marched in the septarch's funeral procession," she said, "and this one beheld him, with these eyes. And you are he!" The more I protested, the more convinced she was. There was no shifting her mind. Even when I embraced her, she was so awe-smitten at opening herself to a septarch's son that her loins remained dry, and I injured her in entering her.

Late that night, when the revelry had ended, my employer came to me, solemn and uneasy. "One of the girls has made strange talk about you this evening," he said. "If the talk is true, you are endangered, for when she returns to her village she'll spread the news, and the police will be here soon enough."

"Must one flee, then?" I asked.

"The choice is yours. Alarms still are out for this prince; if you are he, no one here can protect you against the authorities."

"Then one must flee. At daybreak—"

"Now," he said. "While the girl still lies here asleep."

He pressed money of Glin into my hand, over and beyond what he owed me in current wages; I gathered my few belongings, and we went outside together. The night was moonless and the winter wind was savage. By starlight I saw the glitter of lightly falling snow. My employer silently drove me down the slope, past the foothills village from which the whores came, and out along a back-country road which we followed for some hours. When dawn met us we were in south-central Glin, not overly far from the River Huish. He halted, at last, in a village that proclaimed itself to be Klaek, a winterbound place of small stone cottages bordering on broad snowy fields. Leaving me in the truck, he entered the first of the cottages, emerging after a moment accompanied by a wizened man who poured forth a torrent of instructions and gesticulations; with the aid of this guidance we found our way to the place my employer was seeking, the cottage of a certain farmer named Stumwil. This Stumwil was a fair-haired man of about my own height, with washed-out blue eyes and an apologetic smile. Maybe he was some kinsman of my employer's, or, more probably, he owed him a debt—I never asked. In any case the farmer readily agreed to my employer's request, and accepted me as a lodger. My employer embraced me and drove off into the gathering snow; I saw him never again. I hope the gods were kind to him, as he was to me.

18

THE COTTAGE was one large room, divided by flimsy curtains into areas. Stumwil put up a new curtain, gave me straw for my mattress, and I had my living quarters. There were seven of us under that roof: Stumwil and myself, and Stumwil's wife, a weary wench whom I could have been persuaded was his mother, and three of their children—two boys some years short of manhood and a girl in mid-adolescence—and the bondsister of the girl, who was lodging with them that year. They were sunny, innocent, trusting folk. Though they knew nothing about me, they all instantly adopted me as a member of the family, some unknown uncle unexpectedly returned from far voyaging. I was not prepared for the easy way they accepted me, and credited it at first to some net of obligation in which my former employer had bound them to me, but no: they were kindly by nature, unquestioning, unsuspicious. I took my meals at their table; I sat among them by their fire; I joined in their games. Every fifth night Stumwil filled a huge dented tub with hot water for the entire family, and I bathed with them, two or three of us in the tub at once, though it disturbed me inwardly to rub up against the plump bare bodies of Stumwil's daughter and her friend. I suppose I could have had the daughter or the bondsister if I had cared to, but I kept back from them, thinking such a seduction would be a breach of hospitality. Later, when I understood more about peasants, I realized that it was my abstinence that had been a breach of hospitality, for the girls were of age and surely willing, and I had disdained them. But I saw that only after I had left Stumwil's place. Those girls now have adult children of their own. I suppose by this time they have forgiven me for my lack of gallantry.

I paid a fee for my lodging, and I helped also with the chores, though in winter there was little to do except shovel snow and feed the fire. None of them showed curiosity about my identity or history. They asked me no questions, and I believe that no questions ever passed through their minds. Nor did the other townspeople pry, though they gave me the scrutiny any stranger would receive.

Newspapers occasionally reached this village, and those that did went from hand to hand until all had read them, when they were placed on deposit at the wineshop at the head of the main village thoroughfare. I consulted them there, a file of stained and tattered scraps, and learned what I could of the events of the past year. I found that my brother Stirron's wedding had taken place on schedule, with appropriate regal pomp; his lean troubled face looked up out of a blurry, grease-splotched bit of old paper, and beside him was his radiant bride, but I could not make out her features. There was tension between Glin and Krell over fishing rights in a disputed coastal area, and men had died in border skirmishes. I pitied General Condorit, whose patrol sector was at the opposite end of the boundary, almost, from the Krell-Glin line, and who therefore must have missed the fun of somehow involving Salla in the shooting. A sea monster, golden-scaled and sinuous, more than ten times the length of a man's body, had been sighted in the Gulf of Sumar by a party of Mannerangi fishermen, who had sworn a mighty oath in the Stone Chapel as to the authenticity of their vision. The prime septarch of Threish, a bloody old brigand if the tales they tell of him are true, had abdicated, and was dwelling in a godhouse in the western mountains not far from Stroin Gap, serving as a drainer for pilgrims bound to Manneran. Such was the news. I found no mention of myself. Perhaps Stirron had lost interest in having me seized and returned to Salla.

It might therefore be safe for me to try to leave Glin.

Eager as I was to get out of that frosty province, where my own kin rebuffed me and only strangers showed me love, two things held me back. For one, I meant to stay with Stumwil until I could help him with his spring planting, in return for his kindness to me. For another, I would not set forth undrained on so dangerous a journey, lest in some mishap my spirit go to the gods still full of poisons. This village of Klaek had no drainer of its own, but depended for its solace on itinerant drainers who passed now and then through the country-side. In the winter these wanderers rarely came by, and so perforce I had gone undrained since the late summer, when a member of that profession had visited the logging camp. I felt the need.

There came a late-winter snow, a storm of wonders that coated every branch with a fiery skin of ice, and immediately thereafter there came a thaw. The world melted. Klaek was surrounded by oceans of mud. A drainer driving a battered and ancient groundcar came to us through this slippery sea and set up shop in an old shack, doing fine business among the villagers. I went to him on the fifth day of his visit, when the lines were shorter, and unburdened my-self for two hours, sparing him nothing, neither the truth about my identity nor my subversive new philosophy of kingship nor the usual grimy little repressed lusts and prides. It was more of a dose, evidently, than a country drainer expected to receive, and he seemed to puff and swell as I poured out my words; at the end he was shaking as much as I, and could barely speak. I wondered where it was that drainers went to unload all the sins and sorrows they absorbed from their clients. They are forbidden to talk to ordinary men of anything they have learned in the confessional; did they therefore have drainer-drainers, servants of the servants, to whom they might de-liver that which they could not mention to anyone else? I did not see how a drainer could carry such a bundle of sadnesses for long unaided, as he got from any dozen of his customers in a day's lis-tening.

With my soul cleansed, I had only to wait for planting-time, and it was not long in coming. The growing season in Glin is short; they get their seeds into the ground before winter's grip has fully slipped, so that they can catch every ray of spring sunlight. Stumwil waited until he felt certain that the thaw would not be followed by one last tumult of snow, and then, with the land still a sucking quagmire, he and his family went out into the fields to plant breadseed and spice-flower and blueglobe.

The custom was to go naked to the planting. On the first morning

I looked out of Stumwil's cottage and beheld the neighbors on all sides walking bare toward the furrows, children and parents and grandparents stripped to the skin with sacks of seed slung over their shoulders—a procession of knobby knees, sagging bellies, dried-out breasts, wrinkled buttocks, illuminated here and there by the smooth firm bodies of the young. Thinking I was in some waking dream, I looked around and saw Stumwil and his wife and their daughter already disrobed, and beckoning to me to do the same. They took their sacks and left the cottage. The two young sons scampered after them, leaving me with the bondsister of Stumwil's daughter, who had overslept and had just appeared. She shucked her garments too; a supple saucy body she had, with small high dark-nippled breasts and slender well-muscled thighs. As I dropped my clothes I asked her, "Why is it done to be naked outdoors in such a cold time?"

"The mud gives cause for slipping," she explained, "and it is easier to wash raw skin than garments."

There was truth enough in that, for the planting was a comic show, with peasants skidding in the tricky muck every tenth step they took. Down they went, landing on hip or haunch and coming up smeared with brown; it was a matter of skill to grasp the neck of one's seed-sack as one toppled, so that no precious seeds would be scattered. I fell like the rest, learning the knack of it quickly, and indeed there was pleasure in slipping, for the mud had a voluptuous oozy feel to it. So we marched on, staggering and lurching, slapping flesh to mud again and again, laughing, singing, pressing our seeds into the cold soft soil, and not one of us but was covered from scalp to tail with muck within minutes. I shivered miserably at the outset, but soon I was warmed by laughter and tripping, and when the day's work was done, we stood around shamelessly naked in front of Stumwil's cottage and doused one another with buckets of water to clean ourselves. By then it seemed reasonable to me that they should prefer to expose their skins rather than their clothing to such a day's labor, but in fact the girl's explanation was incorrect: I learned from Stumwil later that week that the nakedness was a religious matter, a sign of humility before the gods of the crops, and nothing else.

Eight days it took to finish the planting. On the ninth, wishing Stumwil and his people a hearty harvest, I took my leave of the village of Klaek, and began my journey to the coast.

19

A NEIGHBOR of Stumwil's took me eastward the first day in his cart. I walked most of the second, begged a ride on the third and fourth, and walked again on the fifth and sixth. The air was cool but the crackle of spring was in it, as buds unfolded and birds returned. I bypassed the city of Glain, which might have been dangerous for me, and without any events that I can clearly recall I made my way swiftly to Biumar, Glin's main seaport and second most populous city.

It was a handsomer place than Glain, though hardly beautiful: a greasy gray sprawl of an oversized town, backed up against a gray and menacing ocean. On my first day there I learned that all passenger service between Glin and the southern provinces had been suspended three moontimes before, owing to the dangerous activities of pirates operating out of Krell, for Glin and Krell were now engaged in an undeclared war. The only way I could reach Manneran, it seemed, was overland via Salla, and I hardly wished to do that. I was resourceful, though. I found myself a room in a tavern near the docks and spent a few days picking up maritime gossip. Passenger service might be suspended, but commercial seafaring, I discovered, was not, since the prosperity of Glin depended upon it; convoys of merchant vessels, heavily armed, went forth on regular schedules. A limping seaman who stayed in the same tavern told me, when blue wine of Salla had oiled him sufficiently, that a merchant convoy of this sort would leave in a week's time, and that he had a berth aboard one of the ships. I considered drugging him on the eve of sailing and borrowing his identity, as is done in pirate tales for children, but a less dramatic method suggested itself to me: I bought his shipping-papers. The sum I offered him was more than he would have earned by shipping out to Manneran and back, so he was happy to take my money and let me go in his place. We spent a long drunken night conferring about his duties on the ship, for I knew nothing of seamanship. At the coming of dawn I still knew nothing, but I saw ways I could bluff a minimal sort of competence.

I went unchallenged on board the vessel, a low-slung air-powered craft heavily laden with Glinish goods. The checking of papers was perfunctory. I picked up my cabin assignment, installed myself, reported for duty. About half the jobs they asked me to do, over the first few days, I managed to carry out reasonably well by imitation and experiment; the other things I merely muddled with, and soon my fellow sailors recognized me for a bungler, but they kept knowledge of that from the officers. A kind of loyalty prevailed in the lower ranks. Once again I saw that my dark view of mankind had been overly colored by my boyhood among aristocrats; these sailors, like the loggers, like the farmers, had a kind of hearty good fellowship among themselves that I had never found among those more strict to the Covenant. They did for me the jobs I could not do myself, and I relieved them of dull work that was within my narrow skills, and all went well. I swabbed decks, cleaned filters, and spent endless hours manning the guns against pirate attacks. But we got past Krell's dreaded pirate coast without incident, and slipped easily down the coast of Salla, which already was green with spring.

Our first port of call was Cofalon, Salla's chief seaport, for five days of selling and buying. I was alarmed at this, for I had not known we planned to halt anywhere in my homeland. I thought at first to announce myself ill and hide belowdecks all our time in Cofalon; but then I rejected the scheme as cowardly, telling myself that a man must test himself frequently against risk, if he would keep his manhood. So I boldly went wenching and wining in town with my shipmates, trusting that time had sufficiently changed my face, and that no one would expect to find Lord Stirron's missing brother in a sailor's rough clothes in such a town as this. My gamble succeeded: I went unvexed the full five days. From newspapers and careful overhearing I learned all I could about events in Salla in the year and a half since my leaving. Stirron, I gathered, was popularly held to be a good ruler. He had brought the province through its winter of famine by purchasing surplus food from Manneran on favorable terms, and our farms had since then had better fortune. Taxes had been cut. The people were content. Stirron's wife had been delivered of a son, the Lord Dariv, who now was heir to the prime septarchy, and another son was on the way. As for the Lord Kinnall, brother to the septarch, nothing was said of him; he was forgotten as though he had never been.

We made other stops here and there down the coast, several in southern Salla, several in northern Manneran. And in good time we came to that great seaport at the southeastern corner of our continent, the holy city of Manneran, capital of the province that bears the same name. It was in Manneran that my life would begin anew.

20

MANNERAN THE PROVINCE was favored by the gods. The air is mild and sweet, filled all the year through with the fragrance of flowers. Winter does not reach so far south, and the Mannerangi, when they would see snow, go as tourists to the Huishtor peaks and gape at the strange cold coating of whiteness that passes for water in other lands. The warm sea that borders Manneran on east and south yields food enough to feed half the continent, and to the southwest there is the Gulf of Sumar as well, with further bounty. War has rarely touched Manneran, protected as it is by a shield of mountains and water from the peoples of the western lands, and separated from its neighbor to the north, Salla, by the immense torrent of the River Woyn. Now and again we have attempted to invade Manneran by sea, but never with any conviction that we would be successful, nor has there been any success; when Salla engages seriously in war, the foe is always Glin.

Manneran the city must also have enjoyed special divine blessings. Its site is the finest natural harbor in all Velada Borthan, a deep-cut bay framed by two opposing fingers of land, jutting toward one another in such a way that no breakwaters are needed there, and ships sit easily at anchor. This harbor is one mighty source of the province's prosperity. It constitutes the chief link between the eastern and western provinces, for there is little landborne commerce across the continent by way of the Burnt Lowlands, and since our world lacks natural fuels, so far as we know, airborne traffic is never likely to amount to much here. So ships of the nine western provinces travel eastward through the Strait of Sumar to the port of Manneran, and ships from Manneran make regular calls on the western coast. The Mannerangi then retail western goods to Salla, Glin, and

Krell in their own vessels, reaping the usual profits of go-betweens. The harbor of Manneran is the only place on our world where men of all thirteen provinces mingle and where all thirteen flags may be seen at once; and this busy commerce spills an unending flow of wealth into the coffers of the Mannerangi. In addition, their inland districts are rich in fertility, even up to the Huishtor slopes, which in their latitudes are unfrozen except at the summits. The farms of Manneran have two or three harvests a year, and, by way of Stroin Gap, the Mannerangi have access to the Wet Lowlands and all the strange and valuable fruits and spices produced there. Small wonder, then, that those who love luxuries seek their fortunes in Manneran.

As if all this good fortune were not enough, the Mannerangi have persuaded the world that they live in the holiest spot on Borthan, and multiply their revenues by maintaining sacred shrines as magnets for pilgrims. One might think that Threish, on the western coast, where our ancestors first settled and the Covenant was drawn up, would put itself forward as a place of pilgrimage second to none. Indeed, there is some sort of shrine in Threish, and westerners too poor to travel to Manneran visit it. But Manneran has established itself as the holy of holies. The youngest of all our provinces, too, except only the breakaway kingdom of Krell; yet by a show of inner conviction and energetic advertisement has Manneran managed to make itself sacred. There is irony in this, for the Mannerangi hold more loosely to the Covenant than any of us in the thirteen provinces; their tropical life has softened them somewhat, and they open their souls to one another to a degree that would get them ostracized as self-barers in Glin or Salla. Still, they have the Stone Chapel, where miracles are reliably reported to have occurred, where the gods supposedly came forth in the flesh only seven hundred years ago, and it is everyone's hope to have his child receive his adult name in the Stone Chapel on Naming Day. From all over the continent they come for that festival, to the vast profit of the Mannerangi hostelkeepers. Why, I was named in the Stone Chapel myself.

21

WHEN WE WERE DOCKED in Manneran and the longshoremen were at work unloading our cargo, I collected my pay and left ship to enter town. At the foot of the pier I paused to pick up a shore pass from the Mannerangi immigration officials. "How long will you be in town?" I was asked, and blandly I replied that I meant to stay among them for three days, although my real intent was to settle for the rest of my years in this place.

Twice before had I been in Manneran: once just out of my infancy, to be bonded to Halum, and once when I was seven, for my Naming Day. My memories of the city amounted to nothing more than vague and random patterns of colors: the pale pink and green and blue tones of the buildings, the dark green masses of the heavy vegetation, the black solemn interior of the Stone Chapel. As I walked away from the waterfront those colors bombarded me again, and glowing images out of my childhood shimmered before my dazzled eyes. Manneran is not built of stone, as our northern cities are, but rather of a kind of artificial plaster, which they paint in light pastel hues, so that every wall and façade sings joyfully, and billows like a curtain in the sunlight. The day was a bright one, and the beams of light bounced gaily about, setting the streets ablaze and forcing me to shade my eyes. I was stunned also by the complexity of the streets. Mannerangi architects rely greatly on ornament; the buildings are decked with ornate ironwork balconies, fanciful scrollings, flamboyant rooftiles, gaudy window-draperies, so that the northern eye beholds at first glance a monstrous baffling clutter, which resolves itself only gradually into a vista of elegance and grace and proportion. Everywhere, too, there are plants: trees lining both sides of each street, vines cascading from window boxes, flowers bursting forth in curbside gardens, and the hint of lush vegetation in the sheltered courtyards of the houses. The effect is refined and sophisticated, an interplay of jungle profusion and disciplined urban textures. Manneran is an extraordinary city, subtle, sensuous, languorous, overripe.

My childhood recollections did not prepare me for the heat. A steamy haze enveloped the streets. The air was wet and heavy. I felt I could almost touch the heat, could seize it and grasp it, could wring it like water from the atmosphere. It was raining heat and I was drenched in it. I was clad in a coarse, heavy gray uniform, the usual wintertime issue aboard a Glinish merchant ship, and this was a sweltering spring morning in Manneran; two dozen paces in that stifling humidity and I was ready to rip off my chafing clothes and go naked.

A telephone directory gave me the address of Segvord Helalam, my bondsister's father. I hired a taxi and went there. Helalam lived just outside the city, in a cool leafy suburb of grand homes and glistening lakes; a high brick wall shielded his house from the view of passersby. I rang at the gate and waited to be scanned. My taxi waited too, as if the driver knew certainly that I would be turned away. A voice within the house, some butler, no doubt, queried me over the scanner line and I replied, "Kinnall Darival of Salla, bondbrother to the daughter of the High Justice Helalam, wishes to call upon the father of his bondsister."

"The Lord Kinnall is dead," I was informed coldly, "and so you are some impostor."

I rang again. "Scan this, and judge if he be dead," I said, holding up to the machine's eye my royal passport, which I had kept so long concealed. "This is Kinnall Darival before you, and it will not go well with you if you deny him access to the High Justice!"

"Passports may be stolen. Passports may be forged."

"Open the gate!"

There was no reply. A third time I rang, and this time the unseen butler told me that the police would be summoned unless I departed at once. My taxi driver, parked just across the road, coughed politely. I had not reckoned on any of this. Would I have to go back to town, and take lodgings, and write Segvord Helalam for an appointment, and offer evidence that I still lived?

By good fortune I was spared those bothers. A sumptuous black groundcar drew up, of a kind used generally only by the highest aristocracy, and from it stepped Segvord Helalam, High Justice of the Port of Manneran. He was then at the height of his career, and he carried himself with kingly grace: a short man, but well constructed, with a fine head, a florid face, a noble mane of white hair, a look of strength and purpose. His eyes, an intense blue, were capable of flashing fire, and his nose was an imperial beak, but he canceled all his look of ferocity with a warm, ready smile. He was recognized in Manneran as a man of wisdom and temperance. I went immediately toward him, with a glad cry of "Bondfather!" Swinging about, he stared at me in bewilderment, and two large young men who had been with him in his groundcar placed themselves between the High Justice and myself as though they believed me to be an assassin.

"Your bodyguard may relax," I said. "Are you unable to recognize Kinnall of Salla?"

"The Lord Kinnall died last year," Segvord replied quickly.

"That comes as grievous news to Kinnall himself," I said. I drew myself tall, resuming princely mien for the first time since my sad exit from the city of Glain, and gestured at the High Justice's protectors with such fury that they gave ground, slipping off to the side. Segvord studied me carefully. He had last seen me at my brother's coronation; two years had gone by since then, and the last softness of childhood had been stripped from me. My year of felling logs showed in the contours of my frame, and my winter among the farmers had weathered my face, and my weeks as a sailor had left me grimy and unkempt, with tangled hair and a shaggy beard. Segvord's gaze cut gradually through these transformations until he was convinced of my identity; then suddenly he rushed at me, embracing me with such fervor that I nearly lost my footing in surprise. He cried my name, and I cried his; then the gate was opening, and he was hurrying me within, and the lofty cream-colored mansion loomed before me, the goal of all my wanderings and turmoil.

22

I WAS CONDUCTED to a pretty chamber and told that it was to be mine, and two servant-girls came to me, plucking off my sweaty seaman's garb; they led me, giggling all the while, to a huge tiled tub, and bathed and perfumed me, and cropped my hair and beard somewhat, and let me pinch and tumble them a bit. They brought me clothes of fine fabric, of a sort I had not worn since my days as royalty, all sheer and white and flowing and cool. And they offered me jewelry, a triple ring set with—I later learned—a sliver of the Stone Chapel's floor, and also a gleaming pendant, a tree-crystal from the land of Threish, on a leather thong. At length, after several hours of polishing, I was deemed fit to present to the High Justice. Segvord received me in the room he called his study, which actually was a great hall worthy of a septarch's palace, in which he sat enthroned even as a ruler would. I recall feeling some annoyance at his pretensions, for not only was he not royal, but he was of the lower aristocracy of Manneran, who had been of no stature whatever until his appointment to high office had put him on the road to fame and wealth.

I asked at once after my bondsister Halum.

"She fares well," he said, "though her soul was darkened by the tidings of your supposed death."

"Where is she now?"

"On holiday, in the Sumar Gulf, on an island where we have another home."

I felt a chill. "Has she married?"

"To the regret of all who love her, she has not."

"Is there anyone, though?"

"No," Segvord said. "She seems to prefer chastity. Of course, she is very young. When she returns, Kinnall, perhaps you could speak to her, pointing out that she might think now about making a match, for now she might have some fair lord, while in a few years' time there will be new maidens ahead of her in line."

"How soon will she be back from this island?"

"At any moment," said the High Justice. "How amazed she will be to find you here!"

I asked him concerning my death. He replied that word had come, two years earlier, that I was mad and had wandered, helpless and deluded, into Glin. Segvord smiled as though to tell me that he knew right well why I had left Salla, and that there had been nothing of insanity about my motives. "Then," he said, "there were reports that the Lord Stirron had sent agents into Glin after you, so that you could be brought back for treatment. Halum feared greatly for your safety at that time. And lastly, this summer past, one of your brother's ministers gave it out that you had gone roaming in the Glinish Huishtors in the pit of winter, and had been lost in the snows, in a blizzard no man could have survived."

"But of course the Lord Kinnall's body was not recovered in the warm months of the year gone by, and was left to wither in the

Huishtors, instead of being brought back to Salla for a proper burial."

"There was no news of finding the body, no."

"Then obviously," I said, "the Lord Kinnall's body awakened in the springtime, and trekked about on a ghostly parade, and went its way southward, and now at last has presented itself on the doorstep of the High Justice of the Port of Manneran."

Segvord laughed. "A healthy ghost!"

"A weary one, as well."

"What befell you in Glin?" he asked.

"A cold time, in more ways than one." I told him of my snubbing at the hands of my mother's kin, of my stay in the mountains, and all the rest. When he had heard that, he wished to know what my plans were in Manneran; to this I replied that I had no plans other than to find some honorable enterprise, and succeed in it, and marry, and settle down, for Salla was closed to me and Glin held no temptations. Segvord nodded gravely. There was, he said, a clerkship open at this very moment in his office. The job carried little pay and less prestige, and it was absurd to ask a prince of Salla's royal line to accept it, but still it was clean work, with a fine chance of advancement, and it might serve to give me a foothold while I acclimated myself to the Mannerangi way of life. Since I had had some such opportunity in mind all along, I told him at once that I would gladly enter his employ, with no heed to my royal blood, since all that was behind me now, done with, and imaginary besides. "What one makes of himself here," I said soberly, " will depend wholly on his merits, not on the circumstances of rank and influence." Which was, of course, pure piffle: instead of trading on my high birth, I would instead here make capital out of being bondbrother to the High Justice of the Port's daughter, a connection that had come to me because of my high birth alone, and where was the effect of merit in any of that?

23

THE SEARCHERS are getting closer to me all the time. Yesterday, while on a long walk through this zone of the Burnt Lowlands, I found, well south of here, the fresh track of a groundcar impressed deep in the dry and fragile crust of the red sand. And this morning, idly strolling in the place where the hornfowl gather—drawn there by some suicidal impulse, maybe?—I heard a droning in the sky, and looked up to see a plane of the Sallan military passing overhead. One does not often see sky-vehicles here. It swooped and circled, hornfowl-fashion, but I huddled under a twisted erosion-knoll, and I think I went unnoticed.

I might be mistaken about these intrusions: the groundcar just some hunting party casually passing through the region, the plane merely out on a training flight. But I think not. If there are hunters here, it is I they hunt. The net will close about me. I must try to write more quickly, and be more concise; too much of what I need to say is yet untold, and I fear being interrupted before I am done. Stirron, let me be for just a few more weeks!

24

THE HIGH JUSTICE of the Port is one of Manneran's supreme officials. He holds jurisdiction over all commercial affairs in the capital; if there are disputes between merchants, they are tried in his court, and by treaty he has authority over the nationals of every province, so that a seacaptain of Glin or Krell, a Sallan or a westerner, when hailed before the High Justice, is subject to his verdicts with no rights of appeal to the courts of his homeland. This is the High Justice's ancient function, but if he were nothing but an arbiter of mercantile squabbles he would hardly have the grandeur that he does. However, over the centuries other responsibilities have fallen to him. He alone regulates the flow of foreign shipping into the harbor of Manneran, granting trade permits for so many Glinish vessels a year, so many from Threish, so many from Salla. The prosperity of a dozen provinces is subject to his decisions. Therefore he is courted by septarchs, flooded with gifts, buried in kindnesses and praise, in the hope that he will allow this land or that an extra ship in the year to come. The High Justice, then, is the economic filter of Velada Borthan, opening and closing commercial outlets as he pleases; he does this not by whim but by consideration of the ebb and flow of wealth across the continent, and it is impossible to over-estimate his importance in our society.

The office is not hereditary, but the appointment is for life, and a High Justice can be removed only through intricate and well-nigh impracticable impeachment procedures. Thus it comes to pass that a vigorous High Justice, such as Segvord Helalam, can become more powerful in Manneran than the prime septarch himself. The septarchy of Manneran is in decay in any case; two of the seven seats have gone unfilled for the past hundred years or more, and the occupants of the remaining five have ceded so much of their authority to civil servants that they are little more than ceremonial figures. The prime septarch still has some shreds of majesty, but he must consult with the High Justice of the Port on all matters of economic concern, and the High Justice has entangled himself so inextricably in the machinery of Manneran's government that it is difficult to say truly who is the ruler and who the civil servant.

On my third day in Manneran, Segvord took me to his courthouse to contract me into my job. I who was raised in a palace was awed to see the headquarters of the Port Justiciary; what amazed me was not its opulence (for it had none) but its great size. I beheld a broad yellow-colored brick structure, four stories high, squat and massive, that seemed to run the entire length of the waterfront two blocks inland from the piers. Within it at worn desks in high-ceilinged offices were armies of drudging clerks, shuffling papers and stamping receipts, and my soul quivered at the thought that this was how I was to spend my days. Segvord led me on an endless march through the building, receiving the homage of the workers as he passed their dank and sweaty offices; he paused here and there to greet someone, to glance casually at some half-written report, to study a board on which, apparently, the movements of every vessel within three days' journey of Manneran were being charted. At length we entered a noble suite of rooms, far from the bustle and hurry I had just seen. Here the High Justice himself presided. Showing me a cool and splendidly furnished room adjoining his own chamber, Segvord told me that this was where I would work.

The contract I signed was like a drainer's: I pledged myself to reveal nothing of what I might learn in the course of my duties, on pain of terrible penalties. For its part the Port Justiciary promised me

70

lifetime employment, steady increases of salary, and various other privileges of a kind princes do not normally worry about.

Quickly I discovered that I was to be no humble inkstained clerk. As Segvord had warned me, my pay was low and my rank in the bureaucracy almost nonexistent, but my responsibilities proved to be great ones; in effect, I was his private secretary. All confidential reports intended for the High Justice's eyes would cross my desk first. My task was to discard those that were of no importance and to prepare abridgments of the others, all but those I deemed to be of the highest pertinence, which went to him complete. If the High Justice is the economic filter of Velada Borthan, I was to be the filter's filter, for he would read only what I wished him to read, and make his decisions on the basis of what I gave him. Once this was clear to me I knew that Segvord had placed me on the path to great power in Manneran.

25

IMPATIENTLY I awaited Halum's return from her isle in the Gulf of Sumar. Neither bondsister nor bondbrother had I had for over two years, and drainers could not take their place; I ached to sit up late at night with Halum or Noim, as in the old days, opening self to self. Noim was somewhere in Salla, I supposed, but I knew not where, and Halum, though she was said to be due back imminently from holidaying, did not appear in my first week in Manneran, nor the second. During the third, I left the Justiciary office early one day, feeling ill from the humidity and the tensions of mastering my new role, and was driven to Segvord's estate. Entering the central courtyard on my way to my room, I caught sight of a tall, slender girl at the far end, plucking from a vine a golden flower for her dark glossy hair. I could not see her face, but from her figure and bearing I had no doubt of her, and joyfully I cried, "Halum!" and rushed across the courtyard. She turned frowning to me, halting me in mid-rush. Her brow was furrowed and her lips were tight together; her gaze was chilly and remote. What did that cold glance mean? Her face was Halum's face—dark eyes, fine slim proud nose, firm chin, bold cheekbones—and yet her face was strange to me. Could two years have changed my bondsister so greatly? The main differences between the Halum I remembered and the woman I saw were subtle ones, differences of expression, a tilt of the eyebrows, a flicker of the nostrils, a quirking of the mouth, as though the whole soul itself within her had altered. Also there were some minor differences of feature, I saw as I drew nearer, but these could be ascribed to the passing of time or to the faults of my memory. My heart sped and my fingers trembled and an odd heat of confusion spread across my shoulders and back. I would have gone to her and embraced her, but suddenly I feared her in her transformations.

"Halum?" I said uncertainly, hoarse-voiced, dry-throated.

"She is not yet here." A voice like falling snow, deeper than Halum's, more resonant, colder.

I was stunned. Like enough to Halum to be her twin! I knew of only one sister to Halum, then still a child, not yet sprouting her breasts. It was not possible for her to have concealed from me all her life a twin, or a sister somewhat older. But the resemblance was extraordinary and disturbing. I have read that on old Earth they had ways of making artificial beings out of chemicals, that could deceive even a mother or a lover with the likeness to some real person, and I could well have been persuaded that moment that the process had come down to us, across the centuries, across the gulf of night, and that this false Halum before me was a devilishly clever synthetic image of my true bondsister.

I said, "Forgive this foolish error. One mistook you for Halum."

"It happens often."

"Are you some kin of hers?"

"Daughter to the brother of the High Justice Segvord."

She gave her name as Loimel Helalam. Never had Halum spoken to me of this cousin, or if she had, I had no recollection of it. How odd that she had hidden from me the existence of this mirror-Halum in Manneran! I told her my name, and Loimel recognized it as that of Halum's bondbrother, of whom she had evidently heard a good deal; she softened her stance a little, and some of the chill that was about her now thawed. For my part I was over the shock of finding the supposed Halum to be another, and I was beginning to warm to Loimel, for she was beautiful and desirable, and—unlike Halum herself!—available. I could by looking at her out of one eye pretend to myself that she was indeed Halum, and I even managed to deceive myself into accepting her voice as my bondsister's. Together we strolled the courtyard, talking. I learned that Halum would come home this evening, and that Loimel was here to arrange a hearty reception for her; I learned also some things about Loimel, for, in the injudicious fashion of many Mannerangi, she guarded her privacy less sternly than a northerner would. She told me her age: a year older than Halum (and I also). She told me she was unmarried, having recently terminated an unpromising engagement to a prince of an old but unfortunately impoverished family of Mannerangi nobility. She explained her resemblance to Halum by saying that her mother and Halum's were cousins, as well as her father being brother to Halum's, and five minutes later, when we walked arm in arm, she hinted scandalously that in fact the High Justice had invaded his elder brother's bridal couch long ago, so that she was properly half-sister to Halum, not cousin. And she told me much more.

I could think only of Halum, Halum, Halum, Halum. This Loimel existed for me solely as a reflection of my bondsister. An hour after we first met, Loimel and I were together in my bedroom, and when her gown had dropped from her I told myself that Halum's skin must be creamy as this, that Halum's breasts must be much like these, that Halum's thighs could be no less smooth, that Halum's nipples would also turn to turrets when a man's thumbs brushed their tips. Then I lay naked beside Loimel and made her ready for taking with many cunning caresses; soon she gasped and pumped her hips and cried out, and I covered her with my body, but an instant before I would have thrust myself into her the thought came coldly to me, *Why, this is forbidden, to have one's bondsister*, and my weapon went limp as a length of rope. It was only a momentary embarrassment: looking down at her face, I told myself brusquely that this was Loimel and not Halum who waited for my thrust, and my manhood revived, and our bodies joined. But another humiliation awaited me. In the moment of entering her my traitor mind said to me, *You cleave Halum's flesh*, and my traitor body responded with an instantaneous explosion of my passions. How intricately our loins are linked to our minds, and how tricky a thing it is when we embrace a woman while pretending she is another! I sank down on Loimel in shame and disgust, hiding my face in the pillow; but she, gripped by urgent needs, thrashed about against me until I found new vigor, and this time I carried her to the ecstasy she sought.

That evening my bondsister Halum at last returned from her holiday in the Gulf of Sumar, and wept with happy surprise to see me alive and in Manneran. When she stood beside Loimel I was all the more amazed by their near twinship: Halum's waist was more slender, Loimel's bosom deeper, but one finds these variations even in true sisters, and in most ways of the body Halum and her cousin seemed to have been stamped from the same mold. Yet I was struck by a profound and subtle difference also, most visible in the eyes, through which, as the poem says, there shines the inner light of the soul. The radiance that came from Halum was tender and gentle and mild, like the first soft beams of sunlight drifting through a summer morning's mist; Loimel's eyes gave a colder, harsher glow, that of a sullen winter afternoon. As I looked from one girl to the other, I formed a quick intuitive judgment: *Halum is pure love, and Loimel is pure self.* But I recoiled from that verdict the instant it was born. I did not know Loimel; I had not found her thus far to be anything but open and giving; I had no right to disparage her in that way.

The two years had not aged Halum so much as burnished her, and she had come to the full radiance of her beauty. She was deeply tanned, and in her short white sheath she seemed like a bronzed statue of herself; the planes of her face were more angular than they had been, giving her a delicate look of almost boyish charm; she moved with floating grace. The house was full of strangers for this her homecoming party, and after our first embrace she was swept away from me, and I was left with Loimel. But toward the end of the evening I claimed my bondright and took Halum away to my chamber, saying, "There is two years' talking to do." Thoughts tumbled chaotically in my mind: how could I tell her all that had happened to me, how could I learn from her what she had done, all in the first rush of words? I could not arrange my thinking. We sat down facing one another at a prim distance, Halum on the couch where only a few hours before I had coupled with her cousin, pretending then to myself that she was Halum. A tense smile passed between us. "Where can one begin?" I said, and Halum, at the same instant, said the same words. That made us laugh and dissolved the tension. And then I heard my own voice asking, without preamble, whether Halum thought that Loimel would accept me as her husband.

26

LOIMEL AND I were married by Segvord Helalam in the Stone Chapel at the crest of the summer, after months of preparatory rituals and purifications. We made these observances by request of Loimel's father, a man of great devoutness. For his sake we undertook a rigorous series of drainings, and day after day I knelt and yielded up the full contents of my soul to a certain Jidd, the best-known and most costly drainer in Manneran. When this was done Loimel and I went on pilgrimage to the nine shrines of Manneran, and I squandered my slender salary on candles and incense. We even performed the archaic ceremony known as the Showing, in which she and I stepped out on a secluded beach one dawn, chaperoned by Halum and Segvord, and, screened from their eyes by an elaborate canopy, formally disclosed our nakedness to one another, so that neither of us could say afterward that we had gone into marriage concealing defects from the other.

The rite of union was a grand event, with musicians and singers. My bondbrother Noim, summoned from Salla, stood up as pledgeman for me, and did the ring-linking. Manneran's prime septarch, a waxen old man, attended the wedding, as did most of the local nobility. The gifts we received were of immense value. Among them was a golden bowl inlaid with strange gems, manufactured on some other world, and sent to us by my brother Stirron, along with a cordial message expressing regret that affairs of state required him to remain in Salla. Since I had snubbed his wedding, it was no surprise for him to snub mine. What did surprise me was the friendly tone of his letter. Making no reference to the circumstances of my disappearance from Salla, but offering thanks that the rumor of my death had proven false, Stirron gave me his blessing and asked me to come with my bride for a ceremonial visit to his capital as soon as we were able. Apparently he had learned that I meant to settle permanently in Manneran, and so would be no rival for his throne; therefore he could think of me warmly again.

I often wondered, and after all these years still do wonder, why

75

Loimel accepted me. She had just turned down a prince of her own realm because he was poor: here was I, also a prince, but an exiled one, and even poorer. Why take me? For my charm in wooing? I had little of that; I was still young and thick-tongued. For my prospects of wealth and power? At that time those prospects seemed feeble indeed. For my physical appeal? Certainly I had some of that, but Loimel was too shrewd to marry just for broad shoulders and powerful muscles; besides, in our very first embrace I had shown her my inadequacies as a lover, and rarely did I improve on that bungled performance in the couplings that followed. I concluded, finally, that there were two reasons why Loimel took me. First, that she was lonely and troubled after the breakup of her other trothing, and, seeking the first harbor that presented itself, went to me, since I was strong and attractive and of royal blood. Second, that Loimel envied Halum in all things, and knew that by marrying me she would gain possession of the one thing Halum could never have.

My own motive for seeking Loimel's hand needs no deep probing to uncover. It was Halum I loved; Loimel was Halum's image; Halum was denied me, therefore I took Loimel. Beholding Loimel, I was free to think I beheld Halum. Embracing Loimel, I might tell myself I embraced Halum. When I offered myself to Loimel as husband, I felt no particular love for her, and had reason to think I might not even like her; yet I was driven to her as the nearest proxy to my true desire.

Marriages contracted for such reasons as Loimel's and mine do not often fare well. Ours thrived poorly; we began as strangers and grew ever more distant the longer we shared a bed. In truth I had married a secret fantasy, not a woman. But we must conduct our marriages in the world of reality, and in that world my wife was Loimel.

27

MEANWHILE IN MY OFFICE at the Port Justiciary I struggled to do the job my bondfather had given me. Each day a formidable stack of reports and memoranda reached my desk; each day I tried to decide which must go before the High Justice and which were to be ignored. At first, naturally, I had no grounds for judgment. Segvord helped me, though, as did several of the senior officials of the Justiciary, who rightly saw that they had more to gain by serving me than by trying to block my inevitable rise. I took readily to the nature of my work, and before the full heat of summer was upon Manneran I was operating confidently, as if I had spent the last twenty years at this task.

Most of the material submitted for the guidance of the High Justice was nonsense. I learned swiftly to detect that sort by a quick scanning, often by looking at just a single page. The style in which they were written told me much: I found that a man who cannot phrase his thoughts cleanly on paper probably has no thoughts worth notice. The style is the man. If the prose is heavy-footed and sluggish, so too, in all likelihood, is the mind of its author, and then what are his insights into the operations of the Port Justiciary worth? A coarse and common mind offers coarse and common perceptions. I had to do a great deal of writing myself, summarizing and condensing the reports of middling value, and whatever I have learned of the literary art may be traced to my years in the service of the High Justice. My style too reflects the man, for I know myself to be earnest, solemn, fond of courtly gestures, and given to communicating more perhaps than others really want to know; all these traits I find in my own prose. It has its faults, yet am I pleased with it: I have my faults, yet am I pleased with me.

Before long I realized that the most powerful man in Manneran was a puppet whose strings I controlled. I decided which cases the High Justice should handle, I chose the applications for special favor that he would read, I gave him the capsuled commentaries on which his verdicts were based. Segvord had not accidentally allowed me to attain such power. It was necessary for someone to perform the screening duties I now handled, and until my coming to Manneran the job had been done by a committee of three, all ambitious to hold Segvord's title some day. Fearing those men, Segvord had arranged to promote them to positions of greater splendor but lesser responsibilities. Then he slid me into their place. His only son had died in boyhood; all his patronage therefore fell upon me. Out of love of Halum he had coolly chosen to make a homeless Sallan prince one of the dominant figures of Manneran.

It was widely understood, by others long before by me, how important I was going to be. Those princes at my wedding had not been there out of respect for Loimel's family, but to curry favor with me. The soft words from Stirron were meant to insure I would show no hostility to Salla in my decisionmaking. Doubtless my royal cousin Truis of Glin now was wondering uneasily if I knew that it was his doing that the doors of his province had closed in my face; he too sent a fine gift for my marriage-day. Nor did the flow of gifts cease with the nuptial ceremony. Constantly there came to me handsome things from those whose interests were bound up in the doings of the Port Justiciary. In Salla we would call such gifts by their rightful name, which is *bribes*; but Segvord assured me that in Manneran there was no harm in accepting them, so long as I did not let them interfere with my objectivity of judgment. Now I realized how, on the modest salary of a judge, Segvord had come to live in such princely style. In truth I did try to put all this bribery from my mind while at my official duties, and weigh each case on its merits alone.

So I found my place in Manneran. I mastered the secrets of the Port Justiciary, developed a feel for the rhythms of maritime commerce, and served the High Justice ably. I moved among princes and judges and men of wealth. I purchased a small but sumptuous house close by Segvord's, and soon had the builders out to increase its size. I worshiped as only the mighty do, at the Stone Chapel itself, and went to the celebrated Jidd for my drainings. I was taken into a select athletic society, and displayed my skills with the feathered shaft in Manneran Stadium. When I visited Salla with my bride the springtime after our wedding, Stirron received me as if I were a Mannerangi septarch, parading me through the capital before a cheering multitude and feasting me royally at the palace. He said not a word to me about my flight from Salla, but was wholly amiable in a reserved and distant fashion. My first son, who was born that autumn, I named for him.

Two other sons followed, Noim and Kinnall, and daughters named Halum and Loimel. The boys were straightbodied and strong; the girls promised to show the beauty of their namesakes. I took great pleasure in heading a family. I longed for the time when I could have my sons with me hunting in the Burnt Lowlands, or shooting the rapids of the River Woyn; meanwhile I went hunting without them, and the spears of many hornfowl came to decorate my home.

Loimel, as I have said, remained a stranger to me. One does not expect to penetrate the soul of one's wife as deeply as that of one's bondsister, but nevertheless, despite the customs of self-containment we observe, one expects to develop a certain communion with some-one one lives with. I never penetrated anything of Loimel's except her body. The warmth and openness she had showed me at our first meeting vanished swiftly, and she became as aloof as any coldbelly wife of Glin. Once in the heat of lovemaking I used "I" to her, as I sometimes did with whores, and she slapped me and twisted her hips to cast me from her loins. We drifted apart. She had her life, I mine; after a time we made no attempt to reach across the gulf to one another. She spent her time at music, bathing, sunsleeping, and piety, and I at hunting, gaming, rearing my sons, and doing my work. She took lovers and I took mistresses. It was a frosty marriage. We scarcely ever quarreled; we were not close enough even for that.

Noim and Halum were with me much of the time. They were great comforts to me.

At the Justiciary my authority and responsibility grew year by year. I was not promoted from my position as clerk to the High Justice, nor did my salary increase by any large extent; yet all of Manneran knew that I was the one who governed Segvord's decisions, and I enjoyed a lordly income of "gifts." Gradually Segvord withdrew from most of his duties, leaving them to me. He spent weeks at a time on his island retreat in the Gulf of Sumar, while I initialed and stamped documents in his name. In my twenty-fourth year, which was his fiftieth he gave up his office altogether. Since I was not a Man-nerangi by birth, it was impossible for me to become High Justice in his place; but Segvord arranged for the appointment of an amiable nonentity as his successor, one Noldo Kalimol, with the understand-ing that Kalimol would retain me in my place of power.

You would be right to assume that my life in Manneran was one of ease and security, of wealth and authority. Week flowed serenely into week, and, though perfect happiness is given to no man, I had few reasons for discontent. The failings of my marriage I accepted placidly since deep love between man and wife is not often en-countered in our kind of society; as for my other sorrow, my hopeless love for Halum, I kept it buried deep within me, and when it rose painfully close to the surface of my soul I soothed myself by a visit to the drainer Jidd. I might have gone on uneventfully in that fashion to the end of my days, but for the arrival in my life of Schweiz the Earthman.

28

EARTHMEN come rarely to Borthan. Before Schweiz, I had seen only two, both in the days when my father held the septarchy. The first was a tall redbearded man who visited Salla when I was about five years old; he was a traveler who wandered from world to world for his own amusement, and had just crossed the Burnt Lowlands alone and on foot. I remember studying his face with intense concentration, searching for the marks of his otherworldly origin—an extra eye, perhaps, horns, tendrils, fangs.

He had none of these, of course, and so I openly doubted his story of having come from Earth. Stirron, with the benefit of two years' more schooling than I, was the one who told me, in a jeering tone, that all the worlds of the heavens, including our own, had been settled by people from Earth, which was why an Earthman looked just like any of us. Nevertheless, when a second Earthman showed up at court a few years later, I still searched for fangs and tendrils. This one was a husky, cheerful man with light brown skin, a scientist making a collection of our native wildlife for some university in a far part of the galaxy. My father took him out into the Burnt Lowlands to get hornfowl; I begged to go along, and was whipped for my nagging.

I dreamed of Earth. I looked it up in books and saw a picture of a blue planet with many continents, and a huge pockmarked moon going around it, and I thought, This is where we all came from. This is the beginning of everything. I read of the kingdoms and nations of old Earth, the wars and devastation, the monuments, the tragedies. The going-forth into space, the attainment of the stars. There was a time when I even imagined I was an Earthman myself, born on that ancient planet of wonders, and brought to Borthan in babyhood to be exchanged for a septarch's true son. I told myself that when I grew up I would travel to Earth and walk through cities ten thousand years old, retracing the line of migration that had led my forefathers' forefathers from Earth to Borthan. I wanted to own a piece of Earth, too, some potsherd, some bit of stone, some battered coin, as a tangible link to the world at the heart of man's wanderings. And I longed for some other Earthman to come to Borthan, so that I could ask him ten thousand thousand questions, so that I could beg a slice of Earth for myself, but none came, and I grew up, and my obsession with the first of man's planets faded.

Then Schweiz crossed my way.

Schweiz was a man of commerce. Many Earthmen are. At the time I met him he had been on Borthan a couple of years as representative of an exporting firm based in a solar system not far from our own; he dealt in manufactured goods and sought our furs and spices in return. During his stay in Manneran, he had become entangled in controversy with a local importer over a cargo of stormshield furs from the northwestern coast; the man tried to give Schweiz poor quality at a higher-than-contracted price, Schweiz sued, and the case went to the Port Justiciary. This was about three years ago, and a little more than three years after the retirement of Segvord Helalam.

The facts of the case were clear-cut and there was no doubt about the judgment. One of the lower justices approved Schweiz's plea and ordered the importer to make good on his contract with the swindled Earthman. Ordinarily I would not have become involved in the matter. But when the papers on the case came to High Justice Kalimol for routine review just prior to affirmation of verdict, I glanced at them and saw that the plaintiff was an Earthman.

Temptation speared me. My old fascination with that race—my delusion of fangs and tendrils and extra eyes—took hold of me again. I had to talk with him. What did I hope to get from him? The answers to the questions that had gone unanswered when I was a boy? Some clue to the nature of the forces that had driven mankind to the stars? Or merely amusement, a moment of diversion in an overly placid life?

I asked Schweiz to report to my office.

He came in almost on the run, a frantic, energetic figure in clothes of flamboyant style and tone. Grinning with a manic glee, he slapped my palm in greeting, dug his knuckles into my desktop, pushed himself back a few steps, and began to pace the room.

"The gods preserve you, your grace!" he cried.

I thought his odd demeanor, his coiled-spring bounciness and his wild-eyed intensity, stemmed from fear of me, for he had good reason to worry, called in by a powerful official to discuss a case that he thought he had won. But I found later that Schweiz's mannerisms were expressions of his own seething nature, not of any momentary and specific tension.

He was a man of middle height, very sparely built, not a scrap of fat on his frame. His skin was tawny and his hair was the color of dark honey; it hung down in a straight flow to his shoulders. His eyes were bright and mischievous, his smile quick and sly, and he radiated a boyish vigor, a dynamic enthusiasm, that charmed me just then, though it would eventually make him an exhausting companion for me. Yet he was no boy: his face bore the first lines of age and his hair, abundant though it was, was starting to go thin at the crown.

"Be seated," I said, for his capering was disturbing me. I wondered how to launch the conversation. How much could I ask him before he claimed Covenant at me and sealed his lips? Would he talk about himself and his world? Had I any right to pry into a foreigner's soul in a way that I would not dare do with a man of Borthan? I would see. Curiosity drove me. I picked up the sheaf of documents on his case, for he was looking at the file unhappily, and held them toward him, saying, "One places the first matters first. Your verdict has been affirmed. Today High Justice Kalimol gives his seal and within a moonrise you'll have your money."

"Happy words, your grace."

"That concludes the legal business."

"So short a meeting? It seems hardly necessary to have paid this call to exchange only a moment's talk, your grace."

"One must admit," I said, "that you were summoned here to discuss things other than your lawsuit."

"Eh, your grace?" He looked baffled and alarmed.

"To talk of Earth," I said. "To gratify the idle inquisitiveness of a bored bureaucrat. Is that all right? Are you willing to talk a while, now that you've been lured here on the pretense of business? You know, Schweiz, one has always been fascinated by Earth and by Earthmen." To win some rapport with him, for he still was frowning and mistrustful, I told him the story of the two other Earthmen I had known, and of my childhood belief that they should be alien in form. He relaxed and listened with pleasure, and before I was through he was laughing heartily. "Fangs!" he cried. "Tendrils!" He ran his hands over his face. "Did you really think that, your grace? That Earthmen were such bizarre creatures? By all the gods, your grace, I wish I had some strangeness about my body, that I could give you amusement!"

I flinched each time Schweiz spoke of himself in the first person. His casual obscenities punctured the mood I had attempted to build. Though I tried to pretend nothing was amiss, Schweiz instantly realized his blunder, and, leaping to his feet in obvious distress, said, "A thousand pardons! One tends to forget one's grammar sometimes, when one is not accustomed to—"

"No offense is taken," I said hastily.

"You must understand, your grace, that old habits of speech die hard, and in using your language one sometimes slips into the mode most natural for himself, even though—"

"Of course, Schweiz. A forgivable lapse." He was trembling. "Besides," I said, winking, "I'm a grown man. Do you think I'm so easily shocked?" My use of the vulgarities was deliberate, to put him at his ease. The tactic worked; he subsided, calming. But he took no license from the incident to use gutter talk with me again that morning, and in fact was careful to observe the niceties of grammatical etiquette for a long time thereafter, until such things had ceased to matter between us.

I asked him to tell me now about Earth, the mother of us all.

"A small planet," he said. "Far away. Choked in its own ancient wastes; the poisons of two thousand years of carelessness and overbreeding stain its skies and its seas and its land. An ugly place."

"In truth, ugly?"

"There are still some attractive districts. Not many of them, and nothing to boast about. Some trees, here and there. A little grass. A lake. A waterfall. A valley. Mostly the planet is a dunghole. Earthmen often wish they could uncover their early ancestors, and bring them to life again, and then throttle them. For their selfishness. For their lack of concern for the generations to come. They filled the world with themselves and used everything up."

"Is this why Earthmen built empires in the skies, then, to escape the filth of their home world?"

"Part of it is that, yes," Schweiz said. "There were so many billions of people. And those who had the strength to leave all went out and up. But it was more than running away, you know. It was a hunger to see strange things, a hunger to undertake journeys, a hunger to make fresh starts. To create new and better worlds of man. A string of Earths across the sky."

"And those who did not go?" I asked. "Earth still has those other billions of people?" I was thinking of Velada Borthan and its sparse forty or fifty millions.

"Oh, no, no. It's almost empty now, a ghost-world, ruined cities, cracking highways. Few live there any longer. Fewer are born there every year."

"But you were born there?"

"On the continent called Europe, yes. One hasn't seen Earth for almost thirty years, though. Not since one was fourteen."

"You don't look that old," I said.

"One reckons time in Earthlength years," Schweiz explained. "By your figuring one is only approaching the age of thirty."

"Also this one," I said. "And here also is one who left his homeland before reaching manhood." I was speaking freely, far more freely than was proper, yet I could not stop myself. I had drawn out Schweiz, and felt an impulse to offer something of my own in return. "Going out from Salla as a boy to seek his fortune in Glin, then finding better luck in Manneran after a while. A wanderer, Schweiz, like yourself."

"It is a bond between us, then."

Could I presume on that bond? I asked him, "Why did you leave Earth?"

"For the same reasons as everyone else. To go where the air is clean and a man stands some chance to become something. The only ones who spend their whole lives there are those who can't help but stay."

"And this is the planet that all the galaxy reveres!" I said in wonder. "The world of so many myths! The planet of boys' dreams! The center of the universe—a pimple, a boil!"

"You put it well."

"Yet it is revered."

"Oh, revere it, revere it, certainly!" Schweiz cried. His eyes were aglow. "The fountain of mankind! The grand originator of the species! Why not revere it, your grace? Revere the bold beginnings that were made there. Revere the high ambitions that sprang from its mud. And revere the terrible mistakes, too. Ancient Earth made mistake after mistake, and choked itself in error, so that you would be spared from having to pass through the same fires and torments." Schweiz laughed harshly. "Earth died to redeem you starfolk from sin. How's that for a religious notion? A whole liturgy could be composed around that idea. A priestcraft of Earth the redeemer." Suddenly he leaned forward and said, "Are you a religious man, your grace?"

I was taken back by the thrusting intimacy of his question. But I put up no barriers.

"Certainly," I said.

"You go to the godhouse, you talk to the drainers, the whole thing?"

I was caught. I could not help but speak.

"Yes," I said. "Does that surprise you?"

"Not at all. Everyone on Borthan seems to be genuinely religious. Which amazes one. You know, your grace, one isn't religious in the least, oneself. One tries, one has always tried, one has worked so *hard* to convince oneself that there are superior beings out there who guide destiny, and sometimes one almost makes it, your grace, one almost believes, one breaks through into faith, but then skepticism shuts things down every time. And one ends by saying, No, it isn't possible, it can't be, it defies logic and common sense. Logic and common sense!"

"But how can you live all your days without a closeness to something holy?" I asked.

"Most of the time, one manages fairly well. Most of the time."

"And the rest of the time?"

"That's when one feels the impact of knowing one is entirely alone in the universe. Naked under the stars, and the starlight hitting the exposed skin, burning, a cold fire, and no one to shield one from it, no one to offer a hiding place, no one to pray to, do you see? The sky is ice and the ground is ice and the soul is ice, and who's to warm it? There isn't anyone. You've convinced yourself that no one exists who can give comfort. One wants some system of belief, one wants to submit, to get down and kneel, to be governed by metaphysics, you know? To believe, to have faith! And one can't. And

85

that's when the terror sets in. The dry sobs. The nights of no sleeping." Schweiz's face was flushed and wild with excitement; I wondered if he could be entirely sane. He reached across the desk, clamped his hand over mine—the gesture stunned me, but I did not pull back—and said hoarsely, "Do you believe in gods, your grace?"

"Surely."

"In a literal way? You think there's a god of travelers, and a god of fishermen, and a god of farmers, and one who looks after septarchs, and—"

"There is a force," I said, "that gives order and form to the universe. The force manifests itself in various ways, and for the sake of bridging the gap between ourselves and that force, we regard each of its manifestations as a 'god,' yes, and extend our souls to this manifestation or that one, as our needs demand. Those of us who are without learning accept these gods literally, as beings with faces and personalities. Others realize that they are metaphors for the aspects of the divine force, and not a tribe of potent spirits living overhead. But there is no one in Velada Borthan who denies the existence of the force itself."

"One feels such fierce envy of that," said Schweiz. "To be raised in a culture that has coherence and structure, to have such assurance of ultimate verities, to feel yourself part of a divine scheme—how marvelous that must be! To enter into a system of belief—it would almost be worth putting up with this society's great flaws, to have something like that."

"Flaws?" Suddenly I found myself on the defensive. "What flaws?"

Schweiz narrowed his gaze and moistened his lips. Perhaps he was calculating whether I would be hurt or angered by what he meant to say. "*Flaws* was possibly too strong a word," he replied. "One might say instead, this society's limits, its—well, its narrowness. One speaks now of the necessity to shield one's self from one's fellow men that you impose. The taboos against reference to self, against frank discourse, against any opening of the soul—"

"Has one not opened his soul to you today in this very room?"

"Ah," Schweiz said, "but you've been speaking to an alien, to one who is no part of your culture, to someone you secretly suspect of having tendrils and fangs! Would you be so free with a citizen of Manneran?"

"No one else in Manneran would have asked such questions as you have been asking."

"Maybe so. One lacks a native's training in self-repression. These questions about your philosophy of religion, then—do they intrude on your privacy of soul, your grace? Are they offensive to you?"

"One has no objections to talking of such things," I said, without much conviction.

"But it's a taboo conversation, isn't it? We weren't using naughty words, except that once when one slipped, but we were dealing in naughty ideas, establishing a naughty relationship. You let your wall down a little way, eh? For which one is grateful. One's been here so long, years now, and one hasn't ever talked freely with a man of Borthan, not once! Until one sensed today that you were willing to open yourself a bit. This has been an extraordinary experience, your grace." The manic smile returned. He moved jerkily about the office. "One had no wish to speak critically of your way of life here," he said. "One wished in fact to praise certain aspects of it, while trying to understand others."

"Which to praise, which to understand?"

"To understand your habit of erecting walls about yourselves. To praise the ease with which you accept divine presence. One envies you for that. As one said, one was raised in no system of belief at all, and is unable to let himself be overtaken by faith. One's head is always full of nasty skeptical questions. One is constitutionally unable to accept what one can't see or feel, and so one must always be *alone*, and one goes around the galaxy seeking for the gateway to belief, trying this, trying that, and one never finds—" Schweiz paused. He was flushed and sweaty. "So you see, your grace, you have something precious here, this ability to let yourselves become part of a larger power. One would wish to learn it from you. Of course, it's a matter of cultural conditioning. Borthan still knows the gods, and Earth has outlived them. Civilization is young on this planet. It takes thousands of years for the religious impulse to erode."

"And," I said, "this planet was settled by men who had strong religious beliefs, who specifically came here to preserve them, and who took great pains to instill them in their descendants."

"That too. Your Covenant. Yet that was—what, fifteen hundred, two thousand years ago? It could all have crumbled by now, but it hasn't. It's stronger than ever. Your devoutness, your humility, your denial of self—"

"Those who couldn't accept and transmit the ideals of the first settlers," I pointed out, "were not allowed to remain among them. That had its effect on the pattern of the culture, if you'll agree that such traits as rebelliousness and atheism can be bred out of a race. The consenters stayed; the rejecters went."

"You're speaking of the exiles who went to Sumara Borthan?"

"You know the story, then?"

"Naturally. One picks up the history of whatever planet one happens to be assigned to. Sumara Borthan, yes. Have you ever been there, your grace?"

"Few of us visit that continent," I said.

"Ever thought of going?"

"Never."

"There are those who do go there," Schweiz said, and gave me a strange smile. I meant to ask him about that, but at that moment a secretary entered with a stack of documents, and Schweiz hastily rose. "One doesn't wish to consume too much of your grace's valuable time. Perhaps this conversation could be continued at another hour?"

"One hopes for the pleasure of it," I told him.

29

WHEN SCHWEIZ was gone I sat a long while with my back to my desk, closing my eyes and replaying in my mind the things we had just said to one another. How readily he had slipped past my guard! How quickly we had begun to speak of inner matters! True, he was an otherworlder, and with him I did not feel entirely bound by our customs. Yet we had grown dangerously close so extraordinarily fast. Ten minutes more and I might have been as open as a bondbrother to him, and he to me. I was astounded and dismayed by my easy dropping of propriety, by the way he had drawn me slyly into such intimacy.

Was it wholly his doing? I had sent for him, I had been the first to ask the close questions. I had set the tone. He had sensed from that some instability in me, and he had seized upon it, quickly flipping the conversation about, so that I was the subject and he the interrogator. And I had gone along with it. Reluctantly but yet willingly, I had opened to him. I was drawn to him, and he to me. Schweiz the tempter! Schweiz the exploiter of my weakness, hidden so long, hidden even from myself! How could he have known I was ready to open?

His high-pitched rapid speech still seemed to echo in the room. Asking. Asking. Asking. And then revealing. *Are you a religious man? Do you believe in literal gods? If only I could find faith! How I envy you. But the flaws of your world. The denial of self. Would you be so free with a citizen of Manneran? Speak to me, your grace. Open to me. I have been alone here so long.*

How could he have known, when I myself did not know?

A strange friendship had been born. I asked Schweiz to dine at home with me; we feasted and we talked, and the blue wine of Salla flowed and the golden wine of Manneran, and when we were warmed by our drinking we discussed religion once more, and Schweiz's difficulties with faith, and my convictions that the gods were real. Halum came in and sat with us an hour, and afterward remarked to me on the power of Schweiz to loosen tongues, saying, "You seemed more drunk than you have ever been, Kinnall. And yet you shared only three bottles of wine, so it must have been something else that made your eyes shine and your words so easy." I laughed and told her that a recklessness came over me when I was with the Earthman, that I found it hard to abide by custom with him.

At our next meeting, in a tavern by the Justiciary, Schweiz said, "You love your bondsister, eh?"

"Of course one loves one's bondsister."

"One means, though, you *love* her." With a knowing snigger.

I drew back, tense. "Was one then so thoroughly wined the other night? What did one say to you of her?"

"Nothing," he replied. "You said it all to her. With your eyes, with your smile. And no words passed."

"May we talk of other things?"

"If your grace wishes."

"This is a tender theme, and painful."

"Pardon, then, your grace. One only meant to confirm one's guess."

"Such love as that is forbidden among us."

"Which is not to say that it sometimes exists, eh?" Schweiz asked, and clinked his glass against mine.

In that moment I made up my mind never to meet with him again. He looked too deep and spoke too freely of what he saw. But four days afterward, coming upon him on a pier, I invited him to dine a second time. Loimel was displeased by the invitation. Nor would Halum come, pleading another engagement; when I pressed her, she said that Schweiz made her uncomfortable. Noim was in Manneran, though, and joined us at the table. We all drank sparingly, and the conversation was a stilted and impersonal one, until, with no perceptible shifting of tone, we found ourselves telling Schweiz of the time when I had escaped from Salla in fear of my brother's jealousies, and Schweiz was telling us of his departure from Earth; when the Earthman went home that night, Noim said to me, not altogether disapprovingly, "There are devils in that man, Kinnall."

30

"THIS TABOO on self-expression," Schweiz asked me when we were together another time. "Can you explain it, your grace?"

"You mean the prohibition against saying 'I' and 'me'?"

"Not that, so much as the whole pattern of thought that would have you deny there are such things as 'I' and 'me,'" he said. "The commandment that you must keep your private affairs private at all times, except only with bond-kin and drainers. The custom of wall-building around oneself that affects even your grammar."

"The Covenant, you mean?"

"The Covenant," said Schweiz.

"You say you know our history?"

"Much of it."

"You know that our forefathers were stern folk from a northern climate, accustomed to hardship, mistrustful of luxury and ease, who came to Borthan to avoid what they saw as the contaminating decadence of their native world?"

"Was it so? One thought only that they were refugees from religious persecution."

"Refugees from sloth and self-indulgence," I said. "And, coming here, they established a code of conduct to protect their children's children against corruption."

"The Covenant."

"The Covenant, yes. The pledge they made each to each, the pledge that each of us makes to all his fellow men on his Naming Day. When we swear never to force our turmoils on another, when we vow to be strong-willed and hardy of spirit, so that the gods will continue to smile on us. And so on and so on. We are trained to abominate the demon that is self."

"Demon?"

"So we regard it. A tempting demon, that urges us to make use of others instead of relying on our own strengths."

"Where there is no love of self, there is neither friendship nor sharing," said Schweiz.

"Perhaps so."

"And thus there is no trust."

"We specify areas of responsibility through contract," I said. "There is no need for knowledge of the souls of others, where law rules. And in Velada Borthan no one questions the rule of law."

"You say you abominate self," said Schweiz. "It seems, rather, that you glorify it."

"How so?"

"By living apart from one another, each in the castle of his skull. Proud. Unbending. Aloof. Uncaring. The reign of self indeed, and no abomination of it!"

"You put things oddly," I said. "You invert our customs, and think you speak wisely."

"Has it always been like this," Schweiz asked, "since the beginning of settlement in Velada Borthan?"

"Yes," I said. "Except among those malcontents you know of, who fled to the southern continent. The rest of us abide by the Covenant. And our customs harden: thus we now may not talk of ourselves in the first person singular, since this is a raw exposure of self, but in medieval times this could be done. On the other hand, some things soften. Once we were guarded even in giving our names to strangers. We spoke to one another only when absolutely necessary. We show more trust nowadays."

"But not a great deal."

"But not a great deal," I admitted.

"And is there no pain in this for you? Every man sealed against all others? Do you never say to yourselves that there must be a happier way for humans to live?"

"We abide by the Covenant."

"With ease or with difficulty?"

"With ease," I said. "The pain is not so great, when you consider that we have bond-kin, with whom we are exempted from the rule of selflessness. And the same with our drainers."

"To others, though, you may not complain, you may not unburden a sorrowful soul, you may not seek advice, you may not expose your desires and needs, you may not speak of dreams and fantasies and romance, you may not talk of anything but chilly, impersonal things." Schweiz shuddered. "Pardon, your grace, but one finds this a harsh way to live. One's own search has constantly been for warmth and love and human contact, for sharing, for opening, and this world here seems to elevate the opposite of what one prizes most highly."

"Have you had much luck," I asked, "finding warmth and love and human contact?"

Schweiz shrugged. "It has not always been easy."

"For us there is never loneliness, since we have bond-kin. With Halum, with Noim, with such as these to offer comfort, why does one need a world of strangers?"

"And if your bond-kin are not close at hand? If one is wandering, say, far from them in the snows of Glin?"

"One suffers, then. And one's character grows tougher. But that is an exceptional situation. Schweiz, our system may force us into isolation, yet it also guarantees us love."

"But not the love of husband for wife. Not the love of father for child."

"Perhaps not."

"And even the love of bond-kin is limited. For you yourself, eh, have admitted that you feel a longing for your bondsister Halum that cannot be—"

I cut him off, telling him sharply, "Speak of other things!" Color flared in my cheeks; my skin grew hot.

Schweiz nodded and smiled a chastened smile. "Pardon, your grace. The conversation became too intense; there was loss of control, but no injury meant."

"Very well."

"The reference was too personal. One is abashed."

"You meant no injury," I said, guilty over my outburst, knowing he had stung me at a vulnerable place and that I had overreacted to the bite of truth. I poured more wine. We drank in silence for a time.

Then Schweiz said, "May one make a proposal, your grace? May one invite you to take part in an experiment that may prove interesting and valuable to you?"

"Go on," I said, frowning, ill at ease.

"You know," he began, "that one has long felt uncomfortably conscious of his solitary state in the universe, and that one has sought without success some means of comprehending his relationship to that universe. For you, the method lies in religious faith, but one has failed to reach such faith because of his unfortunate compulsion toward total rationalism. Eh? One cannot break through to that larger sense of *belonging* by words alone, by prayer alone, by ritual alone. This thing is possible for you, and one envies you for it. One finds himself trapped, isolated, sealed up in his skull, condemned to metaphysical solitude: a man apart, a man on his own. One does not find this state of godlessness enjoyable or desirable. You of Borthan can tolerate the sort of emotional isolation you impose on yourselves, since you have the consolations of your religion, you have drainers and whatever mystical mergings-with-the-gods the act of draining gives you; but the one who speaks to you now has no such advantages."

"All this we have discussed many times," I said. "You spoke of a proposal, an experiment."

"Be patient, your grace. One must explain oneself fully, step by step."

Schweiz flashed me his most charming smile, and turned on me eyes that were bright with visionary schemes. His hands roamed the air expressively, conjuring up invisible drama, as he said, "Perhaps your grace is aware that there are certain chemical substances—drugs, yes, call them drugs—that allow one to make an opening into the infinite, or at least to have the illusion that one has made such an opening—to attain a brief and tentative glimpse into the mystic realms of the intangible. Eh? Known for thousands of years, these drugs, used in the days before Earthmen ever went to the stars. Employed in ancient religious rites. Employed by others as a substitute for religion, as a secular means of finding faith, the gateway to the infinite for such as this one, who can get there no other way."

"Such drugs are forbidden in Velada Borthan," I said.

"Of course, of course! For you they offer a means of sidestepping the processes of formal religion. Why waste time at a drainer's if you can expand your soul with a pill? Your law is wise on this point. Your Covenant could not survive if you allowed these chemicals to be used here."

"Your proposal, Schweiz," I said.

"One first must tell you that he has used these drugs himself, and found them not entirely satisfactory. True, they open the infinite. True, they let one merge with the Godhead. But only for moments: a few hours at best. And at the end of it, one is as alone as before. It is the illusion of the soul's opening, not the opening itself. Whereas this planet produces a drug that can provide the real thing."

"What?"

"In Sumara Borthan," said Schweiz, "dwell those who fled the rule of the Covenant. One is told that they are savages, going naked and living on roots and seeds and fish; the cloak of civilization has dropped away from them and they have slipped back into barbarism. So one learned from a traveler who had visited that continent not long ago. One also learned that in Sumara Borthan they use a drug made from a certain powdered root, which has the capacity of opening mind to mind, so that each can read the inmost thoughts of the other. It is the very opposite of your Covenant, do you see? They know one another from the soul out, by way of this drug they eat."

"One has heard stories of the savagery of those folk," I said.

Schweiz put his face close to mine. "One confesses himself tempted by the Sumaran drug. One hopes that if he could ever get inside another mind, he could find that community of soul for which he has searched so long. It might be the bridge to the infinite that he seeks, the spiritual transformation. Eh? In quest of revelations he has tried many substances. Why not this?"

"If it exists."

"It exists, your grace. This traveler who came from Sumara Borthan brought some of it with him to Manneran, and sold some of it to the curious Earthman." Schweiz drew forth from a pocket a small glossy envelope, and held it toward me. It contained a small quantity

94

of some white powder; it could have been sugar. "Here it is," he said.

I stared at it as if he had pulled out a flask of poison.

"Your proposal?" I demanded. "Your experiment, Schweiz?"

"Let us share the Sumaran drug," he said.

31

I MIGHT HAVE SLAPPED the powder from his hand and ordered his arrest. I might have commanded him to get away from me and never come near again. I might at the very least have cried out that it was impossible I would ever touch any such substance. But I did none of those things. I chose instead to be coolly intellectual, to show casual curiosity, to remain calm and play conversational games with him. Thus I encouraged him to lead me a little deeper into the quicksand.

I said, "Do you think that one is so eager to contravene the Covenant?"

"One thinks that you are a man of strong will and inquiring mind, who would not miss an opportunity for enlightenment."

"Illegal enlightenment?"

"All true enlightenment is illegal at first, within its context. Even the religion of the Covenant: were your forefathers not driven out of other worlds for practicing it?"

"One mistrusts such analogy-making. We are not talking of religions now. We talk of a dangerous drug. You ask one to surrender all the training of his lifetime, and open himself to you as he has never done even to bond-kin, even to a drainer."

"Yes."

"And you imagine that one might be willing to do such a thing?"

"One imagines that you might well emerge transformed and cleansed, if you could bring yourself to try," Schweiz said.

"One might also emerge scarred and twisted."

"Doubtful. Knowledge never injures the soul. It only purges that which encrusts and saps the soul."

"How glib you are, Schweiz! Look, though: can you believe it would be possible to give one's inner secrets to a stranger, to a foreigner, to an otherworlder?"

"Why not? Better to a stranger than to a friend. Better to an Earthman than a fellow citizen. You'd have nothing to fear: the Earthman would never try to judge you by the standards of Borthan. There'd be no criticisms, no disapprovals of what's under your skull. And the Earthman will leave this planet in a year or two, on a journey of hundreds of light-years, and what then will it matter that your mind once merged with his?"

"Why are you so eager to have this merger happen?"

"For eight moontimes," he said, "this drug has been in one's pocket, while one hunts for someone to share it with. It looked as though the search would be in vain. Then one met you, and saw your potential, your strength, your hidden rebelliousness—"

"One is aware of no rebelliousness, Schweiz. One accepts his world completely."

"May one bring up the delicate matter of your attitude toward your bondsister? That seems a symptom of a fundamental discontent with the restrictions of your society."

"Perhaps. Perhaps not."

"You would know yourself better after sampling the Sumaran drug. You would have fewer perhapses and more certainties."

"How can you say this, if you haven't had the drug yourself?"

"So it seems to one."

"It is impossible," I said.

"An experiment. A secret pact. No one would ever know."

"Impossible."

"Is it that you fear to share your soul?"

"One is taught that such sharing is unholy."

"The teachings can be wrong," he said. "Have you never felt the temptation? Have you never tasted such ecstasy in a draining that you wished you might undergo the same experience with someone you loved, your grace?"

Again he caught me in a vulnerable place. "One has had such feelings occasionally," I admitted. "Sitting before some ugly drainer, and imagining it was Noim instead, or Halum, and that the draining was a two-way flow—"

"Then you already long for this drug, and don't realize it!"

"No. No."

"Perhaps," Schweiz suggested, "it is the idea of opening to a stranger that dismays you, and not the concept of opening itself. Perhaps you would take this drug with someone other than the Earthman, eh? With your bondbrother? With your bondsister?"

I considered that. Sitting down with Noim, who was to me like a second self, and reaching his mind on levels that had never been available to me before, and he reaching mine. Or with Halum—or with Halum—

Schweiz, you tempter!

He said, after letting me think a while, "Does the idea please you? Here, then. One will surrender his chance with the drug. Take it, use it, share it with one whom you love." He pressed the envelope into my hand. It frightened me; I let it fall to the table as if it were aflame.

I said, "But that would deprive you of your hoped-for fulfillment."

"No matter. One can get more of the drug. One may perhaps find another partner for the experiment. Meanwhile you would have known the ecstasy, your grace. Even an Earthman can be unselfish. Take it, your grace. Take it."

I gave him a dark look. "Would it be, Schweiz, that this talk of taking the drug yourself was only pretense? That what you really look for is someone to offer himself as an experimental subject, so you can be sure the drug is safe before you risk it?"

"You misunderstand, your grace."

"Maybe not. Maybe this is what you've been driving toward." I saw myself administering the drug to Noim, saw him falling into convulsions before my eyes as I made ready to bring my own dose to my lips. I pushed the envelope back toward Schweiz. "No. The offer is refused. One appreciates the generosity, but one will not experiment on his loved ones, Schweiz."

His face was very red. "This implication is unwarranted, your grace. The offer to relinquish one's own share of the drug was made in good faith, and at no little cost to one's own plans. But since you reject it, let us return to the original proposition. The two of us will sample the drug, in secrecy, as an experiment in possibilities. Let us find out together what its powers may be and what doors it can open for us. We would have much to gain from this adventure, one is sure."

"One sees what you would have to gain," I said. "But what purpose is there in it for—"

"Yourself?" Schweiz chuckled. Then he rammed me with the barbed hook. "Your grace, by making the experiment you would learn that the drug is safe, you would discover the proper dosage, you would lose your fear of the mind-opening itself. And then, after obtaining a further supply of the drug, you would be properly prepared to use it for a purpose from which your fears now hold you back. You could take the drug together with the only person whom you truly love. You could use it to open your mind to your bondsister Halum, and to open hers to you."

32

THERE IS A STORY they tell to children who are still learning the Covenant, about the days when the gods had not yet ceased to walk the world in human form, and the first men had not yet arrived on Borthan. The gods at that time did not know they were divine, for they had no mortals about them for comparison, and so they were innocent beings, unaware of their powers, who lived in a simple way. They dwelled in Manneran (this is the source of Manneran's claim to superior holiness, the legend that it was once the home of the gods) and ate berries and leaves, and went without clothing except in the mild Mannerangi winter, when they threw shawls of animal hide loosely over their shoulders. And there was nothing godlike about them.

One day two of these ungodlike gods decided they would go off to see something of the world. The idea for making such a journey came first to the god whose secret name is Kinnall, now the god who looks after wayfarers. (Yes, he for whom I was named.) This Kinnall invited the goddess Thirga to join him, she whose responsibility now is the protection of those who are in love. Thirga shared Kinnall's restlessness and off they went.

From Manneran they walked west along the southern coast until they came to the shores of the Gulf of Sumar. Then they turned north, and passed through Stroin Gap just by the place where the Huishtor Mountains come to an end. They entered the Wet Lowlands, and stayed there a while, and then proceeded to the Burnt

Lowlands, which they found less to their liking, and finally they ventured into the Frozen Lowlands, where they thought they would perish of the cold. So they turned south again, and this time they also walked to the west, and shortly they found themselves staring at the inland slopes of the Threishtor Mountains. There seemed no way for them to cross over this mighty range. They followed its eastern foothills south, but could not get out of the Burnt Lowlands, and they suffered great hardships, until at last they stumbled upon Threish Gate, and made their way through that difficult pass into the cool and foggy province of Threish.

On their first day in Threish the two gods discovered a place where a spring flowed out of a hillside. The opening in the hillside was nine-sided, and the rock surrounding the opening was so bright that it dazzled the eye, for it rippled and iridesced, and glowed with many colors constantly pulsing and changing, red and green and violet and ivory and turquoise and many more. And the water that came forth was of the same shimmering quality, having in it every color anyone ever had seen. The stream flowed only a short distance this way, and then was lost in the waters of a much larger brook, in which all the wondrous colors vanished.

Kinnall said, "We have wandered a long while in the Burnt Lowlands, and our throats are dry from thirst. Shall we drink?" And Thirga said, "Yes, let us drink," and knelt by the opening in the hillside. She cupped her hands and filled them with the glittering water, and poured it into her mouth, and Kinnall drank also, and the taste of the water was so sweet that they thrust their faces right against the flow of the spring, gulping down all they could.

As they did this they experienced strange sensations of their bodies and minds. Kinnall looked toward Thirga and realized that he could see the thoughts within her soul, and they were thoughts of love for him. And she looked toward him, and saw his thoughts as well. "We are different now," Kinnall said, and he did not even need words to convey his meaning, for Thirga understood him as soon as his thought formed. And she replied, "No, we are not different, but are merely able to understand the use of the gifts we have always had."

And it was true. For they had many gifts, and they had never used them before. They could rise in the air and travel like birds; they could change the shapes of their bodies; they could walk through the Burnt Lowlands or the Frozen Lowlands, and feel no discomfort; they could live without taking in food; they could halt

99

the aging of their flesh, and become as young as they pleased; they could speak without saying words. All these things they might have done before coming to the spring, except that they had not known how, and now they were capable of using the skills with which they had been born. They had learned, by drinking the water of the bright spring, how to go about being gods.

Even so, they did not yet know that they were gods.

They drank at the wonderful spring again, but it taught them nothing that the first gulp had not already showed them, and so they moved onward through Threish. Everything they beheld now was transformed, taking on a jeweled beauty, a magical luminous brilliance, and they were stunned by the wonder of their change. And everything they saw they shared with one another, for their souls were in perfect communion and full harmony.

After some time they remembered the others who lived in Manneran, and flew back to tell them about the spring. The journey took only an instant. All their friends crowded round as Kinnall and Thirga spoke of the miracle of the spring, and demonstrated the powers they had mastered. When they were done, everyone in Manneran resolved to go to the spring, and set out in a long procession, through Stroin Gap and the Wet Lowlands and up the eastern slopes of the Threishtors to Threish Gate. Kinnall and Thirga flew above them, guiding them from day to day. Eventually they reached the place of the spring, and one by one they drank of it and became as gods. Then they scattered, some returning to Manneran, some going to Salla, some going even to Sumara Borthan or the far continents of Umbis, Dabis, and Tibis, since, now that they were as gods, there were no limits on the speed of their travel, and they wished to see those strange places. But Kinnall and Thirga settled down beside the spring in eastern Threish and were content to explore one another's soul.

Many years passed, and then the starship of our forefathers came down in Threish, near the western shore. Men had at last reached Borthan. They built a small town and went about the task of collecting food for themselves. A certain man named Digant, who was among these settlers, ventured deep into the forest in search of meat-animals, and became lost, and roamed and roamed until finally he came to the place where Kinnall and Thirga lived. He had never seen any such as they before, nor they anyone such as he.

"What sort of creatures are you?" he asked.

Kinnall replied, "Once we were quite ordinary, but now we do quite well, for we never grow old, and we can fly faster than any bird, and our souls are open to each other, and we can take on any shape we please."

"Why, then, you are gods!" Digant cried.

"Gods? What are gods?"

And Digant explained that he was a man, and had no such powers as theirs, for men must use words to talk, and can neither fly nor change their shape, and grow older with each journey of the world around the sun, until the time of dying comes. Kinnall and Thirga listened with care, comparing themselves to Digant, and when he was done speaking they knew it was true, that he was a man and they were gods.

"Once we were almost like men ourselves," Thirga admitted. "We felt hunger and grew old and spoke only by means of words and had to put one foot in front of the other to get from place to place. We lived like men out of ignorance, for we did not know our powers. But then things changed."

"And what changed them?" Digant asked.

"Why," said Kinnall in his innocence, "we drank from that glistening spring, and the water of it opened our eyes to our powers, and allowed us to become as gods. That was all."

Then Digant's soul surged with excitement, for he told himself that he too could drink from the spring, and then he would join this pair in godhood. He would keep the spring a secret afterward, when he returned to the settlers on the coast, and they would worship him as their living god, and treat him with reverence, or he would destroy them. But Digant did not dare ask Kinnall and Thirga to let him drink from the spring, for he feared that they would refuse him, being jealous of their divinity. So he hatched a scheme to get them away from that place.

"Is it true," he asked them, "that you can travel so fast that you are able to visit every part of this world in a single day?"

Kinnall assured him that this was true.

"It seems difficult to believe," said Digant.

"We will give you proof," Thirga said, and she touched her hand to Kinnall's, and the two gods went aloft. They soared to the highest peak of the Threishtors and gathered snowflowers there; they descended into the Burnt Lowlands and scooped up a handful of the red soil; in the Wet Lowlands they collected herbs; by the Gulf of Sumar they took some liquor from a flesh-tree; on the shores of the Polar Gulf they pried out a sample of the eternal ice; then they leaped over the top of the world to frosty Tibis, and began their journey through the far continents, so that they might bring back to the doubting Digant something from every part of the world.

The moment Kinnall and Thirga had departed on this enterprise, Digant rushed to the spring of miracles. There he hesitated briefly, afraid that the gods might return suddenly and strike him down for his boldness; but they did not appear, and Digant thrust his face into the flow and drank deeply, thinking, Now I too shall be as a god. He filled his gut with the glowing water and swayed and grew dizzy, and fell to the ground. Is this godhood, he wondered? He tried to fly and could not. He tried to change his shape and could not. He tried to make himself younger and could not. He failed in all these things because he had been a man to begin with, and not a god, and the spring could not change a man into a god, but could only help a god to realize his full powers.

But the spring gave Digant one gift. It enabled him to reach into the minds of the other men who had settled in Threish. As he lay on the ground, numb with disappointment, he heard a tiny tickling sound in the middle of his mind, and paid close heed to it and realized he was hearing the minds of his friends. And he found a way of amplifying the sound so that he could hear everything clearly: yes, and this was the mind of his wife, and this was the mind of his sister, and this was the mind of his sister's husband, and Digant could look into any of them and any other mind, reading the innermost thoughts. This is godhood, he told himself. And he probed their minds deeply, flushing out all their secrets. Steadily he increased the scope of his power until every mind at once was connected to his. Forth from them he drew the privacies of their souls, until, intoxicated with his new power, swollen with the pride of his godhood, he sent out a message to all those minds from his mind, saying, "HEAR THE VOICE OF DIGANT. IT IS DIGANT THE GOD THAT YOU SHALL WORSHIP."

When this terrible voice broke into their minds, many of the settlers in Threish fell down dead with shock, and others lost their sanity, and others ran about in wild terror, crying, "Digant has invaded our minds! Digant has invaded our minds!" And the waves of fear and pain coming out of them were so intense that Digant himself suffered greatly, falling into a paralysis and stupor, though his dazed mind continued to roar, "HEAR THE VOICE OF DIGANT. IT IS DIGANT THE GOD THAT YOU SHALL WORSHIP." Each time that great cry went forth, more settlers died and more lost their reason, and Digant, responding to the mental tumults he had caused, writhed and shook in agony, wholly unable to control the powers of his brain.

Kinnall and Thirga were in Dabis when this occurred, drawing forth from a marsh a triple-headed worm to show to Digant. The bellowings of Digant's mind sped around the world even to Dabis, and, hearing those sounds, Kinnall and Thirga left off what they were doing and hurried back to Threish. They found Digant close to death, his brain all but burned out, and they found the settlers of Threish dead or mad; and they knew at once how this had come to pass. Swiftly they brought an end to Digant's life, so that there would be silence in Threish. Then they went among the victims of the would-be god, and raised all the dead and healed all the injured. And lastly they sealed the opening in the hillside with a seal that could not be broken, for it was plain to them that men must not drink of that spring, but only gods, and all the gods had already taken their draughts of it. The people of Threish fell on their knees before those two, and asked in awe, "Who are you?" and Kinnall and Thirga replied, "We are gods, and you are only men." And that was the beginning of the end of the innocence of the gods. And after that time it was forbidden among men to seek ways of speaking mind to mind, because of the harm that Digant had done, and it was written into the Covenant that one must keep one's soul apart from the souls of others, since only gods can mingle souls without destroying one another, and we are not gods.

33

OF COURSE I found many reasons to postpone taking the Sumaran drug with Schweiz. First, High Justice Kalimol departed on a hunting trip, and I told Schweiz that the doubled pressures of my work in his absence made it impossible for me to undertake the experiment just then. Kalimol returned; Halum fell ill; I used my worry over her as the next excuse. Halum recovered; Noim invited Loimel and myself to spend a holiday at his lodge in southern Salla. We came back from Salla; war broke out between Salla and Glin, creating complex maritime problems for me at the Justiciary. And so the weeks went. Schweiz grew impatient. Did I mean to take the drug at all? I could not give him an answer. I did not truly know. I was afraid. But always there burned in me the temptation he had planted there. To reach out, godlike, and enter Halum's soul—

I went to the Stone Chapel, waited until Jidd could see me, and let myself be drained. But I kept back from Jidd all mention of Schweiz and his drug, fearing to reveal that I toyed with such dangerous amusements. Therefore the draining was a failure, since I had not fully opened my soul to the drainer; and I left the Stone Chapel with a congestion of the spirit, tense and morose. I saw clearly now that I must necessarily yield to Schweiz, that what he offered was an ordeal through which I must pass, for there was no escaping it. He had found me out. Beneath my piety I was a potential traitor to the Covenant. I went to him.

"Today," I said. "Now."

34

WE NEEDED SECLUSION. The Port Justiciary maintains a country lodge in the hills two hours northwest of the city of Manneran, where visiting dignitaries are entertained and treaties of trade negotiated. I knew that this lodge was not currently in use, and I reserved it for myself for a three-day span. At midday I picked Schweiz up in a Justiciary car and drove quickly out of the city. There were three servants on duty at the lodge—a cook, a chambermaid, a gardener. I warned them that extremely delicate discussions would be taking place, so that they must on no account cause interruptions or offer distractions. Then Schweiz and I sealed ourselves in the inner living quarters. "It would be best," he said, "to take no food this evening. Also they recommend that the body be absolutely clean."

The lodge had an excellent steambath. We scrubbed ourselves vigorously, and when we came out we donned loose, comfortable silken robes. Schweiz's eyes had taken on the glassy glitter that came over them in moments of high excitement. I felt frightened and uneasy, and began to think that I would suffer some terrible harm out of this evening. Just then I regarded myself as one who was about to undergo surgery from which his chances of recovery were slight. My mood was sullen resignation: I was willing, I was here, I was eager to make the plunge and have done with it.

"Your last chance," Schweiz said, grinning broadly. "You can still back out."

"No."

"You understand that there are risks, though? We are equally inexperienced in this drug. There are dangers."

"Understood," I said.

"Is it also understood that you enter this voluntarily, and under no coercion?"

I said, "Why this delay, Schweiz? Bring out your potion."

"One wishes to assure himself that your grace is fully prepared to meet any consequences."

In a tone of heavy sarcasm I said, "Perhaps there should be a contract between us, then, in the proper fashion, relieving you of any liability in case one wishes later to press a claim for damage to the personality—"

"If you wish, your grace. One does not feel it necessary."

"One wasn't serious," I said. I was fidgety now. "Can it be that you're nervous about it too, Schweiz? That you have some doubts?"

"We take a bold step."

"Let's take it, then, before the moment goes by. Bring out the potion, Schweiz. Bring out the potion."

"Yes," he said, and gave me a long look, his eyes to mine, and clapped his hands in childlike glee. And laughed in triumph. I saw how he had manipulated me. Now I was begging him for the drug! Oh, devil, devil!

From his traveling case he fetched the packet of white powder. He told me to get wine, and I ordered two flasks of chilled Mannerangi golden from the kitchen, and he dumped half the contents of the packet into my flask, half into his. The powder dissolved almost instantly: for a moment it left a cloudy gray wake, and then there was no trace of it. We gripped our flasks. I remember looking across the table at Schweiz and giving him a quick smile; he described it to me later as the pale, edgy smirk of a timid virgin about to open her thighs. "It should all go down at once," Schweiz said, and he gulped his wine and I gulped mine, and then I sat back, expecting the drug to hit me instantly. I felt a faint giddiness, but that was only the wine doing its work in my empty gut. "How long does it take to begin?" I asked. Schweiz shrugged. "It will be some while yet," he replied. We waited in silence. Testing myself, I tried to force my mind to go forth and encounter his, but I felt nothing. The sounds of the room became magnified: the creak of floorboards, the rasping of insects outside the window, the tiny hum of the bright electric light. "Can you explain," I said hoarsely, "the way this drug is thought to operate?" Schweiz answered, "One can tell you only what was told to him. Which is, that the potential power to link one mind to another exists in all of us from birth, only we have evolved a chemical substance in the blood that inhibits the power. A very few are born without the inhibitor, and these have the gift of reaching minds, but most of us are forever blocked from achieving this silent communication, except when for some reason the production of the hormone ceases of its own accord and our minds open for a while. When this occurs it is often mistaken for madness. This drug of Sumara Borthan, they say, neutralizes the natural inhibitor in our blood, at least for a short time, and permits us to make contact with one another, as we would normally do if we lacked the counteracting substance in the blood. So one has heard." To this I answered, "We all might be supermen, then, but we are crippled by our own glands?" And Schweiz, gesturing grandly, said, "Maybe it is that there were good biological reasons for evolving this protection against our own powers. Eh? Or maybe not." He laughed. His face had turned very red. I asked him if he really believed this story of an inhibitory hormone and a counterinhibitory drug, and he said that he had no grounds for making judgment. "Do you feel anything yet?" I asked. "Only the wine," he said. We waited. We waited. Perhaps it will do nothing, I thought, and I will be reprieved. We waited. At length Schweiz said, "It may be beginning now."

35

I WAS AT FIRST GREATLY AWARE of the functioning of my own body: the thud-thud of my heart, the pounding of the blood against the walls of arteries, the movements of fluids deep within my ears, the drifting of corpuscular bodies across my field of vision. I became enormously receptive to external stimuli: currents of air brushing my cheek, a fold of my robe touching my thigh, the pressure of the floor against the sole of my foot. I heard an unfamiliar sound as of water tumbling through a distant gorge. I lost touch with my surroundings, for as my perceptions intensified the range of them also narrowed, and I found myself incapable of perceiving the shape of the room, for I saw nothing clearly except in a constricted tunnel at the other end of which was Schweiz; beyond the rim of this tunnel there was only haze. Now I was frightened, and fought to clear my mind, as one may make a conscious effort to free the brain of the muddle caused by too much wine; but the harder I struggled to return to normal perception, the more rapidly did the pace of change accelerate. I entered a state of luminous drunkenness, in which brilliant radiant rods of colored light streamed past my face, and I was certain I must have sipped from Digant's spring. I felt a rushing sensation, like that of air moving swiftly against my ears. I heard a high whining sound that was barely audible at first, but swept up in crescendo until it took on tangibility and appeared to fill the room to overflowing, yet the sound was not painful. The chair beneath me throbbed and pulsated in a steady beat that seemed tuned to some patient pulsation of our planet itself. Then, with no discernible feeling of having crossed a boundary, I realized that my perceptions had for some time been double: now I was aware of a second heartbeat, of a second spurt of blood within vessels, of a second churning of intestines. But it was not mere duplication, for these other rhythms were different, setting up complex symphonic interplays with the rhythms of my own body, creating percussive patterns that were so intricate that the fibers of my mind melted in the attempt to follow them. I began to sway in time with these beats, to clap my hands against my thighs, to snap my fingers; and, looking down my vision-tunnel, I saw Schweiz also swaying and clapping and snapping, and realized whose bodily rhythms it was I had been receiving. We were locked together. I had difficulty now distinguishing his heartbeat from my own, and sometimes, glancing across the table at him, I saw my own reddened, distorted face. I experienced a general liquefying of reality, a breaking down of walls and restraints; I was unable to maintain a sense of Kinnall Darival as an individual; I thought not in terms of *he* and *I*, but of *we*. I had lost not only my identity but the concept of self itself.

At that level I remained a long while, until I started to think that the power of the drug was receding. Colors grew less brilliant, my perception of the room became more conventional, and I could again distinguish Schweiz's body and mind from my own. Instead of feeling relief that the worst was over, though, I felt only disappointment that I had not achieved the kind of mingling of consciousness that Schweiz had promised.

But I was mistaken.

The first wild rush of the drug was over, yes, yet we were only now coming into the true communion. Schweiz and I were apart but nevertheless together. This was the real selfbaring. I saw his soul spread out before me as though on a table, and I could walk up to the table and examine those things that were on it, picking up this utensil, that vase, these ornaments, and studying them as closely as I wished.

Here was the looming face of Schweiz's mother. Here was a swollen pale breast streaked with blue veins and tipped by an enormous rigid nipple. Here were childhood furies. Here were memories of Earth. Through the eyes of Schweiz I saw the mother of worlds, maimed and shackled, disfigured and discolored. Beauty gleamed through the ugliness. This was the place of his birth, this disheveled city; these were highways ten thousand years old; these were the stumps of ancient temples. Here was the node of first love. Here were disappointments and departures. Betrayals, here. Shared confidences, here. Growth and change. Corrosion and despair. Journeys. Failures. Seductions. Confessions. I saw the suns of a hundred worlds.

And I passed through the strata of Schweiz's soul, inspecting the gritty layers of greed and the boulders of trickery, the oily pockets of maliciousness, the decaying loam of opportunism. Here was self incarnate; here was a man who had lived solely for his own sake.

Yet I did not recoil from the darkness of Schweiz.

I saw beyond those things. I saw the yearning, the god-hunger in the man, Schweiz alone on a lunar plain, splayfooted on a black shield of rock under a purple sky, reaching up, grasping, taking hold of nothing. Sly and opportunistic he might be, yes, but also vulnerable, passionate, honest beneath all his capering. I could not judge Schweiz harshly. He was I. I was he. Tides of self engulfed us both. If I were to cast Schweiz down, I must also cast down Kinnall Darival. My soul was flooded with warmth for him.

I felt him, too, probing me. I erected no barriers about my spirit as he came to explore it. And through his own eyes I saw what he was seeing in me. My fear of my father. My awe of my brother. My love for Halum. My flight into Glin. My choosing of Loimel. My petty faults and my petty virtues. Everything, Schweiz. Look. Look. Look. And it all came back refracted through his soul, nor did I find it painful to observe. Love of others begins with love of self, I thought suddenly.

In that instant the Covenant fell and shattered within me.

Gradually Schweiz and I pulled apart, though we remained in contact some time longer, the strength of the bond ebbing steadily. When it broke at last, I felt a shivering resonance, as if a taut string had snapped. We sat in silence. My eyes were closed. I was queasy in the pit of my stomach and conscious, as I had never been conscious before, of the gulf that keeps each of us forever alone. After some long time I looked across the room at Schweiz.

He was watching me, waiting for me. He wore that demonic look of his, the wild grin, the bright-eyed gleam, only now it seemed to me less a look of madness than a reflection of inner joy. He appeared younger now. His face was still flushed.

"I love you," he said softly.

The unexpected words were bludgeons. I crossed my wrists before my face, palms out, protecting myself.

"What upsets you so much?" he asked. "My grammar or my meaning?"

"Both."

"Can it be so terrible to say, *I love you?*"

"One has never—one does not know how to—"

"To react? To respond?" Schweiz laughed. "I don't mean I love you in any physical way. As if that would be so hideous. But no. I mean what I say, Kinnall. I've been in your mind and I liked what I saw there. I love you."

"You talk in 'I,'" I reminded him.

"Why not? Must I deny self even now? Come on: break free, Kinnall. I know you want to. Do you think what I just said to you is obscene?"

"There is such a strangeness about it."

"On my world those words have a holy strangeness," said Schweiz. "And here they're an abomination. Never to be allowed to say 'I love you,' eh? A whole planet denying itself that little pleasure. Oh, no, Kinnall, no, no, no!"

"Please," I said faintly. "One still has not fully adjusted to the things the drug did. When you shout at one like that—"

But he would not subside.

"You were in my mind too," he said. "What did you find there? Was I so loathsome? Get it out, Kinnall. You have no secrets from me now. The truth. The truth!"

"You know, then, that one found you more admirable than one had expected."

Schweiz chuckled. "And I the same! Why are we afraid of each other now, Kinnall? I told you: I love you! We made contact. We saw there were areas of trust. Now we have to change, Kinnall. You more than me, because you have farther to go. Come. Come. Put words to your heart. Say it."

"One can't."

"Say 'I.'"

"How difficult that is."

"Say it. Not as an obscenity. Say it as if you love yourself."

"Please."

"Say it."

"I," I said.

"Was that so awful? Come, now. Tell me how you feel about me. The truth. From the deepest levels."

"A feeling of warmth—of affection, of trust—"

"Of love?"

"Of love, yes," I admitted.

"Then say it."

"Love."

"That isn't what I want you to say."

"What, then?"

"Something that hasn't been said on this planet in two thousand years, Kinnall. Now: say it. I—"

"I—"

"Love you."

"Love you."

"I love you."

"I—love—you."

"It's a beginning," Schweiz said. Sweat streamed down his face and mine. "We start by acknowledging that we can love. We start by acknowledging that we have selves *capable* of loving. Then we begin to love. Eh? We begin to love."

36

LATER I SAID, "Did you get from the drug what you were looking for, Schweiz?"

"Partially."

"How so, partially?"

"I was looking for God, Kinnall, and I didn't quite find him, but I got a better idea of where to look. What I did find was how not to be alone any more. How to open my mind fully to someone else. That's the first step on the road I want to travel."

"One is happy for your sake, Schweiz."

"Must you still talk to me in that third-person lingo?"

"I can't help myself," I said. I was terribly tired. I was beginning to feel afraid of Schweiz again. The love I bore for him was still there, but now suspicion was creeping back. Was he exploiting me? Was he milking a dirty little pleasure out of our mutual exposures? He had pushed me into becoming a self-barer. His insistence on my speaking in "I" and "me" to him—was that a token of my liberation, was it something beautiful and pure, as he claimed, or was it only a reveling in filth? I was too new to this. I could not sit placidly while a man said, "I love you" to me, and compelled me to say to him, "I love you."

"Practice it," Schweiz said. "I. I. I. I."

"Stop. Please."

"Is it that painful?"

"It's new and strange to me. I need—there, you see?—I need to slide into this more gradually."

"Take your time, then. Don't let me rush you. But don't ever stop moving forward."

"One will try. I will try," I said.

"Good." After a moment he said, "Would you try the drug again, ever?"

"With you?"

"I don't think there's any need for that. I mean with someone like your bondsister. If I offered you some, would you use it with her?"

"I don't know."

"Are you afraid of the drug now?"

I shook my head. "That isn't easy for me to answer. I need time to come to terms with the whole experience. Time to think about it, Schweiz, before getting involved again."

"You've tasted the experience. You've seen that there's only good to be had from it."

"Perhaps. Perhaps."

"Without doubt!" His fervor was evangelical. His zeal tempted me anew.

Cautiously I said, "If more were available, I would seriously consider trying it again. With Halum, maybe."

"Good!"

"Not immediately. But in time. Two, three, four moontimes from now."

"It would have to be farther from now than that."

"Why?"

Schweiz said, "This was my entire stock of the drug that we used this evening. I have no more."

"But you could get some, if you tried?"

"Oh, yes. Yes, certainly."

"Where?"

"In Sumara Borthan," he said.

37

WHEN ONE IS NEW to the ways of pleasure, it is not surprising to find guilt and remorse following first indulgence. So was it with me. In the morning of our second day at the lodge I awoke after troubled sleep, feeling such shame that I prayed the ground to swallow me. What had I done? Why had I let Schweiz goad me into such foulness? Selfbaring! Selfbaring! Sitting with him all night, saying "I" and "me" and "me" and "I," and congratulating myself on my new freedom from convention's strangling hand! The mists of day brought a mood of disbelief. Could I have actually opened myself like that? Yes, I must, for within me now were memories of Schweiz's past, which I had not had access to before. And myself within him, then. I prayed for a way of undoing what I had done. I felt I had lost something of myself by surrendering my apartness. You know, to be a self-barer is not a pretty thing among us, and those who expose themselves gain only a dirty pleasure from it, a furtive kind of ecstasy. I insisted to myself that I had done nothing of that, but had embarked rather on a spiritual quest; but even as I put the phrase to myself it sounded portentous and hypocritical, a flimsy mask for shabby motives. And I was ashamed, for my sake, for my sons' sake, for the sake of my royal father and his royal forefathers, that I had come to this. I think it was Schweiz's *"I love you"* that drove me into such an abyss of regret, more than any other single aspect of the evening, for my old self saw those words as doubly obscene, even while the new self that was struggling to emerge insisted that the Earthman had meant nothing shameful, neither with his *"I"* nor with his *"love."* But I rejected my own argument and let guilt engulf me. What had I become, to trade endearments with another man, an Earthborn merchant, a lunatic? How could I have given my soul to him? Where did I stand, now that I was so wholly vulnerable to him? For a moment I considered killing Schweiz, as a way of recovering my privacy. I went to him where he slept, and saw him with a smile on his face, and I could feel no hatred for him then.

That day I spent mostly alone. I went off into the forest and bathed at a cool pond; then I knelt before a firethorn tree and pretended it was a drainer, and confessed myself to it in shy whispers; afterward I walked through a brambly woods, coming back to the lodge thorned and smudged. Schweiz asked me if I felt unwell. No, I told him, nothing is wrong. I said little that evening, but huddled in a floating-chair. The Earthman, more talkative than ever, a torrent of buoyant words, launched himself into the details of a grand scheme for an expedition to Sumara Borthan to bring back sacks of the drug, enough to transform every soul in Manneran, and I listened without commenting, for everything had become unreal to me, and that project seemed no more strange than anything else.

I hoped the ache of my soul would ease once I was back in Manneran and at my desk in the Justiciary. But no. I came into my house and Halum was there with Loimel, the cousins exchanging clothes with one another, and at the sight of them I nearly turned and fled. They smiled warm woman-smiles at me, secret smiles, the token of the league they had formed between themselves all their lives, and in despair I looked from my wife to my bondsister, from one cousin to the other, receiving their mirrored beauty as a double sword in my belly. Those smiles! Those knowing eyes! They needed no drug to pull the truths from me.

Where have you been, Kinnall?

To a lodge in the forest, to play at selfbaring with the Earthman.

And did you show him your soul?

Oh, yes, and he showed his.

And then?

Then we spoke of love. I love you, he said, and one replied, I love you.

What a wicked child you are, Kinnall!

Yes. Yes. Where can one hide from his shame?

This silent dialogue whirled through my brain in an instant, as I came toward them where they sat beside the courtyard fountain. Formally I embraced Loimel, and formally I embraced my bondsister, but I kept my eyes averted from theirs, so sharp was my guilt. It was the same in the Justiciary office for me. I translated the glances of the underlings into accusing glares. *There is Kinnall Darival, who revealed all our mysteries to Schweiz of Earth. Look at the Sallan self-barer slink by us! How can he stand his own reek?* I kept to myself and did my work poorly. A document concerning some transaction of Schweiz's crossed my desk, throwing me into dismay. The thought of facing Schweiz ever again appalled me. It would have been no great chore for me to revoke his residence permit in Manneran, using the authority of the High Justice; poor payment for the trust he showed me, but I came close to doing it, and checked myself only out of a deeper shame even than I already bore.

On the third day of my return, when my children too had begun to wonder what was wrong with me, I went to the Stone Chapel to seek healing from the drainer Jidd.

It was a damp day of heavy heat. The soft furry sky seemed to hang in looping folds over Manneran, and everything was coated in glistening beads of bright moisture. That day the sunlight was a strange color, almost white, and the ancient black stone blocks of the holy building gave off blinding reflections as though they were edged with prisms; but once inside the chapel, I found myself in dark, cool, quiet halls. Jidd's cell had pride of place in the chapel's apse, behind the great altar. He awaited me already robed; I had reserved his time hours in advance. The contract was ready. Quickly I signed and gave him his fee. This Jidd was no more lovely than any other of his trade, but just then I was almost pleased by his ugliness, his jagged knobby nose and thin long lips, his hooded eyes, his dangling earlobes. Why mock the man's face? He would have chosen another for himself, if he had been consulted. And I was kindly disposed to him, for I hoped he would heal me. Healers were holy men. *Give me what I need from you, Jidd, and I will bless your ugly face!* He said, "Under whose auspices will you drain?"

"The god of forgiving."

He touched a switch. Mere candles were too common for Jidd. The amber light of forgiveness came from some concealed gas-jet and flooded the chamber. Jidd directed my attention toward the mirror, instructing me to behold my face, put my eyes to my eyes. The eyes of a stranger looked back at me. Droplets of sweat clustered in the roots of my beard, where the flesh of my cheeks could be seen. *I love you,* I said silently to the strange face in the mirror. Love of others begins with love of self. The chapel weighed on me; I was in terror of being crushed beneath a block of the ceiling. Jidd was saying the preliminary words. There was nothing of love in them. He commanded me to open my soul to him.

I stammered. My tongue turned upon itself and was knotted. I gagged; I choked; I pulled my head down and pressed it to the cold floor. Jidd touched my shoulder and murmured formulas of comfort until my fit softened. We began the rite a second time. Now I traveled more smoothly through the preliminaries, and when he asked me to speak, I said, as though reciting lines that had been written for me by someone else, "These days past one went to a secret place with another, and we shared a certain drug of Sumara Borthan that unseals the soul, and we engaged in selfbaring together, and now one feels remorse for his sin and would have forgiveness for it."

Jidd gasped, and it is no little task to astonish a drainer. That gasp nearly punctured my will to confess; but Jidd artfully recovered control, coaxing me onward with bland priestly phrases, until in a few moments the stiffness left my jaws and I was spilling everything out. My early discussions of the drug with Schweiz. (I left him unnamed. Though I trusted Jidd to maintain the secrecy of the draining, I saw no spiritual gain for myself in revealing to anyone the name of my companion in sin.) My taking of the drug at the lodge. My sensations as the drug took hold. My exploration of Schweiz's soul. His entry into mine. The kindling of deep affection between us as our union of spirit developed. My feeling of alienation from the Covenant while under the drug's influence. That sudden conviction of mine that the denial of self which we practice is a catastrophic cultural error. The intuitive realization that we should deny our solitude instead, and seek to bridge the gulfs between ourselves and others, rather than glorying in isolation. Also I confessed that I had dabbled in the drug for the sake of eventually reaching the soul of Halum; hearing from me this admission of yearning for my bondsister was old stuff to Jidd by now. And then I spoke of the dislocations I had experienced since coming out of my drug-trance: the guilt, the shame, the doubt. At last I fell silent. There before me, like a pale globe glowing in the dimness, hung the facts of my misdeeds, tangible and exposed, and already I felt cleaner for having revealed them. I was willing now to be brought back into the Covenant. I wanted to be purged of my aberration of selfbaring. I hungered to do penance and resume my upright life. I was eager to be healed, I was begging for absolution and restoration to my community. But I could not feel the presence of the god. Staring into the mirror, I saw only my own face, drawn and sallow, the beard in need of combing. When Jidd began to recite the formulas of absolution, they were merely words to me, nor did my soul lift. I was cut off from all faith. The irony of that distracted me: Schweiz, envying me for my beliefs, seeking through the drug to understand the mystery of submission to the supernatural, had stripped me of my access to the gods. There I knelt, stone knees on stone floor, making hollow responses to Jidd's hollow phrases, while wishing that Jidd and I could have taken the drug together, so there might have been true communion between us. And I knew that I was lost.

"The peace of the gods be with you now," said Jidd.

"The peace of the gods is upon one."

"Seek no more for false succor, and keep your self to yourself, for other paths lead only to shame and corruption."

"One will seek no other paths."

"You have bondsister and bondbrother, you have a drainer, you have the mercies of the gods. You need no more."

"One needs no more."

"Go in peace, then."

I went, but not in his kind of peace, for the draining had been a leaden thing, meaningless and trifling. Jidd had not reconciled me to the Covenant: he had simply demonstrated the degree of my separation from it. Unmoved though I had been by the draining, however, I emerged from the Stone Chapel somehow purged of guilt. I no longer repented my selfbaring. Perhaps this was some residual effect of the draining, this inversion of my purpose in going to Jidd, but I did not try deeply to analyze it. I was content to be myself and to be thinking these thoughts. My conversion at that instant was complete. Schweiz had taken my faith from me, but he had given me another in its place.

38

THAT AFTERNOON a problem came to me concerning a ship from Threish and some false cargo manifests, and I went to a pier to verify the facts. There by chance I encountered Schweiz. Since parting from him a few days before, I had dreaded meeting him again; it would be intolerable, I thought, to look into the eyes of this man who had beheld my entire self. Only by keeping apart from him could I eventually persuade myself that I had not, in fact, done with him what I had done. But then I saw him near me on the pier. He clutched a thick sheaf of invoices in one hand and was shaking the other furiously at some watery-eyed merchant in Glinish dress. To my amazement I felt none of the embarrassment I had anticipated, but only warmth and pleasure at the sight of him. I went to him. He clapped my shoulder; I clapped his. "You look more cheerful now," he said.

"Much."

"Let me finish with this scoundrel and we'll share a flask of golden, eh?"

"By all means," I said.

An hour later, as we sat together in a dockside tavern, I said, "How soon can we leave for Sumara Borthan?"

39

THE VOYAGE to the southern continent was conducted as though in a dream. Not once did I question the wisdom of undertaking the journey, nor did I pause to ask myself why it was necessary for me to take part in person, rather than let Schweiz make the trip alone, or send some hireling to gather the drug on our behalf. I simply set about the task of arranging for our passage.

No commercial shipping goes regularly between Velada Borthan and Sumara Borthan. Those who would travel to the southern continent must charter a vessel. This I did, through the instrumentality of the High Justiciary, using intermediaries and dummy signatories. The vessel I chose was no Mannerangi craft, for I did not care to be recognized when we sailed, but rather a ship of the western province of Velis that had been tied down in Manneran Harbor for the better part of a year by a lawsuit. It seemed there was some dispute over title to the ship going on in its home port, and the thicket of injunctions and counterinjunctions had succeeded in making it impossible for the vessel to leave Manneran after its last voyage there. The captain and crew were bitter over this enforced idleness and had already filed a protest with the Justiciary; but the High Justice had no jurisdiction over a lawsuit that was being fought entirely in the courts of Velis, and we therefore had had to continue the stay on the vessel's departure until word came from Velis that title was clear. Knowing all this, I issued a decree in the High Justice's name that would permit the unfortunate craft temporarily to accept charters for voyages to points "between the River Woyn and the eastern shore of the Gulf of Sumar." That usually was taken to mean any point along the coast of the province of Manneran, but I specified also that the captain might hire himself out for trips to the northern coast of Sumara Borthan. Doubtless that clause left the poor man puzzled, and it must have puzzled him even more when, a few days later, he was approached by my agents and asked to make a voyage to that very place.

Neither Loimel nor Halum nor Noim nor anyone else did I tell of my destination. I said only that the Justiciary required me to go abroad for a short while. At the Justiciary I was even less specific, applying to myself for a leave of absence, granting it at once, and informing the High Justice at the last possible moment that I was not going to be available for the immediate future.

To avoid complications with the collectors of customs, among other things, I picked as our port of departure the town of Hilminor, in southwestern Manneran on the Gulf of Sumar. This is a medium-sized place that depends mainly on the fishing trade, but which serves also as a halfway stop for ships traveling between the city of Manneran and the western provinces. I arranged to meet our chartered captain in Hilminor; he then set out for that town by sea, while Schweiz and I made for it in a groundcar.

It was a two-day journey via the coastal highway, through a countryside ever more lush, ever more densely tropical, as we approached the Gulf of Sumar. Schweiz was in high spirits, as was I. We talked to one another in the first person constantly; to him it was nothing, of course, but I felt like a wicked boy sneaking off to whisper "I" and "me" in a playmate's ear. He and I speculated on what quantity of the Sumaran drug we would obtain, and what we would do with it. No longer was it just a question of my getting some to use with Halum: we were talking now of proselytizing everyone and bringing about a wholesale liberation of my self-stifling countrymen. That evangelical approach had crept gradually into our plans almost without my realizing it, and had swiftly become dominant.

We came to Hilminor on a day so hot the sky itself seemed to break out in blisters. A shimmering dome of heat covered everything, and the Gulf of Sumar, as it lay before us, was golden-skinned in the fierce sunlight. Hilminor is rimmed by a chain of low hills, which are thickly forested on the seaward side and desert on the landward; the highway curved through them, and we stopped at one point so that I could show Schweiz the flesh-trees that covered the parched inland slopes. A dozen of the trees were clustered in one place. We walked through crackling tinder-dry underbrush to reach them: twice the height of men they were, with twisted limbs and thick pale bark, spongy to the touch like the flesh of very old women. The trees were scarred from repeated tapping of their sap, making them look all the more repugnant. "Can we taste the fluid?" Schweiz asked. We had no implements for making the tap, but just then a girl of the town came along, perhaps ten years old, half-naked, tanned a deep brown to hide the dirt; she was carrying an auger and a flask, and evidently had been sent out by her family to collect flesh-tree sap. She looked at us sourly. I produced a coin and said, "One would show his companion the taste of the flesh-tree." Still a sour look; but she jammed her auger into the nearest tree with surprising force, twisted it, withdrew, and caught the gush of clear thick fluid. Sullenly she handed her flask to Schweiz. He sniffed it, took a cautious lick, finally had a gulp. And whooped in delight. "Why isn't this stuff sold all over Velada Borthan?" he asked.

"The whole supply comes from one little area along the Gulf," I told him. "Most of it's consumed locally, and a lot gets shipped to Threish, where it's almost an addiction. That doesn't leave much left over for the rest of the continent. You can buy it in Manneran, of course, but you have to know where to look."

"You know what I'd like to do, Kinnall? I'd like to start a flesh-tree plantation, grow them by the thousands, and get enough juice bottled so we not only could market it all over Velada Borthan, but could set up an export deal. I—"

"*Devil!*" the girl cried, and added something incomprehensible in the coast dialect, and snatched the flask from his hand. She ran off wildly, knees high, elbows outthrust, several times looking back to make a finger-jabbing sign of contempt or defiance at us. Schweiz, bewildered, shook his head. "Is she crazy?" he asked.

"You said 'I' three times," I said. "Very careless."

"I've slipped into bad habits, talking with you. But can it really be such a filthy thing to say?"

"Filthier than you'll ever imagine. That girl is probably on her way to tell her brothers about the dirty old man who obscened at her on the hillside. Come on: let's get into town before we're mobbed."

"Dirty old man," Schweiz murmured. "Me!"

I pushed him into the groundcar and we hurried toward the port of Hilminor.

40

OUR SHIP RODE at anchor, a small squat craft, twin screws, auxiliary sail, hull painted blue and gold. We presented ourselves to the captain—Khrisch was his name—and he greeted us blandly by the names we had assumed. In late afternoon we put out to sea. At no time during the voyage did Captain Khrisch question us about our purposes, nor did any of his ten crewmen. Surely they were fiercely curious about the motives of anyone who cared to go to Sumara Borthan, but they were so grateful to be out of their escrow even for this short cruise that they were chary of offending their employers by too much prying.

The coast of Velada Borthan dipped from sight behind me and ahead lay only the grand open sweep of the Strait of Sumar. No land at all could be seen, neither aft nor fore. That frightened me. In my brief career as a Glinish seaman I had never been far from the coast, and during stormy moments I had soothed myself with the comforting deceit that I might always swim to shore if we capsized. Here, though, the universe seemed all to be of water. As evening approached, a gray-blue twilight settled over us, stitching sky seamlessly to sea, and it became worse for me: now there was only our little bobbing, throbbing ship adrift and vulnerable in this directionless, dimensionless void, this shimmering antiworld where all places melted into a single nonplace. I had not expected the strait to be so wide. On a map I had seen in the Justiciary only a few days before, the strait had had less breadth than my little finger; I had assumed that the cliffs of Sumara Borthan would be visible to us from the earliest hours of the voyage; yet here we were amid nothingness. I stumbled to my cabin and plunged face first onto my bunk, and lay there shaking, calling upon the god of travelers to protect me. Bit by bit I came to loathe myself for this weakness. I reminded myself that I was a septarch's son and a septarch's brother and another septarch's cousin, that in Manneran I was a man of the highest authority, that I was the head of a house and a slayer of hornfowl. All this did me no good. What value is lineage to a drowning man? What use are broad shoulders and powerful muscles and a skill at swimming, when the land itself has been swallowed up, so that a swimmer would have no destination? I trembled. I think I may have wept. I felt myself dissolving into that gray-blue void. Then a hand lightly caught my shoulder. Schweiz. "The ship is sound," he whispered. "The crossing is a short one. Easy. Easy. No harm will come."

If it had been anyone else who had found me like that, any other man except perhaps Noim, I might have killed him or myself, to bury the secret of my shame.

I said, "If this is what it is like to cross the Strait of Sumar, how can one travel between the stars without going mad?"

"One grows accustomed to travel."

"The fear—the emptiness—"

"Come above." Gently. "The night is very beautiful."

Nor did he lie. Twilight was past and a black bowl pocked with fiery jewels lay over us. Near cities one cannot see the stars so well, because of the lights and the haze. I had looked upon the full glory of the heavens while hunting in the Burnt Lowlands, yes, but then I had not known the names of what I saw. Now, Schweiz and Captain Khrisch stood close alongside me on deck, taking turns calling out the names of stars and constellations, vying with each other to display their knowledge, each one pouring his astronomy into my ear as though I were a terrified child who could be kept from screaming only by a constant flow of distractions. See? See? And see, there? I saw. A host of our neighboring suns, and four or five of the neighbor-planets of our system, and even a vagrant comet that night. What they taught me stayed with me. I could step out my cabin now, I believe, here in the Burnt Lowlands, and call off the stars the way Schweiz and the captain called them off to me aboard ship in the Strait of Sumar. How many more nights do I have, I wonder, on which I will be free to look at the stars?

Morning brought an end to fear. The sun was bright, the sky was lightly fleeced, the broad strait was calm, and it did not matter to me that land was beyond sight. We glided toward Sumara Borthan in an almost imperceptible way; I had to study the surface of the sea with care to remind myself we were in motion. A day, a night, a day, a night, a day, and then the horizon sprouted a green crust, for there was Sumara Borthan. It provided a fixed point for me, except that we were the fixed point, and Sumara Borthan was making for it. The southern continent slid steadily toward us, until at last I saw a rim of bare yellow-green rock stretching from east to west, and atop those naked cliffs rose a thick cap of vegetation, lofty trees knitted together by heavy vines to form a closed canopy, stubbier shrubs clustering in the darkness below, everything cut down the side as if to reveal the jungle's edge to us in cross-section. I felt not fear but wonder at the sight of that jungle. I knew that not one of those trees and plants grew in Velada Borthan; the beasts and serpents and insects of this place were not those of the continent of my birth; what lay before us was alien and perhaps hostile, an unknown world awaiting the first footstep. In a tumble of tangled imaginings I dropped down the well of time, and saw myself as an explorer peeling the mystery from a newly found planet. Those gigantic boulders, those slender, high-crowned trees, those dangling snaky vines, all were products of a raw, elemental mystery straight out of evolution's belly, which now I was about to penetrate. That dark jungle was the gate to something strange and terrible, I thought, yet I was not frightened so much as I was stirred, deeply moved, by the vision of those sleek cliffs and tendriled avenues. This was the world that existed before man came. This was as it was when there were no godhouses, no drainers, no Port Justiciary: only the silent leafy paths, and the surging rivers scouring the valleys, and the unplumbed ponds, and the long heavy leaves glistening with the jungle's exhalations, and the unhunted prehistoric beasts turning in the ooze, and the fluttering winged things that knew no fear, and the grassy plateaus, and the veins of precious metals, a virgin kingdom, and over everything brooding the presence of the gods, of the god, of the god, waiting for the time of worshipers. The lonely gods who did not yet know they were divine. The lonely god.

Of course the reality was nothing so romantic. There was a place where the cliffs dipped to sea level and yielded to a crescent harbor, and here a squalid settlement existed, the shacks of a few dozen Sumarnu who had taken to living here so that they might meet the needs of such ships as occasionally did come from the northern continent. I had thought that all the Sumarnu lived somewhere in the interior, naked tribesmen camping down by the volcanic peak Vashnir, and that Schweiz and I would have to hack our way through the whole apocalyptic immensity of this mysterious land, unguided and uncertain, before we found what passed for civilization and made contact with anyone who might sell us that for which we had come. Instead, Captain Khrisch brought his little ship smartly to shore by a crumbling wooden pier, and as we stepped forth a small delegation of Sumarnu came to offer us a sullen greeting.

You know my fantasy of fanged and grotesque Earthmen. So, too, I instinctively expected these people of the southern continent to look in some way alien. I knew it was irrational; they were, after all, sprung from the same stock as the citizens of Salla and Manneran and Glin. But had these centuries in the jungle not transformed them? Had their disavowal of the Covenant not laid them open to infiltration by the vapors of the forest, and turned them into unhuman things? No and no. They looked to me like peasants of any province's back country. Oh, they wore unfamiliar ornaments, odd jeweled pendants and bracelets of an un-Veladan sort, but there was nothing else about them, neither tone of skin nor shape of face nor color of hair, that set them apart from the men I had always known.

There were eight or nine of them. Two, evidently the leaders, spoke the dialect of Manneran, though with a troublesome accent. The others showed no sign of understanding northern languages, but chattered among themselves in a tongue of clicks and grunts. Schweiz found communication easier than I did, and entered into a long conversation, so difficult for me to follow that I soon ceased to pay attention. I wandered off to inspect the village, and was inspected in turn by goggle-eyed children—the girls here walked about naked even after they were of the age when their breasts had sprouted— and when I returned Schweiz said, "It's all arranged."

"What is?"

"Tonight we sleep here. Tomorrow they'll guide us to a village that produces the drug. They don't guarantee we'll be allowed to buy any."

"Is it only sold at certain places?"

"Evidently. They swear there's none at all available here."

I said, "How long a journey will it be?"

"Five days. On foot. Do you like jungles, Kinnall?"

"I don't know the taste of them yet."

"It's a taste you're going to learn," said Schweiz.

He turned now to confer with Captain Khrisch, who was planning to go off on some expedition of his own along the Sumaran coast. Schweiz arranged to have our ship back at this harbor waiting for us when we returned from our trip into the jungle. Khrisch's men unloaded our baggage—chiefly trade-goods for barter, mirrors and knives and trinkets, since the Sumarnu had no use for Veladan currency—and got their ship out into the strait before night fell.

Schweiz and I had a shack for ourselves, on a lip of rock overlooking the harbor. Mattresses of leaves, blankets of animal hide, one lopsided window, no sanitary facilities: this is what the thousands of years of man's voyage through the stars have brought us to. We haggled over the price of our lodgings, finally came to an agreement in knives and heat-rods, and at sundown were given our dinner. A surprisingly tasty stew of spicy meats, some angular red fruits, a pot of half-cooked vegetables, a mug of what might have been fermented milk—we ate what was given us, and enjoyed it more than either of us had expected, though we made edgy jokes about the diseases we were likely to catch. I poured out a libation to the god of travelers, more out of habit than conviction. Schweiz said, "So you still believe, after all?" I replied that I found no reason not to believe in the gods, though my faith in the teachings of men had been greatly weakened.

This close to the equator, darkness came on swiftly, a sudden black curtain rolling down. We sat outside a little while, Schweiz favoring me with some more astronomy, and testing me on what I had already learned. Then we went to bed. Less than an hour later, two figures entered our shack; I was still awake, and sat up instantly, imagining thieves or assassins, but as I groped for a weapon a stray moonbeam showed me the profile of one of the intruders, and I saw heavy breasts swinging. Schweiz, out of the dark far corner, said, "I think they're included in tonight's price." Another instant and warm naked flesh pressed against me. I smelled a pungent odor, and touched a fat haunch and found it coated in some spicy oil: a Sumarnu cosmetic, I found out afterward. Curiosity warred with caution in me. As I had when a boy taking lodgings in Glain, I feared catching a disease from the loins of a woman of a strange race. But should I not experience the southern kind of loving? From Schweiz's direction I heard the slap of meat on meat, hearty laughter, liquid lip-noises. My own girl wriggled impatiently. Parting the plump thighs, I explored, aroused, entered. The girl squirmed into what I suppose was the proper native position, lying on her side, facing me, one leg flung over me and her heel jammed hard against my buttocks. I had not had a woman since my last night in Manneran; that and my old problem of haste undid me, and I unloaded myself in the usual premature volleys. My girl called out something, probably in derision of my manhood, to her moaning and sighing companion in Schweiz's corner, and got a giggled answer. In rage and chagrin I forced myself to revive and, pumping slowly, grimly, I ploughed her anew, though the stink of her breath nearly paralyzed me and her sweat, mingling with her oil, formed a nauseous compound. Eventually I pushed her over the brink of pleasure, but it was cheerless work, a tiresome chore. When it was done she nipped my elbow with her teeth: a Sumarnu kiss, I think it was. Her gratitude. Her apology. I had done her good service after all. In the morning I scanned the village maidens, wondering which lass it was had honored me with her caresses. All of them gaptoothed, sagbreasted, fisheyed: let my couchmate have been none of the ones I saw. For days afterward I kept uneasy watch on my organ, expecting it each morning to be broken out in red spots or running sores; but all I caught from her was a distaste for the Sumarnu style of passion.

41

FIVE DAYS. Six, actually: either Schweiz had misunderstood, or the Sumarnu chieftain was poor at counting. We had one guide and three bearers. I had never walked so much before, from dawn to sunset, the ground yielding and bouncy beneath my feet. The jungle rising, a green wall, on both sides of the narrow path. Astonishing humidity, so that we swam in the air, worse than on the worst day in Manneran. Insects with jeweled eyes and terrifying beaks. Slithering many-legged beasts rushing past us. Strugglings and horrid cries in the underbrush, just beyond sight. The sunlight falling in dappled streaks, barely making it through the canopy high above. Flowers bursting from the trunks of trees: parasites, Schweiz said. One of them a puffy yellow thing that had a human face, goggly eyes, a gaping pollen-smeared mouth. The other even more bizarre, for from the midst of its red and black petals rose a parody of genitalia, a fleshy phallus, two dangling balls. Schweiz, shrieking with amusement, seized the first of these that we found, wrapped his hand around the floral cock, bawdily flirted with it and stroked it. The Sumarnu muttered things; perhaps they were wondering if they had done right to send girls to our shack that night.

We crept up the spine of the continent, emerging from the jungle for a day and a half to climb a good-sized mountain, then more jungle on the other side. Schweiz asked our guide why we had not gone around the mountain instead of over it, and was told that this was the only route, for poison-ants infested all the surrounding lowlands: very cheering. Beyond the mountain lay a chain of lakes and streams and ponds, many of them thick with gray toothy snouts barely breaking the surface. All this seemed unreal to me. A few days' sail to the north lay Velada Borthan, with its banking houses and its groundcars, its customs collectors and its godhouses. That was a tamed continent, but for its uninhabitable interior. Man had made no impact at all, though, on this place where we marched. Its disorderly wildness oppressed me—that and the heavy air, the sounds in the night, the unintelligible conversations of our primitive companions.

On the sixth day we came to the native village. Perhaps three hundred wooden huts were scattered over a broad meadow at a place where two rivers of modest size ran together. I had the impression that there once had been a larger town here, possibly even a city, for on the borders of the settlement I saw grassy mounds and humps, quite plausibly the site of ancient ruins. Or was that only an illusion? Did I need so badly to convince myself that the Sumarnu had regressed since leaving our continent, that I had to see evidences of decline and decay wherever I looked?

The villagers surrounded us: not hostile, only curious. Northerners were uncommon sights. A few of them came close and touched me, a timid pat on the forearm, a shy squeeze of the wrist, invariably accompanied by a quick little smile. These jungle folk seemed not to have the sullen sourness of those who lived in the shacks by the harbor. They were gentler, more open, more childlike. Such little taint of Veladan civilization as had managed to stain the harbor folk had darkened their spirits; not so here, where contact with northerners was less frequent.

An interminable parley began among Schweiz, our guide, and three of the village elders. After the first few moments Schweiz was out of it: the guide, indulging in long cascades of verbal embellishments footnoted by frantic gesticulations, seemed to be explaining the same thing over and over to the villagers, who constantly made the same series of replies to him. Neither Schweiz nor I could understand a syllable of it. At last the guide, looking agitated, turned to Schweiz and poured forth a stream of Sumarnu-accented Mannerangi, which I found almost wholly opaque but which Schweiz, with his tradesman's skill at communicating with strangers, was able to penetrate. Schweiz said finally to me, "They're willing to sell to us. Provided we can show them that we're worthy of having the drug."

"How do we do that?"

"By taking some with them, at a love-ritual this evening. Our guide's been trying to talk them out of it, but they won't budge. No communion, no merchandise."

"Are there risks?" I asked.

Schweiz shook his head. "It doesn't seem that way to me. But the guide has the idea that we're only looking for profit in the drug, that we don't mean to use it ourselves but intend to go back to Manneran and sell what we get for many mirrors and many heat-rods and many knives. Since he thinks we aren't users, he's trying to protect us from exposure to it. The villagers also think we aren't users, and they're damned if they'll turn a speck of the stuff over to anyone who's merely planning to peddle it. They'll make it available only to true believers."

"But we *are* true believers," I said.

"I know. But I can't convince our man of that. He knows enough about northerners to know that they keep their minds closed at all times, and he wants to pamper us in our sickness of soul. But I'll try again."

Now it was Schweiz and our guide who parleyed, while the village chiefs stood silent. Adopting the gestures and even the accent of the guide, so that both sides of the conversation became unintelligible to me, Schweiz pressed and pressed and pressed, and the guide resisted all that the Earthman was telling him, and a feeling of despair came over me so that I was ready to suggest that we give up and go empty-handed back to Manneran. Then Schweiz somehow broke through. The guide, still suspicious, clearly asked Schweiz whether he really wanted what he said he wanted, and Schweiz emphatically said he did, and the guide, looking skeptical, turned once more to the village chiefs. This time he spoke only briefly with them, and then briefly again with Schweiz. "It's been settled," Schweiz told me. "We'll take the drug with them tonight." He leaned close and touched my elbow. "Something for you to remember, when you go under: *be loving*. If you can't love them, all is lost."

I was offended that he had found it necessary to warn me.

42

TEN OF THEM CAME for us at sundown and led us into the forest east of the village. Among them were the three chieftains and two other older men, along with two young men and three women. One of the women was a handsome girl, one a plain girl, and one quite old. Our guide did not go with us; I am not sure whether he was not invited to the ceremony or simply did not feel like taking part.

We marched a considerable distance. No longer could we hear the cries of children in the village or the barking of domestic animals. Our halting-place was a secluded clearing, where hundreds of trees had been felled and the dressed logs laid out in five rows as benches, to form a pentagonal amphitheater. In the middle of the clearing was a clay-lined fire-pit, with a great heap of firewood neatly stacked beside it; as soon as we arrived, the two young men commenced building a towering blaze. On the far side of the woodpile I saw a second clay-lined pit, about twice as wide as a large man's body; it descended diagonally into the ground and gave the appearance of being a passage of no little depth, a tunnel offering access to the depths of the world. By the glow of the firelight I tried to peer into it from where I stood, but I was unable to see anything of interest.

Through gestures the Sumarnu showed us where we should sit: at the base of the pentagon. The plain girl sat beside us. To our left, next to the tunnel entrance, sat the three chiefs. To our right, by the fire-pit, were the two young men. In the far right corner sat the old woman and one of the old men; the other old man and the handsome girl went to the far left corner. Full darkness was upon us by the time we were seated. The Sumarnu now removed what little clothing they wore, and, seeing them obviously beckoning to us to do the same, Schweiz and I stripped, piling our clothes on the benches behind us. At a signal from one of the chiefs the handsome girl rose and went to the fire, poking a bough into it until she had a torch; then, approaching the slanting mouth of the tunnel, she wriggled awkwardly feet-first into it, holding the torch high. Girl and torch disappeared entirely from view. For a little while I could see the flickering light of the firebrand coming from below, but soon it went out, sending up a gust of dark smoke. Shortly the girl emerged, without the torch. In one hand she carried a thick-rimmed red pot, in the other a long flask of green glass. The two old men—high priests?—left their benches and took these things from her. They began a tuneless chant, and one, reaching into the pot, scooped from it a handful of white powder—the drug!—and dropped it into the flask. The other solemnly shook the flask from side to side in a mixing motion. Meanwhile the old woman—a priestess?—had prostrated herself by the mouth of the tunnel and began to chant in a different intonation, a jagged gasping rhythm, while the two young men flung more wood on the fire. The chanting continued for a good many minutes. Now the girl who had descended into the tunnel—a slim high-breasted wench with long silken red-brown hair—took the flask from the old man and brought it to our side of the fire, where the plain girl, stepping forward, received it reverently with both hands. Solemnly she carried it to the three seated chieftains and held it toward them. The chieftains now joined the chanting for the first time. What I thought of as the Rite of the Presentation of the Flask went on and on; I was fascinated at first, finding delight in the strangeness of the ceremony, but soon I grew bored and had to amuse myself by trying to invent a spiritual content for what was taking place. The tunnel, I decided, symbolized the genital opening of the world-mother, the route to her womb, where the drug—made from a root, from something growing underground— could be obtained. I devised an elaborate metaphorical construct involving a mother-cult, the symbolic meaning of carrying a lighted torch into the world-mother's womb, the use of plain and handsome girls to represent the universality of womanhood, the two young fire-warders as guardians of the chieftains' sexual potency, and a great deal more, all of it nonsense, but—so I thought—an impressive enough scheme to be assembled by a bureaucrat like myself of no great intellectual powers. My pleasure in my own musings evaporated abruptly when I realized how patronizing I was being. I was treating these Sumarnu like quaint savages, whose chants and rites were of mild aesthetic interest but could not possibly have any serious content. Who was I to take this lofty attitude? I had come to them, had I not, begging the drug of enlightenment that my soul craved; which of us then was the superior being? I assailed myself for my snobbery. *Be loving.* Put aside courtly sophistication. Share their rite if you can, and at the least show no contempt for it, feel no contempt, *have* no contempt. *Be loving.* The chieftains were drinking now, each taking a sip, handing the flask back to the plain-looking girl, who when all three had sipped began to move about the circle, bringing the flask first to the old men, then to the old woman, then to the handsome girl, then to the young fire-tenders, then to Schweiz, then to me. She smiled at me as she gave me the flask. By the fire's leaping light she seemed suddenly beautiful. The flask contained a warm gummy wine; I nearly gagged as I drank. But I drank. The drug entered my gut and journeyed thence to my soul.

43

WE ALL BECAME ONE, the ten of them and the two of us. First there were the strange sensations of going up, the heightening of perception, the loss of bearings, the visions of celestial light, the hearing of eerie sounds; then came the detecting of other heartbeats and bodily rhythms about me, the doubling, the overlapping of awarenesses; then came the dissolution of self, and we became one, who had been twelve. I was plunged into a sea of souls and I perished. I was swept into the center of all things. I had no way of knowing whether I was Kinnall the septarch's son, or Schweiz the man of old Earth, or the fire-tenders, or the chiefs, or the priests, or the girls, or the priestess, for they were inextricably mixed up in me and I in them. And the sea of souls was a sea of love. How could it be anything else than that? We were each other. Love of self bound us each to each, all to all. Love of self is love of others; love of others is love of self. And I loved. I knew more clearly than ever why Schweiz had said to me, *I love you,* as we were coming out of the drug the first time—that odd phrase, so obscene on Borthan, so incongruous in any case when man is speaking to man. I said to the ten Sumarnu, *I love you,* though not in words, for I had no words that they would understand, and even if I had spoken to them in my own tongue and they had understood, they would have resented the foulness of my words, for among my people *I love you* is an obscenity, and no help for it. *I love you.* And I meant it, and they accepted the gift of my love. I who was part of them. I who not long ago had patronized them as amusing primitives worshiping bonfires in the woods. Through them I sensed the sounds of the forest and the heaving of the tides, and, yes, the merciful love of the great worldmother, who lies sighing and quaking beneath our feet, and who has bestowed on us the drug-root for the healing of our sundered selves. I learned what it is to be Sumarnu and live simply at the meeting-place of two small rivers. I discovered how one can lack groundcars and banking houses and still belong to the community of civilized humanity. I found out what half-souled things the people of Velada Borthan have made of themselves in the name of holiness, and how whole it is possible to be, if one follows the way of the Sumarnu. None of this came to me in words or even in a flow of images, but rather in a rush of received knowledge, knowledge that entered and became part of me after a manner I can neither describe nor explain. I hear you saying now that I must be either lying or lazy, to offer you as little specific detail of the experience as I have done. But I reply that one cannot put into words what never *was* in words. One can deal only in approximations, and one's best effort can be nothing more than a distortion, a coarsening of the truth. But I must transform perceptions into words and set them down as my skills permit, and then you must pick my words from the page and convert them into whatever system of perceptions your mind habitually employs, and at each stage of this transmission a level of density leaches away, until you are left only with the shadow of what befell me in the clearing in Sumara Borthan. So how can I explain? We were dissolved in one another. We were dissolved in love. We who had no language in common came to total comprehension of our separate selves. When the drug at length lost its hold on us, part of me remained in them and part of them remained in me. If you would know more than that, if you would have a glimpse of what it is to be released from the prison of your skull, if you would taste love for the first time in your life, I say to you, Look for no explanations fashioned out of words, but put the flask to your lips. Put the flask to your lips.

44

WE HAD PASSED the test. They would give us what we wanted. After the sharing of love came the haggling. We returned to the village, and in the morning our bearers brought out our cases of trade-goods, and the three chieftains brought out three squat clay pots, with the white powder visible within them. And we heaped up a high stack of knives and mirrors and heat-rods, and they carefully poured quantities of powder from two of the pots into the third. Schweiz did most of the bargaining. The guide we had brought from the coast was of little value, for, though he could talk these chieftains' language, he had never talked to their souls. In fact the bargaining inverted itself suddenly, with Schweiz happily piling still more trinkets into the price, and the chiefs responding by adding more powder to our bowl, everyone laughing in a sort of hysterical good nature as the contest of generosity grew more frenzied. In the end we gave the villagers everything we had, keeping only a few items for gifts to our guide and bearers, and the villagers gave us enough of the drug to snare the minds of thousands.

Captain Khrisch was waiting when we reached the harbor. "One sees you have fared well," he remarked.

"Is it so obvious?" I asked.

"You were worried men when you went into this place. You are happy men coming out of it. Yes, it is obvious."

On the first night of our voyage back to Manneran, Schweiz called me into his cabin. He had the pot of white powder out, and he had broken the seal. I watched as he carefully poured the drug into little packets of the kind in which that first dose had come. He worked in silence, scarcely glancing at me, filling some seventy or eighty packets. When he was done, he counted out a dozen of them and pushed them to one side. Indicating the others, he said, "Those are for you. Hide them well about your luggage, or you'll need all your power with the Port Justiciary to get them safely past the customs collectors."

"You've given me five times as much as you've taken," I protested.

"Your need is greater," Schweiz told me.

45

I DID NOT UNDERSTAND what he meant by that until we were in Manneran again. We landed at Hilminor, paid Captain Khrisch, went through a minimum of inspection formalities (how trusting the port officials were, not very long ago!), and set out in our groundcar for the capital. Entering the city of Manneran by the Sumar Road, we passed through a crowded district of marketplaces and open-air shops, where I saw thousands of Mannerangi jostling, haggling, bickering. I saw them driving their hard bargains and whipping out contract forms to close the deals. I saw their faces, pinched, guarded, the eyes bleak and unloving. And I thought of the drug I carried and told myself, *If only I could change their frosty souls.* I had a vision of myself going among them, accosting strangers, drawing this one aside and that, whispering gently to each of them, "I am a prince of Salla and a high official of the Port Justiciary, who has put such empty things aside to bring happiness to mankind, and I would show you how to find joy through selfbaring. Trust me: I love you." No doubt some would flee from me as soon as I began to speak, frightened by the initial obscenity of my "I am," and others might hear me out and then spit in my face and call me a madman, and some might cry for the police; but perhaps there would be a few who would listen, and feel tempted, and come off with me to a quiet dockside room where we could share the Sumaran drug. One by one I would open souls, until there were ten in Manneran like me—twenty—a hundred—a secret society of self-barers, knowing one another by the warmth and love in their eyes, going about the city unafraid to say "I" or "me" to their fellow initiates, giving up not merely the grammar of politeness but all the poisonous denials of self-love that that grammar implied. And then I would charter Captain Khrisch again for a voyage to Sumara Borthan, and return laden with packets of white powder, and continue on through Manneran, I and those who now were like me, and we would go up to this one and that, smiling, glowing, to whisper, "I would show you how to find joy through selfbaring. Trust me: I love you."

There was no role for Schweiz in this vision. This was not his planet; he had no stake in transforming it. All that interested him was his private spiritual need, his hunger to break through to a sense of the godhood. He had begun that breakthrough already, and could complete it on his own, apart. Schweiz had no need to skulk about the city, seducing strangers. And this was why he had given me the greater share of our Sumaran booty: I was the evangelist, I was the new prophet, I was the messiah of openness, and Schweiz realized that before I did. Until now he had been the leader—drawing me into his confidence, getting me to try the drug, luring me off to Sumara Borthan, making use of my power in the Port Justiciary, keeping me at his side for companionship and reassurance and protection. I had been in his shadow throughout. Now he would cease to eclipse me. Armed with my little packets, I alone would launch the campaign to change a world.

It was a role I welcomed. All my life I had been overshadowed by one man or another, so that for all my strength of body and ability of mind I had come to seem second-rate to myself. Perhaps that is a natural defect of being born a septarch's second son. First there had been my father, whom I could never hope to equal in authority, agility, or might; then Stirron, whose kingship brought only exile for me; then my master in the Glinish logging camp; then Segvord Helalam; then Schweiz. All of them men of determination and prestige, who knew and held their places in our world, while I wandered in frequent bewilderment. Now, in the middle of my years, I could at last emerge. I had a mission. I had purpose. The spinners of the divine design had brought me to this place, had made me who I was, had readied me for my task. In joy I accepted their command.

46

THERE WAS A GIRL I kept for my sport, in a room on the south side
of Manneran, in the tangle of old streets back of the Stone Chapel.
She claimed to be a bastard of the Duke of Kongoroi, spawned when
the duke was on a state visit to Manneran in the days of my father's
reign. Perhaps her story was true. Certainly she believed it. I was
in the habit of going to her twice or thrice each moontime for an
hour of pleasure, whenever I felt too stifled by the routine of my
life, whenever I felt boredom's hand at my throat. She was simple
but passionate: lusty, available, undemanding. I did not hide my
identity from her, but I gave her none of my inner self, and none
was expected; we talked very little, and there was no question of
love between us. In return for the price of her lodgings, she let me
make occasional use of her body, and the transaction was no more
complex than that: a touching of skins, a sneeze of the loins. She
was the first to whom I gave the drug. I mixed it with golden wine.
"We will drink this," I said, and when she asked me why, I replied,
"It will bring us closer together." She asked, in no great curiosity,
what it would do to us, and I explained, "It will open self to self,
and make all walls transparent." She offered no protests—no talk
of the Covenant, no whining about privacy, no lectures of the evils
of selfbaring. She did as she was told, convinced I would bring no
harm to her. We took the dose, and then we lay naked on her couch
waiting for the effects to begin. I stroked her cool thighs, kissed the
tips of her breasts, playfully nibbled her earlobes, and soon the
strangeness started, the buzzing and the rush of air, and we began
to detect one another's heartbeats and pulse. "Oh," she said. "Oh,
one feels so peculiar!" But it did not frighten her. Our souls drifted
together and were fused in the clear white light coming from the
Center of All Things. And I discovered what it is like to have only
a slit between my thighs, and I learned how it is to wriggle one's
shoulders and have heavy breasts slap together, and I felt eggs throbbing and impatient in my ovaries. At the height of our voyage we
joined our bodies. I felt my rod slide into my cavern. I felt myself

moving against myself. I felt the slow sucking oceanic tide of ecstasy beginning to rise somewhere at my dark hot moist core, and I felt the hot prickling tickle of impending ecstasy dancing along my tool, and I felt the hard hairy shield of my chest crushing against the tender globes of my breasts, and I felt lips on my lips, tongue on my tongue, soul in my soul. This union of our bodies endured for hours, or so it seemed. And in that time my self was open to her, so that she could see in it all she chose, my boyhood in Salla, my flight to Glin, my marriage, my love for my bondsister, my weaknesses, my self-deceptions, and I looked into her and saw the sweetness of her, the giddiness, the moment of first finding blood on her thighs, the other blood of a later time, the image of Kinnall Darival as she carries it in her mind, the vague and unformed commandments of the Covenant, and all the rest of her soul's furniture. Then we were swept away by the storms of our senses. I felt her orgasm and mine, mine and mine, hers and hers, the double column of frenzy that was one, the spasm and the spurt, the thrust and the thrust, the rise and the fall. We lay sweaty and sticky and exhausted, the drug still thundering through our joined minds. I opened my eyes and saw hers, unfocused, the pupils dilated. She gave me a lopsided smile. "I—I—I—I—I," she said. "I!" The wonder of it seemed to daze her. "I! I! I!" I planted a kiss between her breasts and felt the brush of my lips myself. "I love you," I said.

47

THERE WAS A CLERK in the Port Justiciary, a certain Ulman, half my age and clearly a man of promise, whom I had come to like. He knew my power and my ancestry and showed no awe of me over that; his respect for me was based entirely on my skills in evaluating and handling the problems of the Justiciary. I kept him late one day and called him into my office when the others were gone. "There is this drug of Sumara Borthan," I said, "that allows one mind freely to enter another." He smiled and said that he had heard of it, yes, but understood it was difficult to obtain and dangerous to use. "There is no danger," I answered. "And as for the difficulty of obtaining it—" I drew forth one of my little packets. His smile did not fade, though dots of color came into his cheeks. We took the drug together in my office. Hours later, when we left for our homes, I gave him some so that he could take it with his wife.

48

IN THE STONE CHAPEL I dared to reach out to a stranger, a short, thickbodied man in princely clothes, possibly a member of the septarch's family. He had the clear serene eyes of a man of good faith and the poise of one who has looked within himself and is not displeased by what he has seen. But when I spoke my words to him, he shoved me away and cursed me with such fury that his anger became contagious; maddened by his words, I nearly struck him in blind frenzy. "Self-barer! Self-barer!" The shout echoed through the holy building, and people emerged from rooms of meditation to stare. It was the worst shame I had known in years. My exalted mission came into another perspective: I saw it as filthy, and myself as something pitiful, a creeping slinking fog of a man driven by who knew what compulsion to expose his shabby soul to strangers. My anger drained from me and fear flowed in: I slipped into the shadows and out a side door, dreading arrest. For a week I walked about on tiptoe, forever looking back over my shoulder. But nothing pursued me except my panging conscience.

49

THE MOMENT of insecurity passed. Again I saw my mission whole, and recognized the merit of what I had pledged myself to do, and felt only sorrow for the man in the Stone Chapel who had spurned my gift. And in a single week I found three strangers who would share the drug with me. I wondered how I could ever have doubted myself. But other seasons of doubt lay ahead.

50

I TRIED TO ARRIVE at a theoretical basis for my use of the drug, to construct a new theology of love and openness. I studied the Covenant and many of its commentaries, attempting to discover why the first settlers of Velada Borthan had found it necessary to deify mistrust and concealment. What did they fear? What were they hoping to preserve? Dark men in a dark time, with mindsnakes creeping through their skulls. In the end I came to no real understanding of them. They were convinced of their own virtue. They had acted for the best. Thou shalt not thrust the inwardness of thy soul upon thy fellow man. Thou shalt not unduly examine the needs of thy own self. Thou shalt deny thyself the easy pleasures of intimate conversation. Thou shalt stand alone before thy gods. And so we had lived, these hundreds of years, unquestioning, obedient, keeping the Covenant. Maybe nothing keeps the Covenant alive now, for most of us, except simple politeness: we are unwilling to embarrass others by baring ourselves, and so we go locked up, our inner wounds festering, and we speak our language of third-person courtliness. Was it time to create a new Covenant? A bond of love, a testament of sharing? Hidden in my rooms at home, I struggled to write one. What could I say that would be believed? That we had done well enough following the old ways, but at grievous personal cost. That the perilous conditions of the first settling no longer obtained among us, and certain customs, having become handicaps rather than assets, could be discarded. That societies must evolve if they are not to decay. That love is better than hate and trust is better than mistrust. But little of what I wrote convinced even me. Why was I attacking the established order of things? Out of profound conviction, or merely out of the hunger for dirty pleasures? I was a man of my own time; I was embedded firmly in the rock of my upbringing even as I toiled to turn that rock to sand. Trapped in the tension between my old beliefs and my still unformed new ones, I swung a thousand times a day from pole to pole, from shame to exaltation. As I labored over the draft of my new Covenant's preamble one evening, my bondsister Halum unexpectedly entered my study. "What are you writing?" she asked pleasantly. I covered one sheet with another. My face must have reflected my discomfort, for hers showed signs of apology for having intruded. "Official reports," I said. "Foolishness. Dull bureaucratic trivia." That night I burned all I had written, in a paroxysm of self-contempt.

51

IN THOSE WEEKS I took many voyages of exploration into unknown lands. Friends, strangers, casual acquaintances, a mistress: companions on strange journeys. But through all the early phase of my time of changes I said not a word to Halum about the drug. To share it with her had been my original goal, that had brought the drug to my lips in the first place. Yet I feared to approach her. It was cowardice that kept me back: what if, by coming to know me too well, she ceased to love me?

52

SEVERAL TIMES I came close to broaching the subject with her. I held myself back. I did not dare to move toward her. If you wish you may measure my sincerity by my hesitation; how pure, you may ask, was my new creed of openness, if I felt that my bondsister would be above such a communion? But I will not pretend there was any consistency in my thinking then. My liberation from the taboos on selfbaring was a willed thing, not a natural evolution, and I had constantly to battle against the old habits of our custom. Though I talked in "I" and "me" with Schweiz and some of the others with whom I had shared the drug, I was never comfortable in doing so. Vestiges of my broken bonds still crept together to shackle me. I looked at Halum and knew that I loved her, and told myself that the only way to fulfill that love was through the joining of her soul and mine, and in my hand was the powder that would join us. And I did not dare. And I did not dare.

53

THE TWELFTH PERSON with whom I shared the Sumaran drug was my bondbrother Noim. He was in Manneran to spend a week as my guest. Winter had come, bringing snow to Glin, hard rains to Salla, and only fog to Manneran, and northerners needed little prodding to come to our warm province. I had not seen Noim since the summer before, when we had hunted together in the Huishtors. In this past year we had drifted apart somewhat; in a sense Schweiz had come to take Noim's place in my life, and I no longer had quite the same need for my bondbrother.

Noim now was a wealthy landowner in Salla, having come into the inheritance of the Condorit family as well as the lands of his wife's kin. In manhood he had become plump, though not fat; his wit and cunning were not hidden deep beneath his new layers of flesh. He had a sleek, well-oiled look, with dark unblemished skin, full, complacent lips, and round sardonic eyes. Little escaped his attention. Upon arriving at my house he surveyed me with great care, as though counting my teeth and the lines about my eyes, and, after the formal bondbrotherly greetings, after the presentation of his gift and the one he had brought from Stirron, after we had signed the contract of host and guest, Noim said unexpectedly, "Are you in trouble, Kinnall?"

"Why do you ask that?"

"Your face is sharper. You've lost weight. Your mouth—you hold it in a quirky grin that doesn't announce a relaxed man within. Your eyes are red-rimmed and they don't want to look directly into other eyes. Is anything wrong?"

"These have been the happiest months of one's life," I said, a shade too vehemently, perhaps.

Noim ignored my disclaimer. "Are you having problems with Loimel?"

"She goes her way, and one goes his own."

"Difficulties with the business of the Justiciary, then?"

"Please, Noim, won't you believe that—"

"Your face has changes inscribed in it," he said. "Do you deny there have been changes in your life?"

I shrugged. "And if so?"

"Changes for the worse?"

"One does not think so."

"You're being evasive, Kinnall. Come: what's a bondbrother for, if not to share problems?"

"There are no problems," I insisted.

"Very well." And he let the matter drop. But I saw him watching me that evening, and again the next day at morning's meal, studying me, probing me. I could never hide anything from him. We sat over blue wine and talked of the Sallan harvest, talked of Stirron's new program of reforming the tax structure, talked of the renewed tensions between Salla and Glin, the bloody border raids that had lately cost me the life of a sister. And all the while Noim watched me. Halum dined with us, and we talked of our childhood, and Noim watched me. He flirted with Loimel, but his eyes did not wander from me. The depth and intensity of his concern preyed on me. He would be asking questions of others, soon, trying to get from Halum or from Loimel some notion of what might be bothering me, and he might stir up troublesome curiosities in them that way. I could not let him remain ignorant of the central experience of his bondbrother's life. Late the second night, when everyone else had retired, I took Noim to my study, and opened the secret place where I stored the white powder, and asked him if he knew anything of the Sumaran drug. He claimed not to have heard of it. Briefly I described its effects to him. His expression darkened; he seemed to draw in on himself. "Do you use this stuff often?" he asked.

"Eleven times thus far."

"Eleven—*why*, Kinnall?"

"To learn the nature of one's own self, through sharing that self with others."

Noim laughed explosively: it was almost a snort. "Selfbaring, Kinnall?"

"One takes up odd hobbies in one's middle years."

"And with whom have you played this game?"

I said, "Their names don't matter. No one you would know. People of Manneran, those with some adventure in their souls, those who are willing to take risks."

"Loimel?"

Now it was my turn to snort. "Never! She knows nothing of this at all."

"Halum, then?"

I shook my head. "One wishes one had the courage to approach Halum. So far one has concealed everything from her. One fears she's too virginal, too easily shocked. It's sad, isn't it, Noim, when one has to hide something as exciting as this, as wonderfully rewarding, from one's bondsister."

"From one's bondbrother too," he observed testily.

"You would have been told in time," I said. "You would have been offered your chance to experience the communion."

His eyes flashed. "Do you think I'd want it?"

His deliberate obscenity earned only a faint smile from me. "One hopes one's bondbrother will share all of one's experiences. At present the drug opens a gulf between us. One has gone again and again to a place you have never visited. Do you see, Noim?"

Noim saw. He was tempted; he hovered at the edge of the abyss; he chewed his lips and tugged at his earlobes, and everything that passed across his mind was as transparent to me as if we had already shared the Sumaran powder. For my sake he was uneasy, knowing that I had seriously strayed from the Covenant and might soon find myself in grave spiritual and legal trouble. For his own sake he was gnawed by curiosity, aware that selfbaring with one's bondbrother was no great sin and half-eager to know the kind of communion he might have with me under the drug. Also his eyes revealed a glint of jealousy, that I had bared myself to this one and this one and that, unimportant strangers, and not to him. I tell you that I comprehended these things at that moment, though I confirmed them later when Noim's soul was open to me.

We said nothing to one another about these matters for several days. He came with me to my office, and watched in admiration as I dealt with matters of the highest national significance. He saw the clerks bowing in and out of my presence, and also the clerk Ulman, who had had the drug, and whose cool familiarity with me touched off suspicious vibrations in Noim's sensitive antennae. We visited with Schweiz, and emptied many a flask of good wine, and discussed religious topics in a hearty, earnest, drunken way. ("All my life," said Schweiz, "has been a quest for plausible reasons to believe in what I know to be irrational.") Noim noticed that Schweiz did not always observe the grammatical niceties. Another night we dined with a group of Mannerangi nobles in a voluptuous house in the hills overlooking the city; small birdlike men, overdressed and fidgety, and huge handsome young wives. Noim was displeased by these effete dukes and barons with their talk of commerce and jewelry, but he grew more irritable yet when the chatter turned to the rumor that a mind-unsealing drug from the southern continent was now procurable in the capital. To this I made only polite interjections of surprise; Noim glared at me for my hypocrisy, and even refused a dish of tender Mannerangi brandy, so tight-strung were his nerves. The day after, we went to the Stone Chapel together, not for draining but merely to view the relics of the early times, for Noim had developed antiquarian interests. The drainer Jidd happened to wander through the cloister at his devotions and smiled oddly at me: I saw Noim at once calculating whether I had drawn even the priest into my subversions. A sizzling tension was building in Noim during those days, for he clearly longed to return to the subject of our early conversation, yet could not bring himself to it. I made no move toward reopening that theme. It was Noim who made the move, finally, on the eve of his departure for his home in Salla. "This drug of yours—" he began hoarsely.

He said he felt he could not regard himself as my true bond-brother unless he sampled it. Those words came from him at great cost. His elegant clothes were rumpled by his restlessness, and a fine line of beaded perspiration stood out on his upper lip. We went to a room where no one could intrude, and I prepared the potion. As he took the flask, he briefly flashed at me his familiar grin, impudent and sly and bold, but his hand was shaking so badly he nearly spilled the drink. The drug took effect quickly for both of us. It was a night of thick humidity, with a dense greasy mist covering the city and its suburbs, and it seemed to me that fingers of that mist were sliding into our room through the partly opened window: I saw shimmering, pulsating strands of cloud groping at us, dancing between my bond-brother and myself. The early sensations of druggedness disturbed

Noim, until I explained that everything was normal, the twinned heartbeats, the cottony head, the high whining sounds in the air. Now we were open. I looked into Noim and saw not only his self but his image of his self, encrusted with shame and self-contempt; there was in Noim a fierce and burning loathing of his imagined flaws, and the flaws were many. He held himself accused of laziness, lack of discipline and ambition, irreligiousness, a casual concern with high obligations, and physical and moral weakness. Why he saw himself in this way I could not understand, for the true Noim was there beside the image, and the true Noim was a tough-minded man, loyal to those he loved, harsh in judgment of folly, clear-sighted, passionate, energetic. The contrast between Noim's Noim and the world's was startling: it was as though he were capable of correctly evaluating everything but his own worth. I had seen such disparities before on these drug voyages; in fact they were universal in all but Schweiz, who had not been trained from childhood in self-denial; yet they were sharper in Noim than in anyone else.

Also I saw, as I had seen before, my own image refracted through Noim's sensibility: a far nobler Kinnall Darival than I recognized. How he idealized me! I was all he hoped to be, a man of action and valor, a wielder of power, an enemy of everything that was frivolous, a practitioner of the sternest inner discipline and devotion. Yet this image bore traces of a new overlay of tarnish, for was I not also now a Covenant-defiling self-barer, who had done this and this and that and that with eleven strangers, and who now had lured his own bondbrother into criminal experimentation? And also Noim found in me the true depth of my feelings for Halum, and upon making that discovery, which confirmed old suspicions, he altered his image of me once again, not for the better. Meanwhile I showed Noim how I had always seen him—quick, clever, capable—and showed him too his own Noim and the objective Noim as well, while he gave me a view of the selves of mine he now could see beside that idealized Kinnall. These mutual explorations continued a long time. I thought the exchanges were immensely valuable, since only with Noim could I attain the necessary depth of perspective, the proper parallax of character, and he only with me; we had great advantages over a pair of strangers meeting for the first time by way of the Sumaran drug. When the spell of the potion began to lift, I felt myself exhausted by the intensity of our communion, and yet ennobled, exalted, transformed.

Not so Noim. He looked depleted and chilled. He could barely lift his eyes to mine. His mood was so frigid that I dared not break in on it, but remained still, waiting for him to recover. At length he said, "Is it all over?"

"Yes."

"Promise one thing, Kinnall. Will you promise?"

"Say it, Noim."

"That you never do this thing with Halum! Is it a promise? Will you promise it, Kinnall? Never. Never. Never."

54

SEVERAL DAYS after Noim's departure some guilty impulse drove me to the Stone Chapel. To fill the time until Jidd could see me, I roamed the halls and byways of the dark building, pausing at altars, bowing humbly to half-blind scholars of the Covenant holding debate in a courtyard, brushing away ambitious minor drainers who, recognizing me, solititiced my trade. All about me were the things of the gods, and I failed to detect the divine presence. Perhaps Schweiz had found the godhood through the souls of other men, but I, dabbling in selfbaring, somehow had lost that other faith, and it did not matter to me. I knew that in time I would find my way back to grace under this new dispensation of love and trust that I hoped to offer. So I lurked in the godhouse of godhouses, a mere tourist.

I went to Jidd. I had not had a draining since immediately after Schweiz first had given me the Sumaran drug. The little crooknosed man remarked on that as I took the contract from him. The pressures of the Justiciary, I explained, and he shook his head and made a chiding sound. "You must be full to overflowing," Jidd said. I did not reply, but settled down before his mirror to peer at the lean, unfamiliar face that dwelled in it. He asked me which god I would have, and I told him the god of the innocent. He gave me a queer look at that. The holy lights came on. With soft words he guided me into the half-trance of confession. What could I say? That I had ignored my pledge, and gone on to use the selfbaring potion with everyone who would take it from me? I sat silent. Jidd prodded me. He did something I had never known a drainer to do before: hearkened back to a previous draining, and asked me to speak again of this drug whose use I had admitted earlier. Had I used it again? I pushed my face close to the mirror, fogging it with my breath. Yes. Yes. One is a miserable sinner and one has been weak once more. Then Jidd asked me how I had obtained this drug, and I said that I had taken it, the first time, in company with one who had purchased it from a man who had been to Sumara Borthan. Yes, Jidd said, and what was the name of this companion? That was a clumsy move: immediately I was on guard. It seemed to me that Jidd's question went far beyond the needs of a draining, and certainly could have no relevance to my own condition of the moment. I refused therefore to give him Schweiz's name, which led the drainer to ask me, a little roughly, if I feared he would breach the secrecy of the ritual.

Did I fear that? On rare occasions I had held things back from drainers out of shame, but never out of fear of betrayal. Naïve I was, and I had full faith in the ethics of the godhouse. Only now, suddenly suspicious, with that suspicion having been planted by Jidd himself, did I mistrust Jidd and all his tribe. Why did he want to know? What information was he after? What could I gain, or he, by my revealing my source of the drug? I replied tautly, "One seeks forgiveness for oneself alone, and how can telling the name of one's companion bring that? Let him do his own confessing." But of course there was no chance that Schweiz would go to a drainer; thus I had come down to playing word-games with Jidd. All value had leaked from this draining, leaving me with an empty husk. "If you would have peace from the gods," Jidd said, "you must speak your soul fully." How could I do that? Confess the seduction of eleven people into selfbaring? I had no need of Jidd's forgiveness. I had no faith in his good will. Abruptly I stood up, a little dizzy from kneeling in the dark, swaying a bit, almost stumbling. The sound of distant hymn-singing floated past me, and a trace of the scent of the precious incense of a plant of the Wet Lowlands. "One is not ready for draining today," I told Jidd. "One must examine one's soul more closely." I lurched toward the door. He looked puzzledly at the money I had given him. "The fee?" he called. I told him he could keep it.

55

THE DAYS BECAME mere vacant rooms, separating one journey with the drug from the next. I drifted idle and detached through all my responsibilities, seeing nothing of what was around me, living only for my next communion. The real world dissolved; I lost interest in sex, wine, food, the doings of the Port Justiciary, the friction between neighboring provinces of Velada Borthan, and all other such things, which to me now were only the shadows of shadows. Possibly I was using the drug too frequently. I lost weight and existed in a perpetual haze of blurred white light. I had difficulties in sleeping, and for hours found myself twisting and shifting, a blanket of muggy tropical air clamping me to my mattress, a haggard insomniac with an ache in his eyeballs and grittiness under his lids. I walked tired through my days and blinking through my evenings. Rarely did I speak with Loimel, nor did I touch her, and hardly ever did I touch any other woman. I fell asleep at midday once while lunching with Halum. I scandalized High Justice Kalimol by replying to one of his questions with the phrase, "It seems to me—" Old Segvord Helalam told me I looked ill, and suggested I go hunting with my sons in the Burnt Lowlands. Nevertheless the drug had the power of bringing me alive. I sought out new sharers, and found it ever more easy to make contact with them, for often now they were brought to me by those who had already made the inner voyage. An odd group they were: two dukes, a marquis, a whore, a keeper of the royal archives, a seacaptain in from Glin, a septarch's mistress, a director of the Commercial and Seafarers Bank of Manneran, a poet, a lawyer from Velis here to confer with Captain Khrisch, and many more. The circle of self-barers was widening. My supply of the drug was nearly consumed, but now there was talk among some of my new friends of outfitting a new expedition to Sumara Borthan. There were fifty of us by this time. Change was becoming infectious; there was an epidemic of it in Manneran.

56

SOMETIMES, unexpectedly, in the blank dead time between one communion and another, I underwent a strange confusion of the self. A block of borrowed experience that I had stowed in the dark depths of my mind might break loose and float up into the higher levels of consciousness, intruding itself into my own identity. I remained aware of being Kinnall Darival, the septarch's son of Salla, and yet there was suddenly among my memories a segment of the self of Noim, or Schweiz, or one of the Sumarnu, or someone else of those with whom I had shared the drug. For the length of that splicing of selves—a moment, an hour, half a day—I walked about unsure of my past, unable to determine whether some event fresh in my mind had really befallen me, or had come to me through the drug. This was disturbing but not really frightening, except the first two or three times. Eventually I learned to distinguish the quality of these unearned memories from that of my genuine past, through familiarity with the textures of each. The drug had made me many people, I realized. Was it not better to be many than to be something less than one?

57

IN EARLY SPRING a lunatic heat settled over Manneran, coupled with such frequent rains that all the city's vegetation went mad, and would have swallowed every street if not given a daily hacking. It was green, green, green, everywhere: green haze in the sky, green rain falling, green sunlight sometimes breaking through, broad glossy green leaves unfurling on every balcony and in every garden plot. A man's own soul can mildew in that. Green, too, were the awnings on the street of the spice-merchants' shops. Loimel had given me a long list of things to purchase, delicacies from Threish and Velis and the Wet Lowlands, and in a docile husbandly way I went to obtain them, since the street of spice was only a short walk from the Justiciary. She was mounting a grand feast to celebrate the Naming Day of our eldest daughter, who was at last going to come into the adult-name we had intended for her: Loimel. All the great ones of Manneran had been invited to look on as my wife acquired a namesake. Among the guests would be several who had covertly sampled the Sumaran drug with me, and I took private pleasure in that; Schweiz, though, had not been invited, since Loimel deemed him coarse, and in any event he had left Manneran on some business trip just as the weather was beginning to go berserk.

I moved through the greenness to the best of the shops. A recent rain had ended and the sky was a flat green plaque resting on the rooftops. To me came delicious fragrances, sweetnesses, pungencies, clouds of tongue-tickling flavors. Abruptly there were black bubbles coursing through my skull and for a moment I was Schweiz haggling on a pier with a skipper who had just brought a cargo of costly produce in from the Gulf of Sumar. I halted to enjoy this tangling of selves. Schweiz faded; through Noim's mind I smelled the scent of newly threshed hay on the Condorit estates, under a delicious late-summer sun; then suddenly and surprisingly I was the bank director with my hand tight on some other man's loins. I cannot convey to you the impact of that last bolt of transferred experience, brief and incandescent. I had taken the drug with the bank director not very long before, and I had seen nothing in his soul, then, of his taste for his own sex. It was not the kind of thing I would overlook. Either I had manufactured this vision gratuitously, or he had somehow shielded that part of his self from me, keeping his predilections sealed until this instant of breaking through. Was such a partial sealing possible? I had thought one's mind lay fully open. I was not upset by the nature of his lusts, only by my inability to reconcile what I had just experienced with what had come to me from him on the day of our drug-sharing. But I had little time to ponder the problem, for, as I stood gaping outside the spice-shop, a thin hand fell on mine and a guarded voice said, "I must talk to you secretly, Kinnall." *I.* The word jolted me from my dreaming.

Androg Mihan, keeper of the archives of Manneran's prime septarch, stood beside me. He was a small man, sharp-featured and gray, the last you would think to seek illegal pleasures; the Duke of Sumar, one of my early conquests, had led him to me. "Where shall we go?" I asked, and Mihan indicated a disreputable-looking lower-class godhouse across the street. Its drainer lounged outside, trying to stir up business. I could not see how we could talk secretly in a godhouse, but I followed the archivist anyway; we entered the godhouse and Mihan told the drainer to fetch his contract forms. The moment the man was gone, Mihan leaned close to me and said, "The police are on their way to your house. When you return home this evening you will be arrested and taken to prison on one of the Sumar Gulf's isles."

"Where do you learn this?"

"The decree was verified this morning and has passed to me for filing."

"What charge?" I asked.

"Selfbaring," Mihan said. "Accusation filed by agents of the Stone Chapel. There is also a secular charge: use and distribution of illegal drugs. They have you, Kinnall."

"Who is the informer?"

"A certain Jidd, said to be a drainer in the Stone Chapel. Did you let the tale of the drug be drained from you?"

"I did. In my innocence. The sanctity of the godhouse—"

"The sanctity of the dunghouse!" Androg Mihan said vehemently. "Now you must flee! The full force of the government is mustered against you."

"Where shall I go?"

"The Duke of Sumar will shelter you tonight," said Mihan. "After that—I do not know."

The drainer now returned, bearing a set of contracts. He gave us a proprietary smile and said, "Well, gentlemen, which of you is to be first?"

"One has remembered another appointment," Mihan said.

"One feels suddenly unwell," I said.

I tossed the startled drainer a fat coin and we left the godhouse. Outside, Mihan pretended not to know me, and we went our separate ways without a word. Not for a moment did I doubt the truth of his warning. I had to take flight; Loimel would have to purchase her own spices. I hailed a car and went at once to the mansion of the Duke of Sumar.

58

Thıs ᴅᴜᴋᴇ ıs one of the wealthiest in Manneran, with sprawling estates along the Gulf and in the Huishtor foothills, and a splendid home at the capital set amidst a park worthy of an emperor's palace. He is hereditary customs-keeper of Stroin Gap, which is the source of his family's opulence, since for centuries they have skimmed a share of all that is brought forth to market out of the Wet Lowlands. In his person this duke is a man of great ugliness or remarkable beauty, I am not sure which: he has a large flat triangular head, thin lips, a powerful nose, and strange dense tightly curled hair that clings like a carpet to his skull. His hair is entirely white, yet his face is unlined. His eyes are huge and dark and intense. His cheeks are hollow. It is an ascetic face, which to me always seemed alternately saintly and monstrous, and sometimes the both at once. I had been close with him almost since my arrival in Manneran so many years before; he had helped Segvord Helalam into power, and he had stood soulbinder to Loimel at our wedding ceremony. When I took up the use of the Sumaran drug, he divined it as if by telepathy, and in a conversation of marvelous subtlety learned from me that I had the drug, and arranged that he should take it with me. That had been four moonrises earlier, in late winter.

Arriving at his home, I found a tense conference in progress. Present were most of the men of consequence whom I had inveigled into my circle of self-barers. The Duke of Mannerangu Smor. The Marquis of Woyn. The bank director. The Commissioner of the Treasury and his brother, the Procurator-General of Manneran. The Master of the Border. And five or six others of similar significance. Archivist Mihan arrived shortly after I did.

"We are all here now," the Duke of Mannerangu Smor said. "They could sweep us up with a single stroke. Are the grounds well guarded?"

"No one will invade us," said the Duke of Sumar, a trifle icily, clearly offended by the suggestion that common police might burst into his home. He turned his huge alien eyes on me. "Kinnall, this will be your last night in Manneran, and no help for it. You are to be the scapegoat."

"By whose choice?" I asked.

"Not ours," the duke replied. He explained that something close to a coup d'etat had been attempted in Manneran this day, and might well yet succeed: a revolt of junior bureaucrats against their masters. The beginning, he said, lay in my having admitted my use of the Sumaran drug to the drainer Jidd. (Around the room faces darkened. The unspoken implication was that I had been a fool to trust a drainer, and now must pay the price of my folly. I had not been as sophisticated as these men.) Jidd, it seemed, had leagued himself with a cabal of disaffected minor officials, hungry for their turn at power. Since he was drainer to most of the great men of Manneran, he was in an extraordinarily good position to aid the ambitious, by betraying the secrets of the mighty. Why Jidd had chosen to contravene his oaths in this fashion was not yet known. The Duke of Sumar suspected that in Jidd familiarity had bred contempt, and after listening for years to the melancholy outpourings of his powerful clients, he had grown to loathe them: exasperated by their confessions, he found pleasure in collaborating in their destruction. (This gave me a new view of what a drainer's soul might be like.) Hence Jidd had, for some months now, been slipping useful facts to rapacious subordinates, who had threatened their masters with them, often to considerable effect. By admitting my use of the drug to him, I had made myself vulnerable, and he had sold me to certain folk of the Justiciary who wished to have me out of office.

"But this is absurd!" I cried. "The only evidence against me is protected by the sanctity of the godhouse! How can Jidd place a complaint against me based on what I've drained to him? I'll have him up on charges for violation of contract!"

"There is other evidence," the Marquis of Woyn said sadly.

"There is?"

"Using what he heard from your own lips," the marquis said, "Jidd was able to guide your enemies into channels of investigation. They have found a certain woman who lives in the hovels behind the Stone Chapel, who has admitted to them that you gave her a strange drink that opened her mind to you—"

"The beasts."

"They have also," the Duke of Sumar said, "been able to link several of us to you. Not all, but several. This morning some of us were presented, by their own subordinates, with demands to resign their offices or face exposure. We met these threats firmly, and those who made them are now under detention, but there is no telling how many allies they have in high places. It is possible that by next moonrise we will all have been cast down and new men will hold our power. However, I doubt this, since, so far as we can determine, the only solid evidence so far is the confession of the slut, who has implicated only you, Kinnall. The accusations made by Jidd will of course be inadmissible, though they can do damage anyway."

"We can destroy her credibility," I said. "I'll claim I never knew her. I'll—"

"Too late," said the Procurator-General. "Her deposition is on record. I've had a copy from the Grand Justiciar. It will stand up. You're hopelessly implicated."

"What will happen?" I asked.

"We will crush the ambitions of the blackmailers," said the Duke of Sumar, "and send them into poverty. We will break Jidd's prestige and drive him from the Stone Chapel. We will deny all of the charges of selfbaring that may be brought against us. You, however, must leave Manneran."

"Why?" I looked at the duke in perplexity. "I'm not without influence. If you can withstand the charges, why not I?"

"Your guilt is on record," the Duke of Mannerangu Smor said. "If you flee, it can be claimed that you alone, and this girl you corrupted, were the only ones involved, and the rest is merely the fabrication of self-serving underlings trying to overthrow their masters. If you stay and try to fight a hopeless case, you'll eventually bring us all down, as your interrogation proceeds."

It was wholly plain to me now.

I was dangerous to them. My strength might be broken in court and their guilt thus exposed. Thus far I was the only one indicted, and I was the only one vulnerable to the processes of Mannerangi justice. They were vulnerable solely through me, and if I went, there was no way of getting at them. The safety of the majority required my departure. Moreover: my naïve faith in the godhouse, which had led me rashly to confess to Jidd, had led to this tempest, which otherwise might have been avoided. I had caused all this; I was the one who must go.

The Duke of Sumar said, "You will remain with us until the dark hours of the night, and then my private groundcar, escorted by bodyguards as though it were I who were traveling, will take you to the estate of the Marquis of Woyn. A riverboat will be waiting there. By dawn you will be across the Woyn and into your homeland of Salla, and may the gods journey at your side."

59

ONCE MORE A REFUGEE. In a single day all the power I had accumulated in fifteen years in Manneran was lost. Neither high birth nor high connections could save me: I might have ties of marriage or love or politics to half the masters of Manneran, yet they were helpless in helping me. I have made it seem as if they had forced me into exile to save their own skins, but it was not like that. My going was necessary, and it brought as much sorrow to them as to me.

I had nothing with me but the clothes I wore. My wardrobe, my weapons, my ornaments, my wealth itself, must remain behind in Manneran. As a boy-prince fleeing from Salla to Glin, I had had the prudence to transfer funds ahead of myself, but now I was cut off. My assets would be sequestered; my sons would be paupered. There had been no time for preparations.

Here at least my friends were of service. The Procurator-General, who was nearly of a size with me, had brought several changes of handsome clothing. The Commissioner of the Treasury had obtained for me a fair fortune in Sallan currency. The Duke of Mannerangu Smor pulled two rings and a pendant from his own body, so that I should not go unadorned into my native province. The Marquis of Woyn pressed on me a ceremonial dagger and his heatrod, with a hilt worked with precious gems. Mihan promised to speak with Segvord Helalam, and tell him the details of my downfall; Segvord would be sympathetic, Mihan believed, and would protect my sons with all his influence, and keep them untainted by their father's indictment. Lastly, the Duke of Sumar came to me at the deepest time of the night, when I sat alone sourly eating the dinner I had had no time for earlier, and handed me a small jeweled case of bright gold, of the sort one might carry medicine in. "Open it carefully," he said. I did, and found it brimming with white powder. In amazement I asked him where he had obtained this; he had lately sent agents secretly to Sumara Borthan, he replied, who had returned with a small supply of the drug. He claimed to have more, but I believe he gave me all he had.

"In an hour's time you will leave," said the duke, to smother my gush of gratitude.

I asked to be allowed to make a call first.

"Segvord will explain matters to your wife," the duke said.

"One did not mean one's wife. One meant one's bondsister." In speaking of Halum I could not drop easily into the rough grammar we self-barers affected. "One has had no chance to make one's farewell to her."

The duke understood my anguish, for he had been within my soul. But he would not grant me the call. Lines might be tapped; he could not risk having my voice go forth from his home this night. I realized then how delicate a position even he must be in, and I did not force the issue. I could call Halum tomorrow, when I had crossed the Woyn and was safe in Salla.

Shortly it was time for me to depart. My friends had already gone, some hours since; the duke alone led me from the house. His majestic groundcar waited, and a corps of bodyguards on individual powercycles. The duke embraced me. I climbed into the car and settled back against the cushions. The driver opaqued the windows, hiding me from view though not interfering with my own vision. The car rolled silently forward, picked up speed, plunged into the night, with my outriders, six of them, hovering about it like insects. It seemed that hours went by before we came even to the main gate of the duke's estate. Then we were on the highway. I sat like a man carved of ice, scarcely thinking of what had befallen me. Northward lay our route, and we went at such a rate that the sun was not yet up when we reached the margin of the Marquis of Woyn's estate, on the border between Manneran and Salla. The gate opened; we shot through; the road cut across a dense forest, in which, by moonlight, I could see sinister parasitic growths like hairy ropes tangling tree to tree. Suddenly we erupted into a clearing and I beheld the banks of the River Woyn. The car halted. Someone in dark robes helped me out, as though I were a dodderer, and escorted me down the spongy bank to a long narrow pier, barely visible in the thick mist rising off the breast of the river. A boat was tied up, no great craft, hardly more than a dinghy. Yet it traveled at great speed across the broad and turbulent Woyn. Still I felt no inner response to my banishment from Manneran. I was like one who has gone forth in battle and had his right leg sliced off at the thigh by a fire-bolt, and who now lies in a tumbled heap, staring calmly at his stump and sensing no pain. The pain would come, in time.

Dawn was near. I could make out the shape of the Sallan side of the river. We pulled up at a dock that jutted out of a grassy bank, plainly some nobleman's private landing. Now I felt my first alarm. In a moment I would step ashore in Salla. Where would I find myself? How would I reach some settled region? I was no boy, to beg rides from passing trucks. But all this had been settled for me hours before. As the boat bumped the shoulder of the pier, a figure emerged in the dimness and extended a hand: Noim. He drew me forth and clasped me in a tight hug. "I know what has happened," he said. "You will stay with me." In his emotion he abandoned polite usage with me for the first time since our boyhood.

60

AT MIDDAY, from Noim's estate in southwestern Salla, I phoned the Duke of Sumar to confirm my safe arrival—it was he, of course, who had arranged for my bondbrother to meet me at the border—and then I put through a call to Halum. Segvord had told her just a few hours earlier of the reasons for my disappearance. "How strange this news is," she said. "You never spoke of the drug. Yet it was so important to you, for you risked everything to use it. How could it have had such a role in your life, and yet be kept a secret from your bondsister?" I answered that I had not dared to let her know of my preoccupation with it, for fear I might be tempted to offer it to her. She said, "Is opening yourself then to your bondsister so terrible a sin?"

61

NOIM TREATED ME with every courtesy, indicating that I could stay with him as long as I wished—weeks, months, even years. Presumably my friends in Manneran would succeed eventually in freeing some of my assets, and I would buy land in Salla and take up the life of a country baron; or perhaps Segvord and the Duke of Sumar and other men of influence would have my indictment quashed, so that I could return to the southern province. Until then, Noim told me, his home was mine. But I detected a subtle coolness in his dealings with me, as if this hospitality was offered only out of respect for our bonding. Only after some days did the source of his remoteness reach the surface. Sitting late past dinner in his great whitewashed feasting-hall, we were talking of childhood days—our main theme of conversation, far safer than any talk of recent events—when Noim suddenly said, "Is that drug of yours known to give people nightmares?"

"One has heard of no such cases, Noim."

"Here's a case, then. One who woke up drenched with chilly sweat night after night, for weeks after we shared the drug in Manneran. One thought one would lose one's mind."

"What kind of dreams?" I asked.

"Ugly things. Monsters. Teeth. Claws. A sense of not knowing who one is. Pieces of other minds floating through one's own." He gulped at his wine. "You take the drug for *pleasure*, Kinnall?"

"For knowledge."

"Knowledge of what?"

"Knowledge of self, and knowledge of others."

"One prefers ignorance, then." He shivered. "You know, Kinnall, one was never a particularly reverent person. One blasphemed, one stuck his tongue out at drainers, one laughed at the god-tales they told, yes? You've nearly converted one into a man of faith with that stuff. The terror of opening one's mind—of knowing that one has no defenses, that you can slide right into one's soul, and are doing it —it's impossible to take."

"Impossible for you," I said. "Others cherish it."

"One leans toward the Covenant," said Noim. "Privacy is sacred. One's soul is one's own. There's a dirty pleasure in baring it."

"Not baring. Sharing."

"Does it sound prettier that way? Very well: there's a dirty pleasure in sharing it, Kinnall. Even though we are bondbrothers, one came away from you last time feeling soiled. Sand and grit in the soul. Is this what you want for everyone? To make us all feel filthy with guilt?"

"There need be no guilt, Noim. One gives, one receives, one comes forth better than one was—"

"Dirtier."

"Enlarged. Enhanced. More compassionate. Speak to others who have tried it," I said.

"Of course. As they come streaming out of Manneran, landless refugees, one will question them about the beauty and wonder of selfbaring. Excuse me: selfsharing."

I saw the torment in his eyes. He wanted still to love me, but the Sumaran drug had shown him things—about himself, perhaps about me—that made him hate the one who had given the drug to him. He was one for whom walls are necessary; I had not realized that. What had I done, to turn my bondbrother into my enemy? Perhaps if we could take the drug a second time, I might make things more clear to him—but no, no hope of that. Noim was frightened by inwardness. I had transformed my blaspheming bondbrother into a man of the Covenant. There was nothing I could say to him now.

After some silence he said, "One must make a request of you, Kinnall."

"Anything."

"One hesitates to place boundaries on a guest. But if you have brought any of this drug with you from Manneran, Kinnall, if you hide it somewhere in your rooms—get rid of it, is that understood? There must be none of it in this house. Get rid of it, Kinnall."

Never in my life had I lied to my bondbrother. Never.

With the jeweled case the Duke of Sumar had given me blazing against my breastbone, I said solemnly to Noim, "You have nothing to fear on that account, Noim."

62

Not many days later the news of my disgrace became public in Manneran, and swiftly reached Salla. Noim showed me the accounts. I was described as the chief adviser to the High Justice of the Port, and openly labeled a man of the greatest authority in Manneran, who, moreover, had blood ties to the prime septarchs of Salla and Glin—and yet, despite these attainments and preferments, I had fallen away from the Covenant to take up unlawful selfbaring. I had violated not merely propriety and etiquette, but also the laws of Manneran, through my use of a certain proscribed drug from Sumara Borthan that dissolves the god-given barriers between soul and soul. Through abuse of my high office, it was said, I had engineered a secret voyage to the southern continent (poor Captain Khrisch! Had he been arrested too?) and had returned with a large quantity of the drug, which I had devilishly forced on a lowborn woman whom I was keeping; I had also circulated the foul stuff among certain prominent members of the nobility, whose names were being withheld because of their thorough repentance. On the eve of my arrest I had escaped to Salla, and good riddance to me: if I attempted to return to Manneran, I would immediately be apprehended. Meanwhile I would be tried in absentia, and, according to the Grand Justiciar, there could be little doubt of the verdict. By way of restitution to the state for the great injury I had done the fabric of social stability, I would be required to forfeit all my lands and property, except only a portion to be set aside for the maintenance of my innocent wife and children. (Segvord Helalam, then, had at least accomplished that.) To prevent my highborn friends from transferring my assets to me in Salla before the trial, all that I possessed was already sequestered in anticipation of the Grand Justiciar's decree of guilt. Thus spake the law. Let others who would make selfbaring monsters of themselves beware!

63

I MADE NO SECRET of my whereabouts in Salla, for I had no reason now to fear the jealousy of my royal brother. Stirron as a boy newly on the throne might have been driven to eliminate me as a potential rival, but not the Stirron who had ruled for more than seventeen years. By now he was an institution in Salla, well loved and an integral part of everyone's existence, and I was a stranger, barely remembered by the older folk and unknown to the younger, who spoke with a Mannerangi accent and who had been publicly branded with the shame of selfbaring. Even if I cared to overthrow Stirron, where would I find followers?

In truth I was hungry for the sight of my brother. In times of storm one turns to one's earliest comrades; and with Noim estranged from me and Halum on the far side of the Woyn, I had only Stirron left. I had never resented having had to flee Salla on his account, for I knew that had our ages been reversed I would have caused him to flee the same way. If our relationship had grown frosty since my flight, it was a frost of his making, arising from his guilty conscience. Some years had passed, now, since my last visit to Salla City: perhaps my adversities would open his heart. I wrote Stirron a letter from Noim's place, formally begging sanctuary in Salla. Under Sallan law I had to be taken in, for I was one of Stirron's subjects and was guilty of no crime committed on Sallan soil: yet I thought it best to ask. The charges lodged against me by the Grand Justiciar of Manneran, I admitted, were true, but I offered Stirron a terse and (I think) eloquent justification of my deviation from the Covenant. I closed the letter with expressions of my unwavering love for him, and with a few reminiscences of the happy times we had had before the burdens of the septarchy had descended on him.

I expected Stirron in return to invite me to visit him at the capital, so that he could hear from my own lips an explanation of the strange things I had done in Manneran. A brotherly reunion was surely in order. But no summons to Salla City came. Each time the telephone chimed, I rushed toward it, thinking it might be Stirron calling. He did not call. Several weeks of tension and gloom passed; I hunted, I swam, I read, I tried to write my new Covenant of love. Noim remained aloof from me. His one experience at soulsharing had thrust him into so deep an embarrassment that he hardly dared to meet my eyes, for I was privy to all his innerness, and that had become a wedge between us.

At last came an envelope bearing the septarch's imposing seal. It held a letter signed by Stirron, but I pray it was some steely minister, and not my brother, who composed that pinch-souled message. In fewer lines than I have fingers, the septarch told me that my request for sanctuary in the province of Salla was granted, but only on the condition that I forswear the vices I had learned in the south. If I were caught just once spreading the use of selfbaring drugs in Salla, I would be seized and driven into exile. That was all my brother had to say. Not a syllable of kindness. Not a shred of sympathy. Not an atom of warmth.

64

AT THE CREST of the summer Halum came unexpectedly to visit us. The day of her arrival, I had gone riding far out across Noim's land, following the track of a male stormshield that had burst from its pen. An accursed vanity had led Noim to acquire a clutch of these vicious furbearing mammals, though they are not native to Salla and thrive poorly there: he kept twenty or thirty of them, all claws and teeth and angry yellow eyes, and hoped to breed them into a profitable herd. I chased the escaped male through woods and plain, through morning and midday, hating it more with each hour, for it left a trail of the mutilated carcasses of harmless grazing beasts. These stormshields kill for sheer love of slaughter, taking but a bite or two of flesh and abandoning the rest to scavengers. Finally I cornered it in a shadowy box-canyon. "Stun it and bring it back whole," Noim had instructed me, conscious of the animal's value: but when trapped it rushed at me with such ferocity that I gave it the full beam, and gladly slew it. For Noim's sake I took the trouble to strip off the precious hide. Then, weary and depressed, I rode without stopping back to the great house. A strange groundcar was parked outside, and beside it was Halum. "You know the summers in Manneran," she explained. "One planned to go as usual to the island, but then one thought, it would be good to take a holiday in Salla, with Noim and Kinnall."

She had by then entered her thirtieth year. Our women marry between fourteen and sixteen, are done bearing their children by twenty-two or twenty-four, and at thirty have begun to slide into middle age, but time had left Halum untouched. Not having known the tempests of marriage and the travails of motherhood, not having spent her energies on the grapplings of the conjugal couch or the lacerations of childbed, she had the supple, pliant body of a girl: no fleshy bulges, no sagging folds, no exploded veins, no thickening of the frame. She had changed only in one respect, for in recent years her dark hair had turned silvery. This was but an enhancement, however, since it gleamed with dazzling brilliance, and offered agreeable contrast to the deep tan of her youthful face.

In her luggage was a packet of letters for me from Manneran: messages from the duke, from Segvord, from my sons Noim and Stirron and Kinnall, from my daughters Halum and Loimel, from Mihan the archivist, and several others. Those who wrote did so in tense, selfconscious style. They were the letters one might write to a dead man if one felt guilty at having survived him. Still, it was good to hear these words out of my former life. I regretted not finding a letter from Schweiz; Halum told me she had heard nothing from him since before my indictment, and thought he might well have left our planet. Nor was there any word from my wife. "Is Loimel too busy to write a line or two?" I asked, and Halum, looking embarrassed, said softly that Loimel never spoke of me these days: "She seems to have forgotten that she was married."

Halum also had brought a trove of gifts for me from my friends across the Woyn. They were startling in their opulence: massy clusters of precious metals, elaborate strings of rare gems. "Tokens of love," Halum said, but I was not fooled. One could buy great estates with this heap of treasure. Those who loved me would not humiliate me by transferring cash to my account in Salla, but they could give me these splendors in the ordinary way of friendship, leaving me free to dispose of them according to my needs.

"Has it been very sad for you, this uprooting?" Halum asked. "This sudden going into exile?"

"One is no stranger to exile," I told her. "And one still has Noim for bondlove and companionship."

"Knowing that it would cost you what it did," she said, "would you play with the drug a second time, if you could turn time backward by a year?"

"Beyond any doubt."

"Was it worth the loss of home and family and friends?"

"It would be worth the loss of life itself," I replied, "if only one could be assured by that that all of Velada Borthan would come to taste the drug."

That answer seemed to frighten her: she drew back, she touched the tips of her fingers to her lips, perhaps becoming aware for the first time of the intensity of her bondbrother's madness. In speaking those words I was not uttering mere rhetorical overstatement, and something of my conviction must have reached Halum. She saw that I believed, and, seeing the depth of my commitment, feared for me.

Noim spent many of the days that followed away from his lands, traveling to Salla City on some family business and to the Plain of Nand to inspect property he was thinking of buying. In his absence I was master of the estate, for the servants, whatever they might think of my private life, did not dare to question my authority to my face. Daily I rode out to oversee the workers in Noim's fields, and Halum rode with me. Actually little overseeing was demanded of me, since this was midway in the seasons between planting and harvest, and the crops looked after themselves. We rode for pleasure, mainly, pausing here for a swim, there for a lunch at the edge of the woods. I showed her the stormshield pens, which did not please her, and took her among the gentler animals of the grazing fields, who came up and amiably nuzzled her.

These long rides gave us hours each day to talk. I had not spent so much time with Halum since childhood, and we grew wonderfully close. We were cautious with one another at first, not wishing to get too near the bone with our questions, but soon we spoke as bond-kin should. I asked her why it was she had never married, and she answered me simply, "One never encountered a suitable man." Did she regret having gone without husband and children? No, she said, she regretted nothing, for her life had been tranquil and rewarding; yet there was wistfulness in her tone. I could not press her further. On her part she questioned me about the Sumaran drug, trying to learn from me what merits it had that had led me to run such risks. I was amused by the way she phrased her inquiries: trying to sound earnest and sympathetic and objective, yet nonetheless unable to hide her horror at what I had done. It was as though her bondbrother had run amok and butchered twenty people in a marketplace, and she now wished to discover, by means of patient and good-humored questioning, just what had been the philosophical basis that had led him to take up mass murder. I also tried to maintain a temperate and dispassionate manner, so that I would not sear her with my intensity as I had done in that first interchange. I avoided all evangelizing, and, as calmly and soberly as I could, I explained to her the effects of the drug, the benefits I gained from it, and my reasons for rejecting the stony isolation of self that the Covenant imposes on us. Shortly a curious metamorphosis came over both her attitude and mine. She became less the highborn lady striving with well-meant warmth to understand the criminal, and more the student attempting to grasp the mysteries revealed by an initiated master. And I became less the descriptive reporter, and more the prophet of a new dispensation. I spoke in flights of lyricism of the raptures of soulsharing; I told her of the strange wonder of the early sensations, as one begins to open, and of the blazing moment of union with another human consciousness; I depicted the experience as something far more intimate than any meeting of souls one might have with one's bond-kin, or any visit to a drainer. Our conversations became monologues. I lost myself in verbal ecstasies, and came down from them at times to see Halum, silver-haired and eternally young, with her eyes sparkling and her lips parted in total fascination. The outcome was inevitable. One scorching afternoon as we walked slowly through the aisles in a field of grain that rose chest-high on her, she said without warning, "If the drug is available to you here, may your bondsister share it with you?" I had converted her.

65

THAT NIGHT I dissolved some pinches of the powder in two flasks of wine. Halum looked uncertain as I handed one to her, and her uncertainty rebounded to me, so that I hesitated to go through with our project; but then she gave me a magical smile of tenderness and drained her flask. "There is no flavor of it," she said, as I drank. We sat talking in Noim's trophy-hall, decked with hornfowl spears and draped with stormshield furs, and as the drug began to take effect Halum started to shiver; I pulled a thick black hide from the wall and draped it about her shoulders, and through it I held her until the chill was past.

Would this go well? Despite all my propagandizing I was frightened. In every man's life there is something he feels driven to do, something that pricks him at the core of his soul so long as it remains undone, and yet as he approaches the doing of it he will know fear, for perhaps to fulfill the obsession will bring him more pain than pleasure. So with me and Halum and the Sumaran drug. But my fear ebbed as the drug took hold. Halum was smiling. Halum was smiling.

The wall between our souls became a membrane, through which we could slide at will. Halum was the first to cross it. I hung back, paralyzed by prudery, thinking even now that it would be an intrusion on my bondsister's maidenhood for me to enter her mind, and also a violation of the commandment against bodily intimacies between bond-kin. So I dangled in this absurd trap of contradictions, too inhibited to practice my own creed, for some moments after the last barriers had fallen; meanwhile Halum, realizing at last that nothing prevented her, slipped unhesitatingly into my spirit. My instant response was to try to shield myself: I did not want her to discover this or this or that, and particularly to learn of my physical desire for her. But after a moment of this embarrassed flurrying I ceased trying to plaster my soul with figleaves, and went across into Halum, allowing the true communion to begin, the inextricable entanglement of selves.

166

I found myself—it would be more accurate to say, I lost myself—in corridors with glassy floors and silvered walls, through which there played a cool sparkling light, like the crystalline brightness one sees reflected from the white sandy bottom of a shallow tropical cove. This was Halum's virginal inwardness. In niches along these corridors, neatly displayed, were the shaping factors of her life, memories, images, odors, tastes, visions, fantasies, disappointments, delights. A prevailing purity governed everything. I saw no trace of the sexual ecstasies, nothing of the fleshly passions. I cannot tell you whether Halum, out of modesty, took care to shield the area of her sexuality from my probings, or had thrust it so far from her own consciousness that I could not detect it.

She met me without fear and joined me in joy. I have no doubt of that. When our souls blended, it was a complete union, without reservation, without qualification. I swam through the glittering depths of her, and the grime of my soul dropped from me: she was healing, she was cleansing. Was I staining her even as she was refining and purifying me? I cannot say. I cannot say. We surrounded and engulfed one another, and supported one another, and interpenetrated one another; and here mingling with my self was the self of Halum, who all my life had been my staff and my courage, my ideal and my goal, this cool incorruptible perfect incarnation of beauty; and perhaps as this corruptible self of mine put on incorruption, the first corrosive plaque sprouted on her shining incorruptibility. I cannot say. I came to her and she came to me. At one point in our journey through one another I encountered a zone of strangeness, where something seemed coiled and knotted: and I remembered that time in my youth, when I was setting out from Salla City on my flight into Glin, when Halum had embraced me at Noim's house, and I had thought I detected in her embrace a tremor of barely suppressed passion, a flicker of the hunger of the body. For me. For me. And I thought that I had found that zone of passion again, only when I looked more closely at it, it was gone, and I beheld the pure gleaming metallic surface of her soul. Perhaps both the first time and the second it was something I manufactured out of my own churning desires, and projected on her. I cannot say. Our souls were twined; I could not have known where I left off and Halum began.

We emerged from the trance. The night was half gone. We blinked, we shook our foggy heads, we smiled uneasily. There is always that moment, coming out of the drug's soul-intimacy, when one feels abashed, one thinks one has revealed too much, and one wants to retract what one has given. Fortunately that moment is usually brief. I looked at Halum and felt my body afire with holy love, a love that was not at all of the flesh, and I started to say to her, as Schweiz had once said to me, *I love you.* But I choked on the word. The "I" was trapped in my teeth, like a fish in a weir. *I. I. I. I love you, Halum. I.* If I could only say it. *I.* It would not come. It was there, but could not get past my lips. I took her hands between mine, and she smiled a serene moonlike smile, and it would have been so easy then to hurl the words out, except that something imprisoned them. *I. I.* How could I speak to Halum of love, and couch my love in the syntax of the gutter? I thought then that she would not understand, that my obscenity would shatter everything. Foolishness: our souls had been one, how then could a mere phrasing of words disturb anything? Out with it! *I love you.* Faltering, I said, "There is —such love in one—for you—such love, Halum—"

She nodded, as if to say, *Don't speak, your clumsy words break the spell.* As if to say, *Yes, there is in one such love for you also, Kinnall.* As if to say, *I love you, Kinnall.* Lightly she got to her feet, and went to the window: cold summer moonlight on the formal garden of the great house, the bushes and trees white and still. I came up behind her and touched her at the shoulders, very gently. She wriggled and made a little purring sound. I thought all was well with her. I was certain all was well with her.

We held no post-mortems on what had taken place between us this evening. That, too, seemed to threaten a puncturing of the mood. We could discuss our trance tomorrow, and all the tomorrows beyond that. I went with her back to her room, not far down the hallway from my own, and kissed her timidly on the cheek, and had a sisterly kiss from her; she smiled again, and closed the door behind her. In my own room I sat awhile awake, reliving everything. The missionary fervor was kindled anew in me. I would become an active messiah again, I vowed, going up and down this land of Salla spreading the creed of love; no more would I hide here at my bondbrother's place, broken and adrift, a hopeless exile in my own nation. Stirron's warning meant nothing to me. How could he drive me from Salla? I would make a hundred converts in a week. A thousand, ten thousand. I would give the drug to Stirron himself, and let the septarch proclaim the new dispensation from his own throne! Halum had inspired me. In the morning I would set out, seeking disciples.

There was a sound in the courtyard. I looked out and saw a groundcar: Noim had returned from his business trip. He entered the house; I heard him in the hallway, passing my room; then there came the sound of knocking. I peered into the corridor. He stood by Halum's door, talking to her. I could not see her. What was this, that he would go to Halum, who was nothing but a friend to him, and fail to greet his own bondbrother? Unworthy suspicions woke in me—unreal accusations. I forced them away. The conversation ended; Halum's door closed; Noim, without noticing me, continued toward his own bedroom.

Sleep was impossible for me. I wrote a few pages, but they were worthless, and at dawn I went out to stroll in the gray mists. It seemed to me that I heard a distant cry. Some animal seeking its mate, I thought. Some lost beast wandering at daybreak.

66

I WAS alone at breakfast. That was unusual but not surprising: Noim, coming home in the middle of the night after a long drive, would have wanted to sleep late, and doubtless the drug had left Halum exhausted. My appetite was powerful, and I ate for the three of us, all the while planning my schemes for dissolving the Covenant. As I sipped my tea one of Noim's grooms burst wildly into the dining-hall. His cheeks were blazing and his nostrils were flared, as if he had run a long way and was close to collapse. "Come," he cried, gasping. "The stormshields—" He tugged at my arm, half dragging me from my seat. I rushed out after him. He was already far down the unpaved road that led to the stormshield pens. I followed, wondering if the beasts had escaped in the night, wondering if I must spend the day chasing monsters again. As I neared the pens I saw no signs of a breakout, no clawed tracks, no torn fences. The groom clung to the bars of the biggest pen, which held nine or ten stormshields. I looked in. The animals were clustered, bloody-jawed, bloody-furred, around some ragged meaty haunch. They were snarling and quarreling over the last scraps of flesh; I could see traces of their feast scattered across the ground. Had some unfortunate farm beast strayed among these killers by darkness? How could such a thing have happened? And why would the groom see fit to haul me from my breakfast to show it to me? I caught his arm and asked him what was so strange about the sight of stormshields devouring their kill. He turned a terrible face to me and blurted in a strangled voice, "The lady—the lady—"

67

Noim was brutal with me. "You lied," he said. "You denied you were carrying the drug, but you lied. And you gave it to her last night. Yes? Yes? Yes? Don't hide anything now, Kinnall. You gave it to her!"

"You spoke with her," I said. I could barely manage words. "What did she tell you?"

"One stopped by her door, because one thought one heard the sound of sobbing," Noim answered. "One inquired if she was well. She came out: her face was strange, it was full of dreams, her eyes were as blank as pieces of polished metal, and yes, yes, she had been weeping. And one asked what was wrong, whether there had been any trouble here. No, she said, all was well. She said you and she had talked all evening. Why was she weeping, then? She shrugged and smiled and said it was a female thing, an unimportant thing—women weep all the time, she said, and need give no explanations. And she smiled again and closed the door. But that look in her eyes—it was the drug, Kinnall! Against all your vows, you gave it to her! And now—and now—"

"Please," I said softly. But he went on shouting, loading me with accusations, and I could not reply.

The grooms had reconstructed everything. They had found the path of Halum's feet in the dew-moist sandy road. They had found the door ajar of the house that gives access to the stormshield pens. They had found marks of forcing on the inner door that leads to the feeding-gate itself. She had gone through; she had carefully opened the feeding-gate, and just as carefully closed it behind her, to loose no killers on the sleeping estate; then she had offered herself to the waiting claws. All this between darkness and dawn, perhaps even while I strolled in a different part. That cry out of the mists—

Why? Why? Why? Why?

68

BY EARLY AFTERNOON such few possessions as I had were packed. I asked Noim for the loan of a groundcar, and he granted it with a brusque wave of his fingers. There was no question of remaining here any longer. Not only were there echoes of Halum resonating everywhere about, but also I had to go apart, into some place where I could think undisturbed, and examine all that I had done and that I hoped to do. Nor did I wish to be here when the district police carried out their inquest into Halum's death.

Had she been unable to face me again, the morning after having given her soul away? She had gone gladly enough into the sharing of selves. But afterward, in that rush of guilty reappraisal that often follows the first opening, she may have felt another way: old habits of reticence reasserting themselves, a sudden cascading sense of horror at what she had revealed. And the quick irreversible decision, the frozen-faced trek to the stormshield pens, the ill-considered passing of the final gate, the moment of regret-within-regret as the animals pounced and she realized she had carried her atonement too far. Was that it? I could think of no other explanation for that plunge from serenity to despair, except that it was a second thought, a reflex of shock that swept her to doom. And I was without a bond-sister, and had lost bondbrother too, for Noim's eyes were merciless when he looked at me. Was this what I had intended, when I dreamed of opening souls?

"Where will you go?" Noim asked. "They'll jail you in Manneran. Take one step into Glin with your drug and you'll be flayed.

Stirron will hound you out of Salla. Where, then, Kinnall? Threish? Velis? Or maybe Umbis, eh? Dabis? No! By the gods, it will be Sumara Borthan, won't it? Yes. Among your savages, and you'll have all the selfbaring you'll need there, yes? Yes?"

Quietly I said, "You forget the Burnt Lowlands, Noim. A cabin in the desert—a place to think, a place of peace—there is so much one must try to understand, now—"

"The Burnt Lowlands? Yes, that's good, Kinnall. The Burnt Lowlands in high summer. A fiery purge for your soul. Go there, yes. Go."

69

ALONE, I drove northward along the flank of the Huishtors, and then westward, on the road that leads to Kongoroi and Salla's Gate. More than once I thought of swerving the car and sending it tumbling over the highway's rim, and making an end. More than once, as the first light of day touched my eyelids in some back-country hostelry, I thought of Halum and had to struggle to leave my bed, for it seemed so much easier to go on sleeping. Day and night and day and night and day, and a few days more, and I was deep into West Salla, ready to go up the mountains and through the gate. While resting one night in a town midway into the uplands I discovered that an order was out in Salla for my arrest. Kinnall Darival, the septarch's son, a man of thirty years, of this height and having these features, brother to the Lord Stirron, was wanted for monstrous crimes: selfbaring, and the use of a dangerous drug, which against the explicit orders of the septarch he was offering to the unwary. By means of this drug the fugitive Darival had driven his own bondsister insane, and in her madness she had perished in a horrible way. Therefore all citizens of Salla were enjoined to apprehend the evildoer, for whom a heavy reward would be paid.

If Stirron knew why Halum had died, then Noim had told him everything. I was lost. When I reached Salla's Gate, I would find officers of the West Sallan constabulary waiting for me, for my destination was known. Yet in that case why had the announcement not informed the populace that I was heading for the Burnt Lowlands? Possibly Noim had held back some of what he knew, so that I could make an escape.

I had no choice but to go forward. It would take me days to reach the coast, and I would find all of Salla's ports alerted for me when I got there; even if I slipped on board a vessel, where would I go? Glin? Manneran? Similarly it was hopeless thinking of getting somehow across the Huish or the Woyn, into the neighboring provinces: I was already proscribed in Manneran, and surely I would find a chilly greeting in Glin. The Burnt Lowlands it would have to be, then. I would stay there some while, and then perhaps try to make my way out via one of the Threishtor passes, to start a new life on the western coast. Perhaps.

I bought provisions in the town, at a place that serves the needs of hunters entering the Lowlands: dried food, some weapons, and condensed water, enough to last me by careful expansion for several moontimes. As I made my purchases I thought the townsfolk were eyeing me strangely. Did they recognize me as the depraved prince whom the septarch sought? No one moved to seize me. Possibly they knew there was a cordon across Salla's Gate, and would take no risks with such a brute, when there were police in plenty to capture me on top of Kongoroi. Whatever the reason, I got out of the town unbothered, and set out now on the final stretch of the highway. In the past I had come this way only in winter, when snow lay deep; even now there were patches of dirty whiteness in shadowy corners, and as the road rose, the snow thickened, until near Kongoroi's double summit everything lay mantled in it. Timing my ascent carefully, I managed things so that I came to the great pass well after sundown, hoping that darkness would protect me in case of a roadblock. But the gate was unguarded. My car's lights were off as I drove the last distance—I half expected to go over the edge—and I made the familiar left turn, which brought me into Salla's Gate, and I saw no one there. Stirron had not had time to close the western border, or else he did not think I would be so mad as to flee that way. I went forward, and through the pass, and slowly down the switchbacks on the western face of Kongoroi, and when dawn overtook me I was into the Burnt Lowlands, choking in the heat, but safe.

70

NEAR THE PLACE where the hornfowl nest I found this cabin, about where I remembered it to be. It was without plumbing, nor were the walls even whole, yet it would do. It would do. The awful heat of the place would be my purge. I set up housekeeping inside, laying out my things, unpacking the journal-paper I had bought in the town for this record of my life and deeds, setting the jeweled case containing the last of the drug in a corner, piling my clothing above it, sweeping away the red sand. On my first full day of residence I busied myself camouflaging my groundcar, so that it would not betray my presence when searchers came: I drove it into a shallow ravine, so that its top barely broke the level of the ground, and collected woody ground-plants to make a covering for it, throwing sand atop the interwoven stems of the plants. Only sharp eyes would see the car when I was done. I made careful note of the place, lest I fail to find it myself when I was ready to leave.

For some days I simply walked the desert, thinking. I went to the place where the hornfowl struck my father down, and had no fear of the sharp-beaked circling birds: let them have me too. I considered the events of my time of changes, asking myself, *Is this what you wanted, Is this what you hoped to bring about, Does this satisfy you?* I relived each of my many soulsharings, from that with Schweiz to that with Halum, asking, *Was this good? Were there mistakes that could have been avoided? Did you gain, or did you lose, by what you did?* And I concluded that I had gained more than I had lost, although my losses had been terrible ones. My only regrets were for poor tactics, not for faulty principles. If I had stayed with Halum until her uncertainties had fled, she might not have given way to the shame that destroyed her. If I had been more open with Noim—if I had stayed in Manneran to confront my enemies—if—if—if—and yet, I had no regrets for having done my changing, but just that I had bungled my revolution of the soul. For I was convinced of the wrongness of the Covenant and of our way of life. Your way of life. That Halum had seen fit to kill herself after two hours of experiencing human love was the most scathing possible indictment of the Covenant.

And finally—not too many days ago—I began to write what you have been reading. My fluency surprised me; perhaps I verged even on glibness, though it was hard for me at first to use the grammar I imposed on myself. *I am Kinnall Darival and I mean to tell you all about myself.* So I began my memoir. Have I been true to that intent? Have I concealed anything? Day upon day my pen has scratched paper, and I have put myself down whole for you, with no cosmetic alterations of the record. In this sweatbox of a cabin have I laid myself bare. Meanwhile I have had no contact with the outside world, except for occasional hints, possibly irrational, that Stirron's agents are combing the Burnt Lowlands for me. I believe that guards are posted at the gates leading into Salla, Glin, and Manneran; and probably at the western passes as well; and also in Stroin Gap, in case I try to make my way to the Gulf of Sumar through the Wet Lowlands. My luck has held well, but soon they must find me. Shall I wait for them? Or shall I move on, trusting to fortune, hoping to find an unguarded exit? I have this thick manuscript. I value it now more than my life itself. If you could read it, if you could see how I have stumbled and staggered toward knowledge of self, if you could receive from it the vibrations of my mind—I have put everything down, I think, in this autobiography, in this record of self, in this document unique in the history of Velada Borthan. If I am captured here, my book will be captured with me, and Stirron will have it burned.

I must move on, then. But—

A sound? Engines?

A groundcar coming swiftly toward my cabin over the flat red land. I am found. It is done. At least I was able to write this much.

71

FIVE DAYS HAVE PASSED since the last entry, and I am still here. The groundcar was Noim's. He came not to arrest me but to rescue me. Cautiously, as if expecting me to open fire on him, he crept about my cabin, calling, "Kinnall? Kinnall?" I went outside. He tried to smile, but he was too tense to manage it. He said, "One thought you would be somewhere near this place. The place of the hornfowl—it still haunts you, eh?"

"What do you want?"

"Stirron's patrols are searching for you, Kinnall. Your path was traced as far as Salla's Gate. They know you're in the Burnt Lowlands. If Stirron knew you as well as your bondbrother does, he'd come straight here with his troops. Instead they're searching to the south, on the theory that you mean to go into the Wet Lowlands to the Gulf of Sumar, and get a ship to Sumara Borthan. But they're bound to start hunting for you in this region once they discover you haven't been down there."

"And then?"

"You'll be arrested. Tried. Convicted. Jailed or executed. Stirron thinks you're the most dangerous man on Velada Borthan."

"I am," I said.

Noim gestured toward the car. "Get in. We'll slip through the blockade. Into West Salla, somehow, and down to the Woyn. The Duke of Sumar will meet you and put you aboard some vessel heading out. You can be in Sumara Borthan by next moonrise."

"Why are you helping me, Noim? Why should you bother? I saw the hate in your eyes when I left you."

"Hate? Hate? No, Kinnall, no hate, only sorrow. One is still your—" He paused. With an effort, he said, "*I'm* still your bondbrother. I'm pledged to your welfare. How can I let Stirron hunt you like a beast? Come. Come. I'll get you safely out of here."

"No."

"No?"

"We're certain to be caught. Stirron will have you, too, for aiding a fugitive. He'll seize your lands. He'll break your rank. Don't make a useless sacrifice for me, Noim."

"I came all the way into the Burnt Lowlands to fetch you. If you think I'll go back without—"

"Let's not quarrel over it," I said. "Even if I escape, what is there for me? To spend the rest of my life hiding in the jungles of Sumara Borthan, among people whose language I can't speak and whose ways are alien to me? No. No. I'm tired of exile. Let Stirron take me."

Persuading Noim to leave me here was no little task. We stood in the midday fire for eternal minutes, arguing vehemently. He was determined to effect this heroic rescue, despite the almost certain probability that we would both be captured. This he was doing out of a sense of duty, not out of love, for I could see that he still held Halum's death to my account. I would not have his disgrace scored against me as well, and told him so: he had done nobly to make this journey, but I could not go with him. Finally he began to yield, but only when I swore I would at least make some effort to save myself. I promised that I would set out for the western mountains, instead of sitting here where Stirron would surely find me. If I reached Velis or Threish safely, I said, I would notify Noim in some way, so that he would cease to fear my fate. And then I said, "There is one thing you can do for me." I brought my manuscript out of the cabin—a great heap of paper, red scribbling on grayish rough sheets. In this, I said, he would find the whole story: my entire self encapsulated, and all the events that had brought me to the Burnt Lowlands. I asked him to read it, and to pass no judgment on me until he had. "You will find things in here that will horrify and disgust you," I warned him. "But I think you'll also find much that will open your eyes and your soul. Read it, Noim. Read it with care. Think about my words." And I asked one last vow of him, by our oath of bonding: that he keep my book safely preserved, even if the temptation came over him to burn it. "These pages hold my soul," I told him. "Destroy the paper and you destroy me. If you loathe what you read, hide the book away, but do no harm to it. What shocks you now may not shock you a few years from now. And someday you may want to show my book to others, so that you can explain what manner of man your bondbrother was, and why he did what he did." *And so that you may change them as I hope my book will change you,* I said silently. Noim vowed this vow. He took my sheaf of pages and stored them in the hold of his groundcar. We embraced; he asked me again if I would not ride away with him; again I refused; I made him say once more that he would read my book and preserve it; once more he swore he would; then he entered the groundcar and drove slowly toward the east. I entered the cabin. The place where I had kept my manuscript was empty, and I felt a sudden hollowness, I suppose much like that of a woman who has carried a child for the full seven moontimes and now finds her belly flat again. I had poured all of myself into those pages. Now I was nothing, and the book was all. Would Noim read it? I thought so. And would he preserve it? Very likely he would, though he might hide it in the darkest corner of his house. And would he someday show it to others? This I do not know. But if you have read what I have written, it is through the kindness of Noim Condorit; and if he has let it be read, then I have prevailed over his soul after all, as I hope to prevail over yours.

72

I HAD SAID to Noim that I would remain in the cabin no longer, but would set out for the west in an attempt to save myself. Yet I found myself unwilling to leave. The sweltering shack had become my home. I stayed a day, and another day, and a third, doing nothing, wandering the blazing solitude of the Burnt Lowlands, watching the hornfowl circle. On the fifth day, as you perhaps are able to see, I fell into the habit of autobiography again, and sat down at the place where I had lately spent so many hours sitting, and wrote a few new pages to describe my visit from Noim. Then I let three days more go by, telling myself that on the fourth I would dig my groundcar out of the red sand and head westward. But on the morning of that fourth day Stirron and his men found my hiding place, and now it is the evening of that day, and I have an hour or two more to write, by the grace of the Lord Stirron. And when I have done with this, I will write no more.

73

THEY CAME in six well-armed groundcars, and surrounded my cabin, and called on me through loudspeakers to surrender. I had no hope of resisting them, nor any desire to try. Calmly—for what use was fear? —I showed myself, hands upraised, at the cabin door. They got out of their cars, and I was amazed to find Stirron himself among them, drawn out of his palace into the Lowlands for an out-of-season hunting party with his brother as quarry. He wore all his finery of office. Slowly he walked toward me. I had not seen him in some years, and I was appalled by the signs of age on him: shoulders rounded, head thrust forward, hair thinning, face deeply lined, eyes yellowed and dim. The profits of half a lifetime of supreme power. We regarded one another in silence, like two strangers seeking a point of contact. I tried to find in him that boy, my playmate, my elder brother, whom I had loved and lost so long ago, and I saw only a grim old man with trembling lips. A septarch is trained to mask his inner feelings, yet Stirron was able to hold nothing secret from me, nor could he keep one consistent expression: I saw in his face, one look tumbling across the other, tokens of imperial rage, bewilderment, sorrow, contempt, and something that I took to be a sort of suppressed love. At length I spoke first, inviting him into my cabin for a conference. He hesitated, perhaps thinking I had assassination in mind, but after a moment he accepted in right kingly manner, waving to his bodyguard to wait outside. When we were alone within, there was another silent spell, which this time he broke, saying, "One has never felt such pain, Kinnall. One scarcely believes what one has heard about you. That you should stain our father's memory—"

"Is it such a stain, lord septarch?"

"To foul the Covenant? To corrupt the innocent—your bondsister among the victims? What have you been doing, Kinnall? *What have you been doing?*"

A terrible fatigue came over me, and I closed my eyes, for I scarcely knew where to begin explaining. After a moment I found strength. I reached toward him, smiling, taking his hand, and said, "I love you, Stirron."

"How sick you are!"

"To talk of love? But we came out of the same womb! Am I not to love you?"

"Is this how you talk now, only in filth?"

"I talk as my heart commands me."

"You are not only sick but sickening," said Stirron. He turned away and spat on the sandy floor. He seemed a remote medieval figure to me, trapped behind his dour kingly face, imprisoned in his jewels of office and his robes of state, speaking in gruff, distant tones. How could I reach him?

I said, "Stirron, take the Sumaran drug with me. I have a little left. I'll mix it for us, and we'll drink it together, and in an hour or two our souls will be one, and you'll understand. I swear, you'll understand. Will you do it? Kill me afterward, if you still want to, but take the drug first." I began to bustle about, making ready the potion. Stirron caught my wrist and halted me. He shook his head with the slow, heavy gesture of one who feels an infinite sadness. "No," he said. "Impossible."

"Why?"

"You will not fuddle the mind of the prime septarch."

"I'm interested in *reaching* the mind of my brother Stirron!"

"As your brother, one wishes only that you may be healed. As prime septarch, one must avoid harm, for one belongs to one's people."

"The drug is harmless, Stirron."

"Was it harmless for Halum Helalam?"

"Are you a frightened virgin?" I asked. "I've given the drug to scores of people. Halum is the only one who reacted badly—Noim too, I suppose, but he got over it. And—"

"The two people in the world closest to you," said Stirron, "and the drug harmed them both. Now you offer it to your brother?"

It was hopeless. I asked him again, several times, to risk an experiment with the drug, but of course he would not touch it. And if he had, would it have availed me anything? I would have found only iron in his soul.

I said, "What will happen to me now?"

"A fair trial, followed by an honest sentence."

"Which will be what? Execution? Imprisonment for life? Exile?"

Stirron shrugged. "It is for the court to decide. Do you take one for a tyrant?"

"Stirron, why does the drug frighten you so? Do you know what it does? Can I make you see that it brings only love and understanding? There's no need for us to live as strangers to each other, with blankets around our souls. We can speak ourselves out. We can reach forth. We can say 'I,' Stirron, and not have to apologize for having selves. I. I. I. We can tell each other what gives us pain, and help each other to escape that pain." His face darkened; I think he was sure I was mad. I went past him, to the place where I had put down the drug, and quickly mixed it, and offered a flask to him. He shook his head. I drank, impulsively gulping it, and offered the flask again to him. "Go on," I said. "Drink. Drink! It won't begin for a while. Take it now, so we'll be open at the same time. Please, Stirron!"

"I could kill you myself," he said, "without waiting for the court to act."

"Yes! Say it, Stirron! I! Myself! Say it again!"

"Miserable self-barer. My father's son! If I talk to you in 'I,' Kinnall, it's because you deserve no better than filth from me."

"It doesn't need to be filth. Drink, and understand."

"Never."

"Why do you oppose it, Stirron? What frightens you?"

"The Covenant is sacred," he said. "To question the Covenant is to question the whole social order. Turn this drug of yours loose in the land and all reason collapses, all stability is lost. Do you think our forefathers were villains? Do you think they were fools? Kinnall, they understood how to create a lasting society. Where are the cities of Sumara Borthan? Why do they still live in jungle huts, while we have built what we have built? You'd put us on their road, Kinnall. You'd break down the distinctions between right and wrong, so that in a short while law itself would be washed away, and every man's hand would be lifted against his fellow, and where would be your love and universal understanding then? No, Kinnall. Keep your drug. One still prefers the Covenant."

"Stirron—"

"Enough. The heat is intolerable. You are arrested; now let us go."

74

BECAUSE THE DRUG was in me, Stirron agreed to let me have a few hours alone, before we began the journey back to Salla, so that I would not have to travel while my soul was vulnerable to external sensations. A small mercy from the lord septarch: he posted two men as guards outside my cabin, and went off with the others to hunt hornfowl until the coming of dusk.

Never had I taken the drug without a sharer. So the strangenesses came upon me and I was alone with them, to hear the throbbings and the whinings and the rushings, and then, as the walls fell away from my soul, there was no one for me to enter, and no one to enter me. Yet I could detect the souls of my guards—hard, closed, metallic—and I felt that with some effort I could reach even into them. But I did not, for as I sat by myself I was launched on a miraculous voyage, my self expanding and soaring until I encompassed this our entire planet, and all the souls of mankind were merged into mine. And a wondrous vision came upon me. I saw my bondbrother Noim making copies of my memoir, and distributing them to those he could trust, and other copies were made from those, to circulate through the provinces of Velada Borthan. And out of the southern land now came shiploads of the white powder, sought not merely by an elite, not only by the Duke of Sumar and the Marquis of Woyn, but by thousands of ordinary citizens, by people hungry for love, by those who found the Covenant turning to ashes, those who wished to reach one another's souls. And though the guardians of the old order did what they could to halt the movement, it could not be stopped, for the former Covenant had run its course, and now it was clear that love and gladness could no longer be suppressed. Until at last a network of communication existed, shining filaments of sensory perception linking one to one to one to all. Until at last even the septarchs and the justiciars were swept up in the tide of liberation, and all the world joined in joyous communion, each of us open to all, and the time of changes was complete; the new Covenant was established. I saw all this from my shabby cabin in the Burnt Lowlands. I saw the bright glow encompassing the world, shimmering, flickering, gaining power, deepening in hue. I saw walls crumbling. I saw the brilliant red blaze of universal love. I saw new faces, changed and exultant. Hands touching hands. Selves touching selves. This vision blazed in my soul for half a day, filling me with joy such as I had never experienced at any time, and my soaring spirit wandered in realms of dream. And only as the drug began to ebb from me did I realize that it was nothing but a fantasy.

Perhaps it will not always be a fantasy. Perhaps Noim will find readers for what I have written, and perhaps others will be persuaded to follow my path, until there are enough like me, and the changes become irreversible and universal. It has happened before. I will disappear, I the forerunner, I the anticipator, I the martyred prophet. But what I have written will live, and through me you will be changed. It may yet be that this is no idle dream.

This final page has been set down as twilight descends. The sun hastens toward the Huishtors. Soon, as Stirron's prisoner, I will follow it. I will take this little manuscript with me, hidden somewhere about me, and if I have good fortune I will find some way of giving it to Noim, so that it can be joined to the pages he has already had from me. I cannot say if I will succeed, nor do I know what will become of me and of my book. And you who read this are unknown to me. But I can say this: if the two parts have become one, and you read me complete, you may be sure that I have begun to prevail. Out of that joining can come only changes for Velada Borthan, changes for all of you. If you have read this far, you must be with me in soul. So I say to you, my unknown reader, that I love you and reach my hand toward you, I who was Kinnall Darival, I who have opened the way, I who promised to tell you all about myself, and who now can say that that promise has been fulfilled. Go and seek. Go and touch. Go and love. Go and be open. Go and be healed.